Freaks of Greenfield High

Book One of the Freaks series

Maree Anderson

ISBN-13: 978-0-9941160-1-7
ISBN-10: 0-9941160-1-2

FREAKS OF GREENFIELD HIGH

First print edition, 2015

Publisher: Maree Anderson

Cover Design: Rob Anderson

Freaks

of

Greenfield High

Also by Maree Anderson:

The Crystal Warriors Series

The Crystal Warrior

Ruby's Dream

Jade's Choice

Opal's Wish

***

The Seer Trilogy

Seer's Hope

Seer's Promise

Seer's Choice

***

Lightning Rider

***

Young Adult books:

The Freaks Series

Freaks of Greenfield High

Freaks in the City

Freaks Under Fire

***

The Liminals Series

Liminal

Phase (coming soon!)

***

Dedication

This one's for my kids.

PROLOGUE

DR. ALEXANDER JAY DURHAM squinted through a gap in the blinds at the convoy snaking up the dirt road. The dying light painted the black Hummers with crimson-hued menace, making them appear as though they'd been dipped in blood. Foolish, greedy men. Alex could not find it in him to regret their fate.

The shadows haunting the study resolved into a teenage girl. She glided over to take his arm. "Come away from the window, Father. It is not safe."

Bah. He was dying. Worrying about *his* safety was futile. Nevertheless, he allowed her to help him to his favorite armchair and settle him into its comforting cushions.

His gaze skittered about, finally coming to rest on a framed photo atop the mantelpiece. It captured a young woman wearing a cheerful sun-colored dress, her lips curved in a wide, unrestrained smile. Time rewound and Alex saw himself with her, pulling all manner of ridiculous faces to make her laugh. His hand fisted on his chest, pressing atop his heart to keep the memories safely imprisoned. Now was not the time to become lost in the past.

His gaze cut to the girl, now seated at the computer desk. And, as it always did when he looked at her, the pain of his loss faded to a dull, comforting ache.

She was his legacy. From the facial structure and skin-tone, to the tousled mane of raven hair that resisted all efforts to tame it, she was a younger replica of his dead wife. She had but one unique physical characteristic, something that was hers and only hers. Alex's brows knit into a frown. Perhaps he'd been foolish to experiment. Perhaps the startling cobalt hue of her eyes would make her too remarkable, too memorable. Perhaps he'd endangered her by—

He reined in his fears. She was skilled at subterfuge. She would cope admirably without him. He had to believe that. "We haven't got much time," he said. "Do you know what to do?"

The girl glanced up from the computer. She slanted her brilliantly clear gaze at him, head cocked to one side in a perfect imitation of thoughtfulness as her fingertips flew over the keyboard. "We have seven minutes fifty-one seconds before the attack force reaches the outskirts of the property. They will secure the area before they begin the assault." She tapped out one last combination of keys and her hands stilled. "And yes, Father, I know what to do."

"Of course you do. Please forgive a foolish old man."

She abandoned her chair to take her place at his side. "There is nothing to forgive," she said. "I have enabled the virus. Phase one is now complete." Phase one being the program she had designed to corrupt the network servers and delete all secured off-site backup data, thus destroying decades of meticulous research. Irretrievably.

Alex nodded his approval. "Good."

She tapped pursed lips with her forefinger, the gesture so humanlike Alex's heart twisted with regret. His beloved Mary would have been able to love the girl unreservedly, nurtured her, given her everything she needed to reach her full potential. Mary would have succeeded where he had failed.

"I have scanned the vehicles and the weaponry," the girl reported. "The attack force comprises twenty-five men. I can delete them. No incriminating evidence will be found."

"Of that I have no doubt. But we must proceed as planned. I am your one weakness, and this is the only way you will be safe." He reached out to pat her hand, momentarily forgetting that she needed no comforting from him. Or indeed, anyone.

She sank to her knees, her head bowed. "Why must I do this, Father?"

"You know why," he whispered, stroking the bent head, marveling at the softness of the hair, the physical perfection of his creation. "My knowledge must never fall into their hands. Please believe me, this is the only way."

He sat back in his chair, squared his shoulders and placed his hands on the armrests, waiting.

The girl did not move.

"Must I order you to do this?"

She raised her head.

Her gaze bored into Alex's, stripping him bare of his delusions. The fine hairs on his nape stood to attention. As God was his witness, he felt as though she was peering into the deepest darkest recesses of his soul. He wondered what she would see there. And, coward that he was, found himself grateful that she was incapable of passing judgment on him.

She waited, sitting back on her heels with her hands clasped neatly in her lap, her features a smooth emotionless mask. "Yes, Father," she said. "You must give the order. Please believe me, this is the *only* way."

Alex pinched the bridge of his nose with his fingers and

heaved a shaky sigh. It served him right, he supposed. He'd poured his heart and soul into her, done his utmost to make her as humanlike as possible. And he had been the one to insist she call him "Father". He could hardly blame her for mustering what they both knew was a token resistance to this final solution.

"So be it," Alex said. "Initiating sequence Revelations 13-colon-17, 6-6-6. Cyborg Unit Gamma-Dash-One, this is Alexander Jay Durham. Confirm."

"Running voiceprint analysis. Identity confirmed." Her voice was now flat, machine-like.... Inhuman. Alex's command had shunted her artificial consciousness aside, allowing him to access her core programming. Forcing her to obey.

"Cyborg Unit Gamma-Dash-One, prepare to initiate sequence J-O-H-N-3-colon-16."

"Initiating."

"Commence sequence J-O-H-N-3-colon-16."

The girl stood and placed her cool hands on his shoulders. Alex closed his eyes. He was tired, so very tired. He harbored no fear for what was to come, merely profound relief. God willing, Mary would be waiting for him.

"I. Do. Not. Want... to do this... Father."

Alex's eyelids flew open and he choked on a gasp. Real tears glistened in her eyes. It should have been impossible for her to fight the command, impossible for her to produce tears.

A malfunction or a miracle? Only time would tell. And Alex had run out of time.

He snatched a deep breath and clasped his hands, settling them into his lap. His eyelids drifted closed. "Cyborg Unit Gamma-Dash-One, commence sequence J-O-H-N-3-colon-16."

"COMMENCING SEQUENCE J-O-H-N-3-colon-16," the cyborg repeated. "I love you, Father." And in one swift, efficient movement, she broke the old man's neck.

As humans often liked to do in such circumstances, she closed her eyes, honoring her creator and his contribution to this world with a minute of silence and utter stillness. She would have preferred to bury him but that was not part of the plan. However, there was another way for her to honor his memory.

The man she called "Father" had always balked at choosing a suitable name for her. The significance of a name, choosing the *right* one, had been too overwhelming for him. She now appropriated his middle name. Henceforth she would be known as "Jay".

Jay's sensors registered that the grumbling purr of Hummer engines had ceased. Leaving Father's body slumped in the armchair, she took a replica Gamma unit from a cabinet and placed it in the chair behind the computer desk. As she arranged the thing in a lifelike pose, positioning its hands on the keyboard, a droplet of moisture plopped onto the Enter key.

Jay swiped at her cheeks and examined the wetness on her fingertips. Her tongue darted out to taste and identify.

Tears?

Impossible. A malfunction.

She blotted her face with her sleeve and filed the phenomenon away in her databanks to be analyzed at a more opportune time. Her immediate priority was to increase her core body temperature until it exactly matched the ambient temperature of the room. Once that task had been achieved, she would automatically make adjustments as she passed through each area of the house so that she would not register as an anomaly on their heat sensors.

Jay activated the replica, and as it began to tap away at the keyboard, Jay accessed what appeared to be a standard household alarm set into the wall beside the door. She input an eleven-digit code. A flashing red light indicated the two-minute countdown had commenced.

She exited the study, locked the door behind her, and headed down the corridor. Once inside her bedroom, she stood atop the huge bed she'd never used, reached up to pop open the concealed ceiling hatch, and levered herself upward into the roof cavity. She replaced the hatch cover and jiggled it back into place. The opening would be almost invisible when viewed from the interior of the room—not that it mattered, but she had been programmed to be meticulous.

Two near-simultaneous booms destroyed the unnatural tranquility—frame charges, explosive panels the attack force had used to blow the front and rear doors. They'd opted for the element of surprise, relying on speed rather than subterfuge to achieve their goal.

Jay slid aside a cleverly designed portion of the roof and, moving so quickly that to human eyes she would be nothing but a blur, she climbed outside, flattened herself against the pitched roofline and froze. From her vantage point, her sensory enhancements allowed her to hear footsteps, measured and quick, as the attack force ascended the stairs and headed for the study. The men were military-trained professionals, maintaining radio silence and communicating via hand signals. Her replica had thoroughly fooled their sensors, leading them to believe they knew exactly where their quarry would be found.

The men were now battering the door into the study with a portable ramming device. Jay had insured it would be no easy task to break through the reinforced door. In their place, however, she would have saved considerable time by barging straight through the wall.

They achieved their objective and burst into the study.

Jay blinked and switched to infrared vision. A near soundless whine, audible only to her, indicated that the final countdown was now in progress. Behind its covering panel, the study alarm's indicator light would now have escalated to a distorted crimson line.

Ten. Nine. Eight….

Using electronics to cover her tracks had been a carefully calculated risk. EMP weapons could render even her sophisticated timing device useless. But an EMP weapon could destroy *all* electronic devices within range, including computer hard drives. Jay had based her primary plan on the assumption that obtaining Father's research was their main priority. They would not dare risk destroying that research, for then, if Alexander Durham's creation escaped their grasp, they would be left with nothing.

She observed the fiery silhouettes of the men raising their weapons as they spotted Father's body and what they believed was their target. Their leader signaled two of his men to approach.

Four. Three. Two—

The instant the first of three precisely timed blasts ripped through the stately old country house, Jay launched herself from the rooftop.

The man seated in the armored car parked behind the Hummers shielded his eyes. He yelled into his comms device, far too distracted by this surprising turn of events to notice Jay surfing the outer limits of the first blast wave.

She landed in a flat-footed crouch, thirty feet nine inches beyond the two-story house. It was not her best jump. In calmer wind conditions she had achieved thirty-one feet.

She took off at a run, simultaneously scanning the vicinity for evidence of pursuit. The probability that the covert organization pursuing her would include a chopper in the retrieval attempt had been high, but aside from tersely shouted orders she heard nothing of note.

For whatever reason, they had underestimated her capabilities, leaving her with nothing to challenge her. Nothing to help ease the painful tightness twisting of what Father had insisted was her heart.

Jay entered a heavily wooded area bordering the property, and all trace of her passing was swallowed by the night.

Chapter One

Jay closed the front door of her apartment and engaged the security system she'd personally designed and installed. She'd also installed a new door, as well as reinforcing the strength of the wall. She didn't fear intruders. For her, increasing the security of each new residence was simply a logical course of action.

The apartment took up the entire topmost floor of an old but well-preserved building. The first floor was little more than a large hall, sporadically rented out to community groups. The ground floor housed a number of eclectic stores. The scarcity of regular customers to the stores, and the lack of foot-traffic, were her chief reasons for choosing this particular apartment.

Leasing it had been ridiculously easy despite her apparent youth. She'd deepened her voice to a masculine timbre while conducting the initial transaction by phone, and then finalized the lease arrangements via email and internet transactions. Child's play to then uplift the keys from the leasing agency in person on behalf of her "uncle", who was "away on business".

No one had queried the absence of Jay's fictional guardian in the week since she'd moved in. Her cover story would hold provided no one pried too deeply into her affairs.

At this early hour, the only sounds were the mouse-like

squeaks of Jay's sneakers on the treads of the worn stairs. She slapped the exit button, pushed through the doors, and set off at a measured jog.

The town she had selected this time was unremarkable—as were its white-collar middle class inhabitants. According to a newspaper article written around the time the current mayor had been elected, Snapperton's only claim to fame was its well-established history of mediocrity.

It would be difficult for operatives to infiltrate the town without being noticed. In Snapperton she could hide in plain sight. For now.

Her internal timepiece told her it was 01:00 hours, early enough to provide an excellent opportunity to map wireless hotspots and detect any signal leakages from Wi-Fi networks that she could exploit if required. She would take special note of unexpected power surges or electronic anomalies that might indicate the area had been targeted and was being monitored.

Forty-six minutes into her run, Jay picked up a tail.

She allowed him to shadow her for five minutes before she pulled up and knelt on the sidewalk to fuss with her perfectly tied shoelaces.

The man ran past her, his chest heaving like a bellows, droplets of sweat flicking from his person and his clothing. She scanned him for hidden weapons and electronic surveillance equipment. Nothing.

As if sensing her scrutiny, he slowed and turned back to her, jogging on the spot. "You… 'kay… hon?" he puffed.

"I am fine. Thank you." She stood, and considered her options given the available data. His expression revealed only concern for her wellbeing. His breathing had been labored and his running technique far too inefficient for him to be a regular runner. He had neither the appearance nor the demeanor of a physically fit, trained operative.

Conclusion: Harmless.

He gave up jogging and stood, feet apart, rolling his shoulders and stretching his neck from side to side. "Yanno, a young girl like you shouldn't be out alone at this hour."

Jay cocked her head and considered his statement carefully. "Why? Are you planning on attacking me?"

He blew out a laugh that turned into a wheezing cough. When he'd caught his breath again he said, "Funny girl. This is Snapperton, fergodsakes—safe as houses. 'Sides, I get the feeling you could outrun me with both hands tied behind your back."

"You are correct in that last assumption."

"You oughta head back home before your folks figure out you're AWOL," he said. "If I found *my* daughter missing at this hour, I'd be frantic. And when I found her, she'd be grounded for the term of her natural life."

"May I ask you a question?"

"Shoot."

"Why are *you* out alone at this hour?"

"Couldn't sleep," he said. "Thought going for a run might tire me out."

She nodded. "Me, too." And to alleviate any further concerns he might have, she added, "I'm heading home now."

"Good-o."

He waved at her as he headed off again. And, after reviewing the conversation, Jay concluded it would be prudent to do as he had suggested and return home before she attracted any more attention. In future, she would limit her "exercise" to more acceptable daylight hours.

AT WHAT SHE DEEMED an appropriate hour of the morning, Jay exited her apartment again, this time heading in the direction of the school she'd chosen. Not that she'd truly *had* a choice of high schools because Snapperton boasted only the one: Greenfield High. She adjusted the straps of her backpack and began pumping her arms as she walked, copying the movements of a group of elderly females on the opposite side of the road.

As Jay powered past two girls who were slightly younger than Jay appeared to be, she heard them giggling. They were talking about her—what a "dork" she was, and how "uncool" it was to be seen power-walking, "'Cause, like, my grandma does that!"

Jay replayed the girls' conversation, analyzing intonation, sentence construction and slang usage, along with facial expressions and body language. The speed she was walking, and the manner in which she was swinging her arms, was apparently not acceptable.

She slowed her pace, let her arms hang loosely at her sides, and instructed her body to move in a way that would not attract further comment. Humans were such complex creatures. And the only human she'd extensively interacted with had been Alexander Durham, the man she'd called Father. Instant access to myriad tracts of information was no substitute when it came to blending in with modern-day teens. He should have provided her with suitable subjects to observe and mimic. It was unconscionably careless of him to have put her at risk by neglecting such a crucial part of her education.

An insistent, high-pitched noise intruded on her thought processes, yanking her into the present… and the realization she was standing in the middle of the sidewalk, jaws clamped together, fists tightly clenched at her sides, her entire body tensed, and her skin flushed with heat.

She performed an internal diagnostic and concluded everything was in order. However there had been no imminent danger, not even the vaguest hint of a potential threat. There was no valid reason for her to have reacted in such a way. Odd.

The duration of the anomaly had been one minute thirty-eight seconds—long enough for her behavior to be deemed strange, and perhaps even noteworthy, had she been observed.

She scanned the street and surrounds. The two girls were nowhere to be seen. The probability they'd passed her by, and turned the corner up ahead, was high enough that Jay dismissed them from her mind. Her immediate concern was the elderly man approaching her at a shuffle.

Attached to a lead the man clutched in his hand was a small, scruffy, extremely voluble creature that Jay identified as canine, primarily terrier, intermixed with at least five other breeds.

Humans seemed to find these creatures useful. Jay could understand the value of the larger breeds. She could even appreciate those canines bred primarily for their unique physical characteristics. But this one possessed no pleasing physical characteristics that she could discern. Its primary function seemed to be housing fleas and making an awful lot of noise.

"Are you all right, young lady?" The old man's voice quavered. "Seeing you standing there like some fierce statue gave me a bit of a turn."

"Yes. Thank you for asking, though. I was deep in thought and standing very still helps me to think." She smiled at the man until the frown lines creasing his face eased.

"Penny for them," he cackled.

Jay searched her databases for quotations and sayings. Ah. He referred to her thoughts. She snorted—a useful response in some awkward social situations. "I do not believe my thoughts are worth that much."

Now the normal thing to do would be to pat the canine. This action might also serve to deflect the man's curiosity about her thoughts—and her apparently unusual manner in thinking them. "May I pat your dog?"

"Sure. Fifi don't much like strangers, though. She might nip you."

Jay squatted and held out her left hand. As she'd observed humans do, she clicked her fingers to invite the dog to approach and sniff her scent. "Here, girl," she said, keeping her tone gentle and encouraging. "Here, Fifi."

The little canine inched forward, its entire body wriggling with indecision. Then it whined and leaned back, sticking its rear in the air and waggling its stubby tail. Its antics were so comical Jay found it ridiculously easy to remember to smile.

The dog's acute sense of smell had detected Jay's otherness. Little wonder it was reluctant to approach. Jay tweaked the chemical mix of her pheromones until her pores secreted an odor more appealing to canine creatures.

The dog gave a series of high-pitched yaps. It bounded forward with an enthusiastic bark and buried its nose in her hand. Then it sat on its haunches to scratch behind one ear.

Poor little creature. The fleas must be driving it to distraction.

Jay concocted a specific mix from her body's available chemical compounds. She ruffled the fur on the dog's back and the flea repellent oozed from the pores of her fingertips, transferring onto its skin. "Who's a brave girl?" she crooned.

"Well, I never!" the old man said. "You must be something quite special, young lady."

Jay made her left eyelid droop in a wink. "Oh," she said, "I am."

He cackled again, appreciating her attempt at wit.

Excellent. She was gaining more proficiency at this nebulous skill humans called humor. She gave the dog one last rub, insuring its freedom from fleas for the next four to six weeks. "I have to go or I'll be late for school. See you, Fifi. You be a good girl, now."

The old man grinned back at her, his nut-brown eyes all but disappearing in a sea of wrinkles. "Goodbye, young lady." He and the dog meandered off down the path.

Jay reviewed the interaction and concluded she'd acquitted herself adequately, and done nothing further to raise the old man's suspicions. From what she understood about social interactions at high school, though, any hint of out of the ordinary behavior would not be so easily forgiven. It was imperative she closely mimic the behavior of her peers so she didn't stand out in any way. Still, it should not be beyond her capabilities to seamlessly integrate into high school life. She did not believe attending high school could be anything close to "hell on earth", as was so frequently claimed in the numerous accounts she'd read.

A tight lump settled in her stomach. For a moment she was confused by the sensation, and then she dismissed it as hunger pangs—merely her body's way of reminding her to re-fuel if she wished to maintain her optimum physical condition.

Humans were lamentably prone to exaggeration. How bad could high school possibly be?

TYLER'S GEL-SLIMED FINGERS paused mid-sweep through his shaggy hair. His gaze zeroed in on a reddened blotch. He thrust his chin closer to the mirror to examine the emerging zit. Great. Just freaking great. As if today wasn't gonna suck enough already.

A rattle of the bathroom door was followed by a muffled curse and loud thumping.

"Hurry up, Tyler!" His twin sister's voice was a banshee-worthy screech.

Tyler rinsed his hands, wrapped his towel more securely around his hips, and unlocked the door.

Caro squeezed her eyes shut, counted to five, and then opened them again to gaze at him like she hoped she'd been imagining things. Her gasp reeked of unmitigated horror. "Omigod!"

The lump on Tyler's chin gave an answering throb. His hand crept to his face.

"What have you done to your *hair*?"

She advanced toward him with hands outstretched, a determined expression in her eyes. He grit his teeth and resigned himself to the coming torture, smothering yelps and blinking furiously watering eyes as she combed her fingers through his hair and roughly tugged it into submission.

Caro had gotten one hundred percent of their allocated personal style gene. She shopped at thrift stores and camped out at the mall when the sales were on, but the truth was, no matter what she wore, the popular girls forgave her. And the jocks wanted into her panties.

Tyler knew this because many of his former so-called friends had made a point of telling him so, hoping to provoke him into losing his cool. But Tyler had given up getting pissed about what they said, *and* how they said it. Apart from the major downside of risking getting pummeled for mouthing off, he'd finally realized his sister loved the attention—thrived on it, even.

Mind you, if any girl could keep a bunch of guys with sewers for brains in line, it was his sister. When Caro got seriously riled, she put every evil twin ever portrayed in a horror flick to shame.

Tyler wished she'd turn some of that evil twin mojo on her current boyfriend and quit giving him second chances. Shawn was a douche—among other things.

"There." Caro backed off and eyed him, head tilted to one side, lips pursed. "Yep. You'll do. You know, as much as it kills me to say this, the whole tortured-emo-look suits you. Those dark smudges under your eyes really give it authenticity."

She said it in an admiring way, like he'd deliberately chosen to emulate the living dead.

As if.

Tyler's "look" was a long overdue trip to the barber and plain old insomnia. He'd spent most of the night either pacing the floor and humming to himself, or hunched over his desk scribbling down lyrics. When the muse got vocal, he had no choice but to surrender.

"Go find some clothes before my eyes start bleeding," Caro said. "Unless of course you're planning on going to school wearing that towel?" She threw him a wicked grin. "If nothing else, it would make one heckuva fashion statement."

Tyler glanced at his watch. His stomach somersaulted. "Jeez! Would it have killed you to mention how late it was?"

"You can catch a ride with me and Nessa if you want," she said.

"Thanks, but no thanks." Last thing he needed was being cooped up in a confined space with his sister's BFF, Vanessa. Who also happened to be his ex. And treated him like something she'd scraped off her shoe despite everything he'd done for her.

His sister heaved a long-suffering sigh and shrugged. "Whatever."

Tyler raced into his bedroom. He yanked clothes from drawers, discovered his jeans in the pile on the floor, and threw himself into them. He located one sneaker in the corner by the wardrobe. The other had mysteriously ended up so far beneath his bed, he had to crawl under it to fish it out. He raked his hair out of his eyes. So much for his styling-by-Caro look.

He grabbed his backpack and clomped downstairs. No time for breakfast—not that he could stomach cereal. Not today.

His mother glanced up from her mag. She sucked down a huge gulp of black coffee before giving him a smile that oozed sympathy. "Morning, kiddo. First period, right?" She paused for his nod. "At least the torture will be over and done with first-up."

"Yeah." Provided he didn't disgrace himself and end up the butt of the entire school. At least when he'd been a jock-god, the fallout from the last embarrassing incident had died down pretty quickly. If he succumbed again, this time the fallout would be real bad.

"Gotta go or I'll miss the bus," he mumbled.

"Don't forget your lunch." His mom jerked her chin at the brown paper bags sitting on the kitchen counter. "And you really should eat something, sweetie. Breakfast is—"

"I know, I know. Breakfast is the most important meal of the day." He kissed his mom's cheek, grabbed the bag with the "T" scrawled on it, and snagged an apple from the fruit bowl. "Happy, now?" he managed around a mouthful of apple.

"Ecstatic." His mother rolled her eyes ceiling-ward in eerie imitation of her daughter. Tyler shuddered. Definitely genetic.

"I know better than to say 'Have a good day'," she said. "Just try to get through it without a trip to the nurse, okay?"

"Thanks for reminding me," he muttered, reaching for the door handle.

"Oh, almost forgot," his mom said, raising her voice as he slid through the doorway. "I've got to finish up a proposal for the boss so I'll be late. Probably around half-six. Does your team have practice tonight?"

"No, Mom. Caro's squad practices Mondays, Wednesdays *and* Fridays, because Bettina's a total slave-driver. *My* team practices on Tuesdays. Remember?"

"Oh. Right. I knew that. Then don't forget it's your turn to cook dinner."

"I know!" he yelled as the door slammed behind him. Outstanding. He'd have the house to himself for a bit. Might even have a chance to get the song fermenting inside his head down on paper.

He sauntered down the path, pretending to be oblivious to the annoying yarping of their elderly neighbor's fleabag dog.

Ah, to hell with it. He halted and turned on his heel to confront Fifi, or Fufu, or whatever the mangy little beast was called, and hit it with his fiercest scowl. "Grrrr!"

Fufu yawned, and then squatted to pee on the grass.

Tyler groaned. Pathetic. If he couldn't even face down an upholstered rat of a dog, what chance did he have?

The coughing of an ancient engine caught his attention.

The bus? Crap!

Tyler ditched his apple core and sprinted down the street, skidding to a halt just as the bus doors jerked to a close behind the lone student who'd been waiting at the stop.

"Hey!" He whacked a door with the flat of his hand.

The driver favored him with a sneer that spread all over his fat face.

Crap. Looked like he'd be walking to school. Again. And he'd be late. Again.

"Hold the bus," someone yelled.

Tyler recognized one of his former teammates. "Yeah. Would if I could, dude." He spread his arms palms outward to indicate helplessness in the face of asshole bus drivers who had it in for him.

The guy rushed up to the bus, and as he pushed past to smack both hands on the doors, his pack swung and clouted Tyler in the face. Nice.

"Hey! Open up!" the guy yelled at the driver.

The doors hissed reluctantly open.

"Thanks, dude," Tyler said, rubbing his cheek.

The guy ignored him and boarded the bus.

Huh. Why was he even surprised to be so thoroughly ignored? It was just more of the same old, same old.

He clambered aboard. "Thanks for stopping to let me on, sir," he said to the driver, his voice throbbing with over-the-top politeness, just to really rub it in.

The driver muttered something uncomplimentary and his piggy little eyes flicked to the rearview mirror.

Tyler knew the man was watching his progress, waiting 'til he was just about to take his seat. But Tyler was wise to his nasty-ass tricks. Hell, he was an old hand at this now. It'd taken a humiliating face-plant in a girl's lap, and a butt-sprawl on the bus floor that had scattered the contents of his bag all over the place, but he'd learned. So when the driver shoved the bus in gear and floored the accelerator, Tyler swung into the nearest empty seat and plunked his butt safely down.

Tyler: one. Assholes: nil.

He leaned his cheek against the window and closed his eyes. The song lurking inside him broke free and his fingers tapped out the notes on his denim-clad thigh.

"Freak!" someone in the seat across from him called out, provoking a spate of taunts and insults from a sheeplike bunch of other kids.

Epic fail on the originality of the insults. Was that the best they could come up with? Yawn.

Tyler absorbed their insults and used them, braiding them into lyrics, lancing the spite of their original intent and twisting them into something powerful of his own making. He cranked the volume in his headspace to the max and nodded his head, now wholly oblivious to the snickers and catcalls. Oh yeah. This one was going to be good—real good. The music crashed through him, spiriting him away from the shithole that was his life… at least until the bus ground to a lurching halt, forcing him to open his eyes to reality again.

He couldn't face elbowing his way through the horde of kids, but he made the mistake of hanging back so long he was the last one to scramble from his seat.

The driver drummed his fingers on the steering wheel and fixed Tyler with a black scowl. Dude sure got pissed when he didn't get to snigger over someone's misfortune.

Tyler heeded the warning signs and launched himself from the top step before the driver could close the doors and take a chunk out of his heels. The man graunched the gears as he drove off, and Tyler pictured him grinding his teeth in frustration.

Tyler: two. Assholes: nil. His day was looking up. But as he wandered through the front gates of Greenfield High, his high spirits oozed from his pores and plopped onto the cracked sidewalk.

He had no clue why the school was called *Greenfield* High when the town was called Snapperton, after its founder. And it wasn't like the school had been built in some lushly grassed field, and then finished off with landscaped grounds and a bunch of twittering birds. The school was a concrete jungle. Oh, except for the trampled, yellowing stretch of grass either side of the path, and a few scraggly, tired-looking trees planted by some poor deluded soul in the fond hopes they'd eventually provide some shade for the kids.

He glowered at the uninspiring three-level building and its dull gray entranceway. Pity his other talent leaned toward portraiture and not architecture. How hard could it be to design something better than *this* heap?

Tyler was halfway through his junior year, and though an end to this torture was in sight, it couldn't come quickly enough. The actual education part of school was semi-bearable but the rest royally sucked. He longed to leave it all behind him—start afresh in a place where no one knew him. Reinvent himself.

Chances of that happening any time soon? Sub-zero. He was stuck here until he graduated. He'd foolishly believed things might get better this year but he couldn't have been more wrong. He had no choice but to suck it up and make the best of it.

He trudged through the entrance, steeling himself for another day of torment.

As he neared the office, he slowed. Whoa. Hot-chick alert.

He mentally compared the girl waiting by the admin desk to Vanessa, the first girl he'd ever been serious about—and who, despite all that'd gone down, still topped his private scale of female hotness.

At least, up until about five seconds ago she had.

Vanessa was your ultimate cheerleader chick, polished to perfection and ultra-conscious of her status. *This* chick was Vanessa's opposite in every way. She was slender—all legs, and hardly any curves. And her mane of dark hair looked like she'd just crawled out of bed—a real statement in a school where ultra-straightened blonde reigned supreme. She wore faded and worn jeans, a black midriff-baring t-shirt, and sneakers that were more holes than sneaker. The vibes she gave off screamed that she didn't much care what she threw on so long as they were clothes. And she sure made the "I couldn't care less what you think of me" look work for her.

Tyler's fingers itched to sketch her, to try and capture on paper what he could only describe as her *presence*, some indefinable thing that made her stand out from the other girls he knew.

She glanced his way, paused, and full-on eyeballed him from head to toe.

His stomach flip-flopped. Vanessa's carefully selected blue contacts had nothing on this girl's eyes. They were the most shockingly intense shade of blue he'd ever seen. They weren't just blue, they were deepest sapphire. Or maybe azure. No, cobalt. Or—

Her somewhat hesitant answering smile turned Tyler's brain to mush. He tried to look away, act all nonchalant like he hadn't been checking her out, but he couldn't move. She burned through his brain. And the song took him.

I walk into the room,
And you're there.
I tremble like a lunatic,
But you only smile.
I'm gone.
Half of what I am is yours.
And I'm lost within you—

Someone jostled Tyler as they passed, jolting him back to the present. But rather than hightail it to his homeroom he stood there, absorbing the girl, etching her into his brain until she turned away to answer a question from one of the admin staff, and released him from her spell.

He blinked like a shortsighted owl and shook himself. Then his lips curved and self-satisfied warmth pooled in his belly. She'd smiled at him. And checked him out—definitely checked him out.

A bunch of guys sauntered past. Among them, Tyler spotted his sister's boyfriend, Shawn.

The warmth drained away. Crap. He knew exactly how this was gonna play out.

Sure enough, Shawn spotted the new chick and did a classic check out the hot babe head-to-toe-er. The other guys looked equally impressed but they hung back, waiting for their cues, unwilling to risk getting smacked down by the guy who called the shots.

Shawn sidled up to the admin counter and leaned against the wall to strike a pose. Shoulders back, arms crossed over outthrust chest, high-top-sneakered feet crossed at the ankles, he waited for her to notice him.

Tyler snickered. Dude!

Then reality smacked him like a stinky wet fish. Typical. This girl had been here all of five minutes and Shawn already had her in his sights.

Tyler skulked off down the corridor. The new chick was a lost cause. And when Caro learned her boyfriend was hitting on someone else? No way did Tyler want to be anywhere near the disaster zone when his sister lost it.

Chapter Two

Ten minutes into first period Bio, Tyler wished he were someplace else. Like, anywhere but here. Bad enough he was shortly gonna have to *dissect* a frog, first he had to sit through the gory diagrams and graphic explanations. He tried not to think about what had happened when he'd dissected the cow's eye. If he didn't hold it together this time, his life wouldn't be worth living.

A rap on the door ended Mr. Gilbert's lecture.

Tyler heaved a ragged sigh of relief and slumped across the desktop, burying his nose in the crook of his arm.

Kermit stank. The odor coated Tyler's throat like rancid cream. He closed his eyes, wishing for a lab partner he could bribe into doing the dissection. But after the last episode, and given his current status, kids were hardly beating a path to the empty stool beside him.

Not that he blamed them.

At the adjacent table someone giggled.

Tyler pried open his eyelids and spied his sister's hopefully-soon-to-be-ex boyfriend nudging his lab-partner… who just happened to be cheer captain, and obviously watched far too much TV because she slavishly imitated the whole cheer-captain-who-ruled-the-school stereotype.

Shawn and Bettina. Now *there* was a match made in heaven. Or hell. Take your pick. If there wasn't such a major ick-factor about stepbrothers-and-sisters hooking up, they would have been perfect for each other.

Bettina giggled again, whispered something back to Shawn, and then fished a gold compact from her pocket. She flicked it open and gave a breathy gasp.

Was it too much to hope for a nice juicy zit to mar that perfect complexion?

Apparently so. For Bettina didn't shriek and have a tantrum, she merely reapplied gloss to her already shiny lips, primped her hair and smooched her reflection.

She was one of those inhuman creatures who never got zits. And the gasp was probably because she'd found a hair out of place.

Next, she pulled out a perfume atomizer and sprayed it over her frog.

Huh. Tyler wished *he'd* thought of that. Then again, spraying his mother's perfume around a classroom would hardly enhance his already dubious reputation.

Bettina caught him watching her. She curled her lip into a somehow still-attractive sneer. Took real talent to pull that off.

"What're you staring at?" she said.

"Just comparing you to this highly fascinating, unidentified stain on my desk," he said.

She hissed like a pampered cat denied a cushion. "Shut up, freak!"

"Yeah," Shawn said. "Shut up, freak."

"Wow. Original. Color me impressed." If Shawn ever did have an original thought, his poor underused brain cells would probably go postal.

Tyler pretended to let his eyelids drift closed and watched them, alert for the particular vibe they gave out when they were planning something heinous. Not that Bettina would ruin her manicure by doing the dirty work herself. She'd simply co-opt her peeps to do it for her.

B might not be that snappy on the verbals, but when it came to masterminding public humiliation? Legend. As numerous Greenfield High students who'd done something to piss her or Shawn off had learned to their cost. Tyler had been on the receiving end of an upended paint tray, had soda poured in his lap, and his chair "accidentally" whipped away just as he was about to plant his butt— "Oops! Didn't see you there. Sooo sorry."

Yeah. Riiight. He'd landed on his tailbone. It'd hurt like crazy, and he walked like he had a poker up his butt for the next few days. But that was minor compared to the girl who'd had her bra and panties stolen while showering after Phys Ed. Going commando in a skirt? Yikes. Poor kid was going to need a lifetime of therapy to get past that one.

Yep, beneath B's pampered, pretty exterior lurked an evil-genius brain. And Shawn was all too happy to follow his stepsister's lead. God only knew what Caro saw in him. Sometimes Tyler didn't understand his sister at all.

For now, Bettina and Shawn seemed distracted by some little drama playing out at the front of the room. The tension oozed from Tyler's muscles and a relieved sigh escaped his lips.

Shawn switched his attention to the pair of Bettina wannabes seated behind him. He stared at them so long they squirmed on their stools and started giggling.

Bettina rolled her eyes. "Just pick one of them, Shawn. How hard can it be?"

"Whatever." A pause while he vacillated some more, and

then, "Hey, Ash, do me a favor?"

Ashlee simpered, throwing a triumphant glance at her lab-partner. "'Course, Shawn. Like, anything you want!"

"We're gonna play musical lab-partners, and you scored the jackpot. You get to sit next to emo-freak-boy and partner him for the rest of the semester."

"But—"

"No buts, Ashlee," Bettina said. "Unless you want me to announce just how big *yours* is getting tonight at practice. About time you cut back on those double-mocha lattés, don't you think?"

Ashlee glanced sideways at Tyler. Her face scrunched up and her lower lip did a primo wobble. Even an idiot could tell she thought her life was "like, *so* over!"

Awww, shame. But Tyler had far more important worries than Ashlee's imminent social demise. The girl didn't have a brain cell to call her own, and she barely breathed without first getting Bettina's approval. Tyler would rather kiss Kermit than put up with Ashlee sitting next to him for an entire semester.

He peeled his cheek from the desktop and sat up. Despite his churning stomach, he even managed a credible sneer. "Forget it, Shawn. No way am I getting stuck with Bubble-brain for—"

"Are you talking about me?" someone said.

Tyler jerked, knocking the dissection tray with his elbow. Kermit flopped limply onto his forearm. He swallowed, and shook the frog off onto the desk. Using two fingers like forceps, he picked up one of its froggy legs and eased its limp body back on the tray. When his stomach had quit trying to crawl up his throat, he glanced up at the girl who'd spoken. And almost fell off his stool.

It was the totally hot chick from this morning.

Tyler's head echoed with the pounding of his pulse, and his chest felt so tight it was difficult to breathe. Mr. Gilbert must have assigned her to be his lab-partner. Please, God, he should be so lucky!

Please, God, he didn't do the whole déjà vu thing and pass out cold on the floor the instant he stuck the knife in Kermit's froggy body.

"Well, hiya," Shawn said to the new girl. "Again." He drew the word out for effect, while giving her a blatant once-over that made Tyler want to smack him a good one.

When Shawn got a blank-faced response instead of the expected gush of girly enthusiasm, he blinked. A tiny frown puckered his brow. "Remember me? From this morning. Outside the office. We had a real *connection*. If you know what I mean."

If she was dumb enough to fall for that line, she sure wasn't worth getting worked up over. Shawn could have her—with Bettina's fricking cherry lip balm on top.

Tyler clenched his jaw, waiting for the inevitable.

She opened her mouth to reply but Shawn rushed on, working the charm for all he was worth. Which, considering Shawn's daddy didn't bother drawing his "meager" salary as Snapperton's mayor, was quite a bit. "Hey, wouldn't you know it? Ashlee was just saying to emo-freak-boy, here, how much she'd lurve to be his lab partner. And Bettina's gonna ditch me for whassername." Shawn gestured vaguely at the girl sitting next to Ashlee.

"E-E-Eloise," the newly christened Whassername managed to splutter, overcome with joy, even though the god of jock straps couldn't be assed to remember her name.

Tyler itched to shake some sense into her but it wasn't worth the effort. Shawn spoke. Girls panted and swooned. Sadly, that was the order of the known universe.

Shawn gazed into Hot-Chick's eyes, acting like he was everything she'd ever wanted, and he was just waiting for her to fall into his arms, and sniffle with gratitude. In a most attractive manner, of course. No reddened noses and impassioned blubbering for Shawn's chicks.

Tyler held his breath, wondering whether she would succumb, hoping she'd be the exception to the rule. Needing her to be different.

Hot-Chick's impassive gaze settled on Bettina, sized her up, and then returned to Shawn… who seemed at a loss to understand why she wasn't playing The Game According To Shawn.

Tyler observed the confusion sloshing around in Shawn's brain with increasing glee. Ding-dong. There it was—Shawn's dawning realization that Hot-Chick probably figured he'd hooked up with *Bettina* and was now ditching her in public. The two of them always had their heads together, leaving their respective hook-ups to trot along behind them like so much window-dressing. Now Shawn's reliance on Bettina was coming back to bite him in the ass.

"Hey," Shawn said, a note of panic infusing his voice. "If you're wondering about Bettina and me? As if! You know what I'm saying?"

Dude. Even Tyler couldn't suppress a wince at the brutal dismissal of Bettina's charms.

Bettina threw Shawn a look that would have shriveled his balls if he'd been paying her the slightest bit of attention, and intervened before he could dig himself an even bigger hole. She slid from her stool and sidled over to command the newcomer's attention with a hand on her arm.

"Hi," she said. "I'm Bettina." Cue wide, doll-like eyes and cutesy pursing of gloss-slicked lips. "And isn't that, like, such a coincidence about me and Eloise deciding to partner up? It means you and Shawn can be—"

"Mr. Gilbert has already assigned me a lab partner." Hot-Chick dropped her backpack on the floor and plunked her butt on the stool next to Tyler.

Was it his imagination, or had the whole class gasped with collective shock and the world ground to a halt?

Tyler bit his lip to hide his grin. This new girl was something else. Shawn was many things, but ignored by girls was not one of them. And Bettina? Tyler doubted anyone had dared cut her off since she'd graced the world with her first complete sentence. They were so out of their depth he almost felt sorry for them both. Then again—

Nah. Shawn was a grade-A asshole. And Bettina did a stellar impression of Miss Toxicality. They deserved whatever they got.

The grin slid off Tyler's face. Hot-Chick would soon learn the consequences of not following "The Rules". He wondered how long it would take her to give in to the pressure and conform. And whether he should do the right thing and clue her in that at Greenfield High, dissing Bettina and ignoring Shawn's overtures equaled social suicide. Maybe if he did, she'd be grateful enough not to give him hell if—*when*—she joined Bettina's crew.

"Is your name really Emo-Freak-Boy?" Tyler's totally hot new lab partner asked. "It is a very unusual name."

Hot-Chick either had a weird sense of humor, or she was smart enough to realize the best way to redeem herself in Shawn and Bettina's eyes was to treat Tyler like pond scum.

A lump of disappointment settled in his gut but he managed to force a laugh. "Ah, nope. Just their pathetic idea of a joke."

She cocked her head to one side. "Then you do not listen to emotive hardcore bands, and have lots of kinky sex?"

He gaped at her. "Huh?"

"According to my sources, those are accepted slang definitions of the words 'emo' and 'freak'."

"Explains a lot," Tyler heard Bettina say to Shawn.

He cursed the flush he could feel heating his cheeks. "Not really my scene."

"Oh," she said. "Then why would they call you Emo-Freak-Boy?"

"They call me a lot of stuff—none of it flattering." He bit his tongue before he could clue her in on geek-freak, freakazoid, and a bunch of other unimaginative things he'd been called. Why did he feel so compelled to spill his guts rather than fob her off with an evasion?

Tyler's blush turned into a wave of mortification that spread down his body. Funny how his love of drawing and music—the two things responsible for the "geek" label being added to the list of insults—hadn't been an issue when he'd been a jock at the top of his game.

"Why?" she asked.

"Why?" He scratched his temple. "Uh, it's because I write songs and—"

"*Songs*? That's a stretch. Emo crap no one would be caught dead listening to." Bettina, typically, had made damn sure her "whisper" carried.

Appreciative giggles rippled through the room. Wait for it—

"And don't forget his other little hobby," Shawn said, not to be outdone by his stepsister. "You know what they say: Those who can, *play*. Those who can't, *coach girls*."

"I find it interesting the Raiders haven't won a single match since I left the team," Tyler said, to nobody in particular.

"Since you got booted off the team, you mean," Shawn shot

back.

"Whatever, dude. It's your fairytale world."

Hot-Chick was watching him, head still cocked to one side, a tiny frown pleating her brows. "And?" she said.

"Sorry?"

"You said you write songs *and*. What is the 'and'?"

"Oh. *And* I draw people. Portraits and stuff."

"I do not understand how that makes you a freak, *or* emo," she said, her tone so deadly earnest that she endeared herself to Tyler even more… if that was at all possible.

"Forget it." He plastered a welcoming smile on his face, and hoped she didn't run shrieking from the room. "I'm Tyler Davidson."

"I am pleased to meet you, Tyler. I am Jay Smith."

"Pleased to meet you, too, Jay." He shook her outstretched hand. Her grip was firm. Her skin was on the cool side, and way smooth considering she didn't seem the type to spend a small fortune on fancy skin gunk like Vanessa.

He abruptly realized he was still clasping Jay's hand. He dropped it, and fussed with the sleeves of the old flannel shirt he'd grabbed from his bag, and thrown on to ward off the chill that'd goosed his skin when he spotted the dead frogs. He adjusted the right sleeve by giving it an extra roll. "You, um, English or something?"

"Why do you ask?"

"Just the way you speak. It's kinda formal."

"You are—"

He glanced up in time to witness her grimace. "*You're* very observant, Tyler," she said.

"You all should be finished writing up your introduction, and starting with the dissections now," Mr. Gilbert prompted the class.

Tyler slid his gaze to Shawn and Bettina, who were bickering over who was going to do the honors. Shawn reached for the knife. Tyler's spine prickled. The next few days were likely to be rough. He'd have to watch his back.

"What are we supposed to be doing?" Jay asked. And suddenly Shawn didn't matter anymore because her gaze was so intent, so focused on him, Tyler might have been one of the insects pinned to Mr. Gilbert's display board.

He made a supreme effort to drag some AWOL brain cells out of hiding. "Uh, what're we doing? Uh...." Mental slap upside the head. "Yeah. We're dissecting Kermit."

"Kermit?"

"The frog."

"I see." Jay stared at the dead frog while Tyler stared at her. She was even more gorgeous up close. Perfect, clear skin—even without makeup. And not a single zit in sight.

He fingered the lump on his chin, which felt like it had doubled in size since this morning and was ramping up its quest to be noticed. Great.

"Why must we dissect the frog?" Jay asked.

Good question. "Ummm. To learn about it, I guess."

"Oh?" Her eyebrows arched. "I can think of a number of better methods. Are you going to proceed?"

"Me?" He inched back from the dissection tray. "No way. Uh, there's this rule, see? New kid gets to do the dissections."

"Is that so?"

"Yep." It was worth a shot. Jay seemed unaffected by the gross smell. Maybe she'd be just as unaffected by the even grosser cutting open part.

"Very well." She poked the frog's stomach with her forefinger.

Tyler's stomach twisted.

She picked up the knife and made precise incisions down Kermit's belly and both legs, then carefully peeled back the flaps of skin to expose muscle. "See how developed the muscles are? It is—" She caught her lower lip between her teeth. "*It's* quite impressive."

She began removing said muscle.

Tyler blew out a relieved breath. She really seemed to know what she was doing. He wasn't going to have to hack Kermit up after all. Woot.

"It can be difficult to tell whether a frog is male or female until the organs are removed." Jay probed Kermit's stomach cavity. "The easiest way is to check how many kidneys the specimen has." She lifted up something squishy and slimy and beckoned him closer. "See there? The males have only one."

Tyler screwed up his nose as the stench of dead things hit him. His skin felt clammy beneath his clothes. He heard someone moan. And realized it was him.

The room spun and he clutched his stool.

Oh God. Please don't let me faint this time....

Chapter Three

JAY LAY THE scalpel on the table. She grabbed Tyler's shoulders, steadying him as he wobbled atop his stool. "Are you unwell?" she asked, gorgeous eyes all shiny with concern.

His stomach chose that exact moment to heave.

"Tyler? What is wrong?"

"Gumph!" he said, desperate to warn her that he was going to—

Shee-it. Amazing how much puke came from eating one little apple. Just kill me now. Please?

Tyler wiped his mouth with the back of his hand and seriously considered crawling under the desk and dying. Puking in Bio. How lame was that?

And puking on a *girl*? A thousand times lamer than fainting. He was never going to live this one down.

"God. Jay. I'm so—"

"Nice one!" Bettina didn't sound the slightest bit sorry about Jay being the up-chuck victim. She couldn't have planned it better if she'd actually bribed Tyler to humiliate her potential competition.

Shawn was nothing if not persistent. He materialized beside Jay like he was a mosquito and she was a plump juicy vein.

"Jeez, you poor thing. Look at the mess he's made of you." He leaned toward her, like he was going to brush her down, and then screwed up his face, clothes-pegging his nose with his fingers. But pinching your nostrils isn't a good look when you're trying to suck up to a hot girl. Shawn finally realized that, and removed his hand from his nose to stick it in the pocket of his jeans. Which meant the puke smell got to him again, and caused a repeat of the screwed up face.

Tyler might have found the whole thing highly amusing if *he* hadn't been the one who'd done the puking.

"I'll take you to the bathroom and help you clean up," Shawn pulled himself together enough to say. And the way he said it, all wink-wink nudge-nudge, let's you and me get to know each other better.

Tyler gritted his teeth so hard his jaw ached. Asshole was dating Tyler's *sister*, for crying out loud! It'd be worth the risk of getting expelled. Reeeally worth it.

He clenched his fist, pulled back his elbow and—

He didn't complete the lunge because Jay clamped her hands around his biceps and pushed him back onto his stool, trapping him. She had some impressive "use your opponent's strength against them" mojo going on.

She leaned in to whisper in his ear. "Calm down."

Over her shoulder, Tyler caught Shawn's "you wouldn't freaking dare!" expression and hot-cold-hot relief washed over him. Last thing his mom needed was a call from the principal's office. She'd wig out and ground him for the next ten years. Plus Tyler would be banned from coaching. And his team would hunt him down and kill him… slowly and painfully.

His trembling muscles abruptly relaxed, leaving his limbs noodle-limp. Jay released him, but before he could thank her for saving his butt, she'd waved a hand in the air and attracted Mr.

Gilbert's gimlet eye.

"Back to your seat, Shawn," Mr. Gilbert said.

"But—"

"You're disrupting class. Carry on massacring your frog."

Unlike the other teachers, Mr. Gilbert didn't give a toss that Shawn's daddy was Snapperton's mayor, the self-proclaimed biggest fish in a small pond. Behind the teacher's back, Shawn flipped him off and slunk back to his stool.

Mr. Gilbert puffed up his chest, thrilled by this stellar opportunity to lecture the new student. "How can I help you, Jay? I'm not surprised you're having a bit of trouble, considering you came in after my preliminary talk."

He peered at the dissection tray and his eyebrows turned into bristled peaks of surprise. Leaning closer, he examined the frog's splayed remains. "Nice work! In fact, I can't remember the last time I saw such a neat dissec— Ungh! What *is* that smell?"

Shawn snickered.

Tyler didn't dare glance Shawn's way. That smartass smirk would only make him lose it again, and then Mr. Gilbert would have no choice but to send him to the principal's office. He fisted his hands at his sides. No way was he gonna let Shawn win. Not this time.

"I thought the takeout tasted strange," Jay said.

Tyler appreciated what she was trying to do but her acting skills were dismal. She didn't look the slightest bit like a girl who'd just tossed her cookies.

"Something *you* ate, eh?" Mr. Gilbert's sympathetic gaze drifted to Tyler, and doubtless those were recollections of Tyler's last fainting episode flitting across his face.

"I think it would be best if we got cleaned up now, Mr. Gilbert," Jay said, commanding the teacher's attention again. "Tyler can show me where the bathrooms are."

"Er, good idea." Mr. Gilbert made shooing motions. "Off you go, you two."

Jay grabbed her backpack and Tyler's, too. He snatched it from her grasp. He wasn't so far gone that he needed a girl to carry his stuff.

All eyes followed them as Jay hauled him from his seat, pulled his arm about her waist, and pretended to let him help her from the room. Tyler would normally have refused hers—or anyone's—assistance. Her efforts to shield him wouldn't make any difference once Shawn and Bettina shot their mouths off. But it was hard to give a crap about what a dork he'd made of himself with Jay's body pressed so tight against his.

She felt good there. Like she belonged. And then apple-puke smell wafted from her t-shirt and his stomach rebelled, making him want to heave again.

Jeez. Worst day ever.

Well, maybe not *ever*. The debacle of last year's Homecoming was right up there for sure.

The instant the classroom door clanged shut behind them, Jay laid one cool hand on the back of Tyler's neck.

His nausea abruptly receded. He pulled away from her, sucked in a deep breath and hoped he could keep it light. Because this girl was really doing his head in. The way she made him feel.... It would be real easy to fall hard for her. Too easy. And he didn't trust the power she had over him.

"Hey, sorry about your t-shirt," he said, keeping his voice light and friendly. "And thanks for bailing me out when I lost it back there. You must work out, huh? When you had a hold of my arms I could barely move."

"It is merely a t-shirt," Jay said. "I did not— I didn't think it in your best interests to allow you to take out your frustrations on Shawn, regardless of how irritating he might be. And I'm stronger than I look. How are you feeling now?"

"Duh. Like crap. How else would I be feeling when I just puked over the hot new chick?"

Embarrassment prickled down his spine. God! Had he really said that aloud?

His brain helpfully replayed his last words. Yep. He really had.

Jay gazed at him with those killer blue eyes. A ghost of a smile played on her lips. "I will take that as a compliment."

"You shouldn't have lied to Mr. Gilbert. Not for me."

The assessing look she hit him with made him squirm. "I didn't lie," she said. "The last thing I ate was a leftover takeout meal. And it did not taste as it should."

She was making it really easy to believe she liked him. Too easy.

A girl like Jay shouldn't want to hang with *him*—especially not now, after what he'd done to her. What the hell was her deal?

In Tyler's experience, girls who looked like Jay always had agendas. And even if she was on the level, when she had to deal with the crap the other kids were gonna give her for hanging with him, she'd soon give him the cold shoulder. Best get out before he got screwed over.

"Thanks for everything you tried to do," he said. And walked off without a backward glance, heading for the temporary sanctuary of the guys' bathroom.

TYLER GRIPPED THE edge of the sink and slumped, head hanging, staring at the scuffed linoleum floor, trying to ignore the stomach-churning odor of industrial disinfectant and the rank smell emanating from the urinals.

When he finally dared to look at his reflection in the age-spotted mirror, he winced.

Bad. Real bad. Face white as chalk, big dark smudges under his eyes. Could be worse, he supposed. Caro had caught a stomach bug last year, and thrown up so much she burst a blood vessel in her eye. At least *he* didn't look like some wannabe demon....

Aw, crap. Who was he trying to fool? He didn't look demonic, but he sure did look like death warmed up—and not in a sparkly vamp who makes the girls swoon kinda way, either.

The zit on his chin throbbed and ached. Excellent. It was shaping up to be an abso-freaking-lutely huge one.

He'd rinsed out his mouth, and was reaching for a paper towel when someone appeared behind him. His pulse thrummed. It was Jay. And talk about stepping quietly—he hadn't even heard the door open.

She dropped her pack at her feet. "I am— I'm sorry. I didn't mean to startle you."

Tyler directed his gaze at her reflection, where it was safer. He gnawed on his thumbnail, trying to find the right way to break it to her. "Look. Don't take this the wrong way, 'kay? But you should make tracks. Last thing you need is to hang with me."

Jay yanked off her t-shirt and reached past him to drop it in the sink. "I need to get cleaned up before the next class."

He blinked. Oh. My. God.

His head felt light, skin all warm and tingly. So did his insides. He swallowed and clutched the edge of the sink, trying not to stare at her. Or notice the plain white bra she wore. "Uh, you're um, not supposed to be in here, you know? This is the *guys*' bathroom."

She nudged him aside with her hip so she could turn on the cold water and wash out her top. "Oh, so that's what the picture on the door is supposed to represent. I thought it meant this was the bathroom for people who happened to be wearing trousers."

Huh? Oh. Right. That dry sense of humor again.

"And you're, um, *not*," he managed to say.

"Not what?" She scrubbed at the puke stain.

"Not a guy." He licked suddenly dry lips. Sooo *not* a guy.

"That is a relief." She wrung excess water from her t-shirt. "I would not like to think I'd been laboring under a misapprehension all these years."

He frowned, not following. "Say again?"

"I'm female. I have all the correct parts—to my knowledge, anyway."

"Do you ever," he muttered, and then lost his train of thought completely. It was all that smooth, pale, very feminine bare skin frying his brain. Not that he was truly looking or anything. Just perving at her in the mirror. Which didn't count.

Did it?

Duh. Sure it did.

Jay put her hands behind her back… to the fastening of her bra.

"Stop right there!" He hunched his shoulders as his shout caromed around the bathroom, rebounding off the walls and ceiling until it seemed to be attacking him from all angles. And damned if the bad-guy part of him wasn't secretly regretful that she'd paused and was still clothed. Relatively speaking, of course.

Hey, he was only human.

He sucked in a deep, calming breath. Sort of. "What the *effing hell* do you think you're doing?"

"I would like to wash this bra," she said. "It smells of vomit, which I presume will be offensive to those I encounter throughout the day."

Lord, give me strength! Shawn would be having a field day with this girl right about now. But Tyler didn't get the sense she was deliberately using her feminine wiles to try and whip him into a lust-fueled male frenzy. She sounded matter-of-fact, like the consequences of stripping off in front of a guy—in the guys' bathroom—hadn't even occurred to her.

Hot and very, very, naïve. Not a good combo here at Greenfield High.

Tyler swallowed a few times before he could work up enough saliva to moisten his dry mouth, and speak actual words. "If you take off your bra, it, ah, won't look too good if someone walks in on us. Hell, it already doesn't look too good. Kids talk. Be all over the school in no time flat. You can wear my shirt. It'll be more, er, comfortable than your wet stuff."

Her gaze drifted from his face to the worn, checked flannel shirt he'd discovered shoved in back of his dad's closet. It was hardly the height of fashion. No surprise his dad had left it behind when he took off.

Jay cocked her head to one side. "Why would you give me your shirt?"

"You can't wear a wet t-shirt. People will get the wrong idea."

Silence.

She was staring at him, gauging his every reaction minutely. He didn't mind. He felt warm all over, like his own personal sun had just risen overhead.

"Thank you," she said. "I would appreciate your shirt. I do not— I *don't* wish to draw attention to myself."

"Yeah. Know the feeling." Tyler shucked the shirt and handed it to Jay, feeling strangely bare despite the faded "Toxic Hazard" t-shirt he still wore. "You wash, uh, *whatever* you have to wash. And I'll guard the door—make sure no one wanders in. But make it quick, okay? Our luck won't hold forever."

He turned his back and wedged his hip against the door. He heard the groan of faucets spewing water and the rip of paper towels being yanked from the dispenser. He closed his eyes against the temptation that was Jay, determined not to get all hot and bothered by images of her drool-worthy toned body. Or her pale, blemish-free skin, that didn't have a single freckle or mole that he could see. His thoughts skittered about like crazy things and finally centered on her face. Specifically, her mouth… and what it would be like to kiss her.

What would her lips feel like? Would they be cool and silky-smooth, like her skin?

Someone pushed on the door, yanking Tyler from his fantasies of locking lips and making out with Jay. He braced himself and leaned on it, blocking whoever it was from entering. "Get lost," he growled, and was relieved to hear the guy swear and head for the second floor bathroom.

"I'm done," Jay said, her voice so close to his ear that she had to be standing right behind him.

He turned. Thankfully, she was decent. So decent, in fact, she looked like a hick.

Oh boy. No way could he leave her to the tender mercies of the Greenfield High fashion police. "Uh, can I make a suggestion?"

"Of course."

"You need to undo a few of those top buttons."

"Why?"

"So you don't look so… so…."

He chewed his lip, searching for the right words. Epic fail.

"Buttoned up," he finally said.

She processed that, nodded, and undid the top two buttons.

"One more," he said.

"Is that truly necessary?"

"Yeah." He waited for her to slip the button. "And maybe if you tie the shirttails at your waist."

"Show me."

He did, and hoped she didn't notice his hands shaking whenever he brushed the bare skin of her stomach.

"Better?"

"Oh yeah." It came out all hoarse and again he had to fight the flush that threatened to telegraph how much she affected him.

He cleared his throat and stepped back. "Much better. As Caro would say, now you're wearing the clothes, the clothes aren't wearing you. You're making a statement."

Jay balled up her wet clothes and sank to her haunches to shove them in a side pocket of her pack. "Caro is your sister, correct?"

Tyler had caught a flash of white amongst the bundle. He tore his mind away from the realization she was now braless. "Uh, yeah. Caro and Shawn are kind of an item."

She stared up at him, her head cocked to one side in that cute-as way she had. "Why do you feel compelled to tell me this?"

Why, indeed. Sheesh. He had to quit with this whole blushing thing. It was becoming a habit. "Because she's my sister. And I don't want her getting hurt if you make a play for Shawn, and he dumps her."

Jay straightened in one smooth, graceful movement, and lounged back against the sink, arms crossed over her chest, feet at the ankles. In direct contrast to Shawn's attempt this morning, Jay owned the pose.

"Is that the only reason?" she asked.

His breath hitched. Damn, she was hot.

And so obviously still waiting for his response. "Okay, okay. You got me. Shawn's a douche. And you deserve better."

"What makes you think I deserve better?"

He gazed past her, focusing on the graffitied stall doors, carefully choosing his words. "Look. I used to be one of Shawn's crew. And I was probably a supreme asshole, too. Just like him." He shrugged. "Goes with the territory. I even had a cheerleader girlfriend. I was a walking cliché until I caught her— Well, anyway. Bad stuff went down and Shawn was in on it. You don't want to get involved with him. In an ideal world, my sister wouldn't be involved with him, either. And believe me, you don't want to get caught in the crossfire if Caro finds out he's been hitting on you."

"You're concerned I might get hurt, too."

"Yeah."

"You don't know me. Why should my wellbeing concern you?"

Gah! Did the girl not understand guy-talking-to-hot-chick subtext? She was gonna make him come right out and say it.

But before he could make a complete dumbass of himself, Jay nodded slowly, like she'd finally understood what he was trying not to say.

Tyler sagged with relief, because once he admitted how he felt about her, there was no taking it back. And if he'd read her wrong, and she wasn't into him—wasn't doing anything more than being "nice" to a guy she felt sorry for—he'd be gutted.

When she didn't say anything more, he slanted her an assessing glance. But he couldn't tell what she was thinking at all—not the merest hint.

Weird.

Tyler had become pretty good at reading people's faces. It was a skill he'd perfected, a skill that helped him get by in this clichéd little corner of hell where the jocks and the cheer squad ruled. He knew how to get by without a bunch of peeps to watch his back. He knew when he could get away with mouthing off. Just like he knew when to shut up, suck it up and do a disappearing act. He had it down to a fine art.

The silence stretched.

Tyler's hopes wound tight, strangling him. What was he thinking, falling for a girl he'd just met?

Jeez. He *was* a dumbass. He'd played right into her hands. Any moment now, she'd slink back to Shawn and this whole pathetic little episode would be all over school.

Except she stayed right where she was, her whole focus on him.

There was a light in her eyes that made his gut clench—in a good way. When he inhaled, she was standing so very close that her scent curled through him. His eyelids drifted closed.... And then, layered beneath her fresh, clean smell was something indefinable, something that made his heart clamor. The merest hint of strangeness.

Tyler's eyelids popped open. His gaze locked on hers.

Those remarkable eyes held his, unblinking. Unwavering.

He saw it then, got the feeling she deliberately let him see it. Jay had secrets. Like Tyler did. And he didn't move at all, not a muscle, as she rose up on tiptoes to press her lips against his.

Jay's kiss was excruciatingly gentle, a butterfly kiss, the merest brush of her lips against his before she backed off and considered him through narrowed eyes.

"What's wrong?" he whispered.

"That must be painful." She pressed the pad of her finger to her lips and then stroked it lightly across the spot on his chin.

She was gone as quickly and noiselessly as she'd come, leaving Tyler's face glowing from her attentions. And his heart aglow with something else—something he'd never felt for a girl before. Something more than just a little scary.

Chapter Four

Jay exited the classroom after last period, and allowed herself to be swept up in the rush of kids heading for their lockers to ditch their books.

Her most challenging lesson today had been learning how best to project mediocrity. Unfortunately, nothing in her construction or programming had prepared her for mediocrity, and she'd come perilously close to standing out from the crowd in second period Mathematics.

After observing her classmates' reactions when she'd voiced but a minute portion of her extensive knowledge, she deemed it prudent to pretend she'd merely made a few lucky guesses. The next time she'd been called upon by the teacher, she'd shrugged and appeared confused. The time after that, she'd asked the teacher to repeat the question, and then given an incorrect answer. As the day had progressed, she was satisfied she'd gotten the hang of revealing enough knowledge to convince the teachers she was a good student, while convincing her classmates she was not especially gifted.

An anomaly in the way the crowd was moving demanded Jay's attention. She spotted a couple of girls standing whispering, forcing students to fan out to avoid them. The first girl held herself stiffly, muscles tensed and jaw working. Flags of crimson painted her cheekbones. She had auburn hair cut into a sharp chin-length bob. She wore black leggings and a deep purple scoop-neck tunic, belted at the waist with a gold cord. Her lip tint matched the gold cord. So did her low-heeled sandals. Glued to her side was a girl whose t-shirt was very tight, and whose red shorts were shorter than any other shorts Jay had seen on a female student.

Jay dismissed them and opened her locker.

Purple Tunic Girl marched up to her and said, "First and last warning, sweetie. Keep your paws off my boyfriend."

Jay swept her gaze over the girl, analyzing her bone structure, facial features, and mannerisms. "Hello, Caro," she said, in a pleasant, conversational tone. "I wondered how long it would take you to introduce yourself."

Caro's companion took that statement as a signal to take matters into her own hands. Jay noted the indicators and tensed her stomach muscles in preparation. When the blow came, it was hard enough that if Jay had been a fragile human female, it would have caused a substantial bruise.

Amidst gasps of "Omigod, did you see that?" from kids who'd witnessed the gesture, Jay heard her attacker inhaling with a hiss that indicated pain. She didn't bother to verify how badly the girl might have injured her hand. The girl's pain was not Jay's concern. She was only interested in gauging Caro's reaction to her friend's behavior.

Caro's jaw sagged. "Vanessa!"

From the strangled tone of Caro's voice and her horrified expression, Jay guessed Vanessa's actions had been unexpected, shocking. Apparently Tyler's sister preferred to intimidate with words rather than actions. That was useful to know. Jay switched her full attention back to the girl who'd hit her.

Vanessa flexed her fingers, and as the girl blinked back tears, Jay noted her pupils were abnormally dilated. Abuse of pharmaceuticals would certainly explain Vanessa's misplaced aggression. "You should go now," Jay said to her. "This is none of your concern."

The girl's pink-slicked lips curled into a sneer. "Is that so?"

Jay dulled the hue of her irises, leaching the color until the intense azure faded to a flat, cold, gunmetal gray. She'd done this before to good effect. She couldn't permanently alter her eye color, but she'd discovered that even a brief, temporary alteration unnerved people.

She took a step toward Vanessa. And another. The girl swallowed another whimper, of fear rather than pain this time, and backed off.

"Hey!"

Tyler's sister grabbed Jay's arm. Jay remembered just in time she was supposed to be a "normal" girl, and allowed herself to be dragged around to face Caro. She wasn't programmed to remain passive when someone attacked her, but these sharp little impulses flicking beneath her skin, urging her to retaliate, weren't usual. She ignored them. She wasn't hurt and nor was she in danger. There was no reason to act on those impulses.

Caro raked her gaze over Jay's attire, lingering on the borrowed flannel shirt. A frown puckered her brows, and her eyes narrowed to slits.

The odds that Caro recognized the shirt were high. It would be interesting to note how Caro reacted if she realized the shirt was her brother's, and that he'd loaned it to the new girl who supposedly had designs on Caro's boyfriend.

Shawn, too, had surprised Jay with his observational skills. The very next time he'd seen her, he had immediately recognized the shirt and made the connection with Tyler. His lips had flattened into a tight white line, and he'd made a derogatory comment about Jay's borrowed attire.

As the school day had progressed, Shawn insisted on sitting next to her wherever possible, and continually slipped disparaging remarks about Tyler into the conversation. Jay had finally realized the remarks were because Shawn was angry.

A knot formed in her stomach at the mere thought of Tyler being harassed by Shawn and his cohorts. Tyler had done nothing wrong. He didn't deserve to be punished for being kind, and worrying about her wellbeing.

"I'll say this in plain English so even you can understand," Caro was saying. "Stay away from Shawn, or I'm gonna make you very sorry."

Jay didn't bother responding to Caro's outlandish claim. But Shawn was another matter, an irritation she would happily be rid of. She'd very politely asked him to please stop bothering her, but apparently Shawn was not intelligent enough to understand her request. And Caro appeared to hold Shawn blameless for his actions, placing the fault squarely on Jay, whose only crime was being the unwilling object of Shawn's attention. It made no sense. She'd actively discouraged him. Perhaps being completely honest with Caro would bring about the desired result.

"You have nothing to worry about so far as Shawn is concerned," she said. "I have no interest in him. In fact, after suffering his attentions at the office this morning, and during three classes today, I find myself in total agreement with your brother. Shawn is a douche. And you deserve better."

Caro blinked at her. Her lips twitched. "Speaking of my brother, I heard what happened in Bio. Thanks for looking out for him."

They were statements, not questions, so Jay remained silent.

"He loaned you his shirt, didn't he?" Caro probed.

Jay didn't see any reason to prevaricate. "Yes. I washed out my t-shirt and he was concerned about me wearing a wet top. It was very kind of him to loan me his shirt."

"Yep. Sounds like Tyler, all right—the whole give you the shirt off his back thing, I mean. Hey, it looks way better on you than it did on him, anyway."

Jay glanced down at her shirtfront. "Thank you. Tyler tied the shirt in this fashion. He seemed to think it looked more attractive this way."

Caro's lip-twitching became more pronounced. If she wasn't careful, it might morph into a smile.

Behind Jay, Vanessa uttered a strangled-sounding gargle, and took advantage of Jay's apparent inattention to grab a handful of her hair.

"Cat-fight!" someone yelled.

The kids milling around in the corridor found a common purpose. They pushed and shoved, trying to get closer so they didn't miss out on the promised entertainment.

"What the hell do you think you're doing, Vanessa?" Caro squawked, and then turned to elbow someone who'd jostled her. "Hey! Back off, jerk-face!"

Vanessa yanked harder on her handful of Jay's hair and in response, Jay arched her back until she had an excellent view of the stained, gray ceiling tiles. Having her hair pulled didn't bother Jay. She could have resisted and left Vanessa with a hank of hair as a trophy. Sure, Jay would have had a bald patch on her scalp, but the missing hair would soon re-grow. What bothered Jay right now was that her current position restricted the scope of her vision.

It was time to rectify the situation—without loss of hair. She arched backward in a gymnastics-style bridge, hands reaching for the floor.

The unexpectedness of her actions startled Vanessa into a shocked shriek, and she released Jay's hair to scramble backward.

Jay's hands contacted with the floor. She kicked up to balance on her hands, and resisted the instinctive desire to lash out at Vanessa with her feet. The girl was not a true threat and there was no need to disable her.

For five seconds, Jay remained upside down, balanced on her hands, her body arrow-straight with feet in the air and toes pointed, giving those nearby the opportunity to get clear before she bent her elbows, abruptly straightened them and pushed off with her hands to bounce upright.

"Shee-it!" someone said. "Nice moves."

Before Vanessa could react to this new development, Jay snaked out her hand and grasped Vanessa's wrist. She pulled the girl toward her until they were face-to-face. "What is your issue with me, Vanessa? I've done nothing to you. I told Caro I have no interest in Shawn. There was no reason for you to attack me again. I am inclined to conclude you are either—" she sought the correct slang term "—*high*, or that you have feelings for Tyler and you are jealous that he helped me."

Vanessa's heavily made-up cheeks flushed with uneven blotches that crawled down her neck. "Me, high? That's rich!" Her gaze slid sideways. When she met Caro's raised eyebrows, she flinched and ducked her head, and then tried to pull from Jay's grasp.

Jay held on to Vanessa's wrist, ignoring her pathetic struggles. She gazed at the students who'd gathered, clearly expecting more entertainment. After selecting what seemed to be the most appropriate response, she twisted her face into a sneer. "Go away. There's nothing more to see here."

Staring students suddenly found more interesting things to concern themselves with.

Excellent. Practicing her facial expressions in the mirror had achieved the desired results.

When they were no longer the center of attention, and the noise level in the hallway had resumed its usual boisterous levels, Caro confronted Jay. "Look. I'm really sorry about this. It wasn't supposed to get physical. I just wanted to warn you off Shawn."

The tight strain in Caro's voice was congruent with her overly wide, worried eyes. Jay calibrated Caro's non-verbal physical responses and concluded she meant every word.

"Your apology is accepted," Jay said. Her gaze cut to Vanessa. "I'm still waiting for yours."

"Sorry," Vanessa muttered, tugging on her wrist to free herself from Jay's grip, and sounding anything but apologetic.

For some reason that Jay couldn't define, Vanessa's rudeness irritated her as much as Shawn's persistence. She waited until Vanessa threw her weight backward in an attempt to free herself again, and without warning, released the girl's wrist.

Vanessa overbalanced and landed on her butt, legs sprawled, mouth hanging open in disbelief.

A bunch of kids who'd witnessed the incident snickered and whispered to each other. Vanessa's face turned a shade of red that almost matched her shorts.

"Sorry," Jay said, matching Vanessa's tone exactly. She slammed the door of her locker and walked off, leaving Caro to deal with her companion in whatever way she chose.

"Skanky bitch!" Jay heard Vanessa say.

"You had it coming, Nessa," came Caro's response. "You're

real lucky she didn't smack you a good one after what you pulled. Look, we've got practice and you need to get your head in the game. You know what Bettina's like. She'll drop you from the squad if you screw up again. We'll talk about this later, 'kay?"

"Whatever."

Jay's lips curved. Yes, Vanessa had deserved "it". And strangely enough, her confrontation with Vanessa had eased the hollow feeling in her belly.

She'd endured this strange feeling since eavesdropping on Tyler in the music room at lunchtime. Unseen and unnoticed, Jay had lurked outside the room, spellbound by the guitar riffs spilling from the gap beneath the closed door.

The ability to create a song or an instrumental piece was one of the rare human abilities Jay could not mimic. She could play any instrument, competently recite any piece of music after hearing it only once, but it was beyond her abilities to create anything new. Tyler's music, his voice, and the words he'd sung.... The combination had been raw and powerful. Haunting.

I wake in the dead of night,
And you're not there.
I call your name,
But there's no answer.
You're gone,
Half of what I am is yours.
And I'm lost without you....

As Jay had listened, a vast emptiness had welled up inside her. Logic dictated the hollow feeling was merely a result of her body's requirement for sufficient sustenance. However, eating a snack from a dispensing machine outside the cafeteria had done little to dispel it. She did not comprehend how mere words put to music could have a physical effect on her.... Or why physically bettering an opponent could help alleviate the symptoms. It bore further investigation.

She pushed through the exit doors, blinking once to accustom her eyesight to the brightness after the gloom of the poorly lit corridor. As she cut through the car park, she noticed Tyler lurking amongst the bunch of students who had congregated in the bus bay. She suspected from the stiffening of his posture that he'd spotted her, but was pretending he hadn't.

This must be what was meant by "playing it cool".

Jay didn't understand how to reciprocate, how to project "coolness" in return. Had kissing Tyler this morning been playing it cool?

She didn't know.

She *did* know it had been uncharacteristic, acting on an impulse that had surged through her body and hijacked her brain. Like now, when her arm, seemingly of its own volition, lifted to acknowledge him with a wave.

Tyler waved back.

Jay felt a wave of heat wash over her, forcing her to adjust her core body temperature. She mulled this new anomaly as she waited for the traffic to clear so she could cross the street. When she got back to her apartment, she would run a full diagnostic to discover the root cause of these minor malfunctions.

"Hey, Tyler! Can you spare a minute?"

The shout prompted Jay to glance over her shoulder. She saw a man beckoning from the open window of a classroom, prompting Tyler to jog back toward the entrance doors.

Jay mentally shuffled through the staff photos and identified the man as the school's music teacher, Mr. Whaley. If she waited around for a while, perhaps she could strike up a conversation with Tyler when he'd finished with the teacher. It would be interesting to learn more about his musical abilities.

Bettina's strident voice floated up from the field, haranguing Caro and Vanessa for being five minutes late to practice. Jay drifted over to observe the cheerleaders from the shadows afforded by the overhanging roof of the school hall.

A bunch of guys sauntered over to plant their butts on the bleachers, and ogle the girls in their short skirts. One of them puckered up and blew a noisy kiss at Bettina. "Hey, B! Shake it for me, baby!"

Bettina tossed an evil look over her shoulder. "Get lost," she told him. "And quit gawking at the guy-candy!" she yelled at those of her squad who had dared to giggle. "Next girl who effs up because her mind's not on the routine is getting benched!"

It was obvious that Bettina took her job as cheer captain very seriously.

Jay watched the squad run once through their routine and then turned away. She could do the tricks with her eyes closed. Not that she didn't appreciate the difficulty and the skill involved for humans to perform such maneuvers, but it held no particular fascination for her.

All the buses had arrived and departed before Tyler appeared again. He surveyed the empty bus bay, glanced at his watch. His shoulders slumped.

Jay jogged toward him as he headed out the school gates.

Tyler's head shot up when he heard her approach, and in the instant before he blanked his expression she saw pleasure. "May I walk with you?" she asked.

"Sure. I'm headed this way." He jerked his chin to the left.

"I'm sorry you missed your bus."

He shrugged. "No drama."

"That teacher inconvenienced you. He should have spoken to you during school hours so you didn't miss your bus."

A snort. "Teachers don't think about stuff like that."

"You're not in trouble with him, are you?"

"Me? Nah. Whaley's cool. He was just giving me some feedback about my latest songwriting attempt."

They walked in silence for a few minutes, with Tyler shooting her surreptitious glances beneath his lashes. "I hear Shawn's still bugging you," he finally said.

Jay didn't have to remind herself that a grimace would be appropriate in this instance. It was her body's automatic response to mention of Shawn. "I asked him very politely to leave me alone, but I suspect he thinks I'm playing hard to get. His lack of intelligence is extremely vexing." Even to her own ears she sounded petulant.

Tyler barked a laugh. "You're something else, you know that?"

She clamped her mouth shut against the immediate agreement that hovered on her lips. She was indeed "something else". But she was training herself to decipher the subtext of what was said before she responded, rather than taking people's comments so literally.

"You really don't like him much, do you?" Tyler seemed to have some difficulty with the idea that any girl could dislike Shawn.

Jay couldn't decipher what it was about Shawn that made him so attractive to the opposite sex. So far as appearances went, he was merely one of a number of physically attractive young males she had encountered. His features were symmetrical enough to be pleasing, but his lack of morals, and his inflated idea of his own importance and desirability, repelled her. She found Tyler's lean physique, shaggy hair, chocolate-brown eyes, and slightly crooked smile, far more aesthetically pleasing. Tyler wasn't perfect, and it was his imperfections that captivated her. In addition, he was far more interesting to talk to than the self-involved Shawn.

"No. I don't like him at all," she said. "Can we please not talk about Shawn?"

"What do you want to talk about, then?"

"I heard you playing your guitar and singing at lunchtime," she said. "You're very talented."

"Thanks." He beamed at her, and something tightened in Jay's chest, making it difficult for her to breathe.

"It wasn't my guitar, though," he said. "That one belongs to the music room. It's a bit of a dog but it does the trick. My own guitar's worth a bit—no way I'd bring it to school and risk it being damaged."

Jay nodded her understanding.

"Hey, do you play an instrument or anything?"

Because she did not wish to appear boastful, she shrugged, and said, "Not really."

Car tires squealed and the acrid odor of burning rubber scented the air. Laughter floated to Jay's ears. She separated out the sounds, identified the vehicle's engine as belonging to a Mazda MX-5 Miata, and ran voice analyses. A simple calculation led her to conclude she would be subjected to an unwelcome encounter in approximately thirty-five seconds.

Just as she and Tyler neared a small group of stores, a red MX-5 rounded the corner and pulled up to the curb ahead of them.

Jay hadn't miscalculated. But then, she seldom did.

"Hey, Jaaay." Shawn called out from the driver's seat, completely ignoring Tyler.

She didn't appreciate the way he drew out the syllables of her name. Her name was Jay. Not Jaaay. If she'd wanted to be called Jaaay, she would have spelled her name with extra As.

"Hello, Shawn." She ignored her programming and did not acknowledge his companion. It was getting easier to be rude and unpleasant if the situation called for it.

"Going somewhere?" Shawn's gaze flicked to his reflection in the rearview mirror. He smoothed his hair.

Jay kept on walking. "I would have thought that was quite obvious, but since you ask, yes."

Tyler emitted a peculiar gurgling sound and cleared his throat.

"Hey, wait up, babe!" Shawn called as they passed his car. He shoved the vehicle in gear and crept along the curb, keeping pace. His smile displayed his artificially whitened capped teeth. "Hop in, I'll give you a lift."

"I don't need a lift. And if I did, there are no spare seats in your car."

The boy sitting up front with Shawn dropped Jay a wink. His lips curved into a sly smile and he patted his lap. "Babe, you can sit right here on this good wood."

"Can it, Matt," Shawn said. "If she's sitting on anyone it'll be me. Capiche?"

Matt smirked. "Whatever, dude."

"Niiice," Tyler said, directing his comment to Shawn. "Caro's gonna be thrilled to hear you're making moves on Jay. Again. I'd watch my back if I were you, Shawn. You know what my sister's like when she gets riled. I can just picture her bitch-slapping you into orbit. Hey, I should sell tickets to the event. I'd make a killing."

Shawn slammed his car into park. He hopped out to confront Tyler, hands fisted at his sides, lower lip outthrust. "What I do when your sister isn't looking over my shoulder is none of your fucking business, freak-boy. So keep your effing mouth shut. Or I'll shut it for you."

Jay clamped her hand on Tyler's arm to prevent him lunging at Shawn. "Let me handle this," she murmured. "Apparently I'm going to have to be extremely unpleasant so he will finally get the message."

Tyler's brow pleated as his gaze raked her face. "You sure?"

"I'm sure." She felt a peculiar warmth curling low in her belly. If she'd been human, that warmth might have indicated she enjoyed his concern for her. She dismissed it as a chemical reaction preparing her body for the coming confrontation with Shawn.

"Okay. But I'm here if you need me," he said.

"Thank you. I appreciate that."

Jay moved toward Shawn, who leaned against his car and crossed his arms over his chest. He smiled lazily at her.

Did this young male truly believe himself so irresistible to females?

Apparently so. He was obviously convinced his physical charms had the power to completely overwhelm her good sense. The boy was an idiot.

"So how 'bout you and me hook up later on?" Shawn said. "Pick you up at nine and—"

"I don't think so."

Shawn blinked at her. "Aw, don't be like that, babe. This playing hard to get thing is getting old."

His tone was light, bantering, but his gaze was challenging.

You don't want to mess with me, it seemed to say. Delusional boy. She was going to enjoy thwarting him.

He reached for her.

Ignoring Tyler's shout of protest, Jay let Shawn grab her wrist and tug her toward him. As Shawn bent his head, she realized he was about to kiss her—force her to comply with his wishes. She grasped his chin in her hand and dulled her eyes so her gaze was flat and cold and menacing. "Are you trying to shut *my* effing mouth now, Shawn?"

He froze. The cocky grin slid from his face.

She thrust him away and stared him down. "I would rather not be bothered by two-timing sleaze-bags, Shawn. For some reason they nauseate me."

Behind her, Tyler snorted with laughter.

"Bitch." Shawn's expression darkened. He raised his hand as if to hit her, but seemed to think better of it and dropped his arm.

He was on edge, his heart rate elevated, a pulse throbbing at his temple. It would not take much to provoke him.

Jay reviewed what she knew about Shawn and his family, and debated her options. If he did lose his temper and hit her, there was a high probability it would work in her favor. When it got around that he had hit a girl, Shawn's godlike reputation amongst the students—both male and female—would take a severe hit.

She released the merest whiff of a very specific pheromone into the air and watched Shawn inhale. A fine sweat broke out on his forehead. His fists clenched and unclenched, clenched again.

"You're such a daddy's boy," she said, curling her lip into a sneer. "Without his money to throw around, you're nothing special, Shawn. You should hear what your team says about you behind your back."

His nostrils flared and his eyes narrowed to slits. "What do they say?"

Yes. She'd been correct to base her verbal attack on his male pride. This was going to be ludicrously easy. "Only that your daddy bought your place on the team with a hefty donation. It must be a real blow to your pride to know you wouldn't have been good enough otherwise."

"Jay." Tyler's voice throbbed with anxiety. "I don't think—"

"I'm fine, Tyler." She swept her glance over Shawn. "He's nothing I can't handle."

Shawn's tanned complexion turned a mottled red.

Jay laughed, and made certain it was a derisive, mocking sound. "Poor Shawn. Did I hurt your feelings? Never mind. I'm sure you'll get over it. Oh, and I almost forgot to mention that Caro and I had an enlightening little chat this afternoon. I'm sure it won't take much more effort on my part to convince her to dump your less-than-toned glutes."

Shawn frowned as he processed that last part.

"Are you saying—?"

"Yes, Shawn. You have a—" she sought the most suitable slang phrase "—flabby ass."

He lost it.

Of course Jay saw the blow coming, but she chose not to exert herself by blocking it. Whatever Shawn did to her, it was highly unlikely to cause permanent damage. The logic that had led to this moment was perfectly sound, so she stood perfectly still, relaxed her facial muscles, and allowed his hand to connect with her cheek.

"Jesus!" Matt's shocked voice shattered the silence.

Excellent. Her decision was already having the desired effect.

Unfortunately, Tyler wasn't aware that Jay didn't feel pain as humans did. Or that she had weighed her options and concluded it was in her best interests to let Shawn assault her. Before she could caution him to stay out of it, Tyler grabbed her arm and yanked her from further harm. Then he charged Shawn, smacking him against the side of the car.

Shawn bellowed and retaliated by first shoving Tyler away, then lunging for him, grabbing him around the waist and steamrolling him backward.

Jay was still considering whether or not Tyler would be irritated if she intervened, when she caught a metallic flash at the edge of her vision. She glanced at Matt and found him recording the incident on a sleek black mobile phone.

"Please put the phone away. Now." She refocused her attention on the two combatants.

"You okay?" Matt asked. "There's a spare seat here if you need to sit down. Do you want me to call someone to come get you?"

She kept her gaze on Tyler and Shawn as she answered. "Yes, I'm okay. No, I don't need to sit down. No, I don't want you to call anyone. Thank you for asking, though. The phone, Matt."

He was silent. When she glanced again at him to confirm he'd stopped videoing the fight, Matt had lowered the phone, and was staring at her like he expected her to be doing something other than what she was currently doing. The trouble was, Jay had no idea what that something might be.

"Sure you're okay?" he finally asked. "You're not gonna faint or anything, are you?"

"Yes, I'm sure. No, I'm not going to faint. Or anything."

His frown smacked of disbelief. "Shit. I can actually see a handprint on your cheek. I'm guessing he didn't hold back, huh?"

"He could have punched me, so I believe he did hold back to

some degree. And the mark will fade soon."

"You're one tough chick."

"Yes."

"Better ice it when you get a chance," he told her. "It'll help with the bruising."

"Thank you for the advice. Aren't you going to Shawn's aid?" If Matt chose that course of action, Jay would take steps to stop him. Two against one was patently unfair.

He shrugged and stuck his feet up on the dash. "Nah. Shawn and Tyler have some major history, so this was always gonna happen. And between you and me, I hope Tyler manages a few good punches before he gets creamed. Shawn deserves to get the hurt put on him."

"Why does Shawn deserve it?" she asked. "Isn't he your friend?"

Matt's lips compressed and the residual humor faded from his eyes. "Lately, that's up for debate. And guys just don't hit girls, okay?"

"Is it okay for girls to hit guys?"

He eyed her, his gaze speculative, gauging the seriousness of her question. "After what that asshole did to you? Duh. Absofricking-lutely."

"Thank you. I wasn't sure of the protocol in a situation like this."

She heard Matt mutter, "This I gotta see," as she turned her gaze back to Tyler and Shawn.

She observed the fight for a moment. Shawn's heavier body mass was proving problematic for Tyler. He did manage to hook one of Shawn's ankles with a sweep of his foot and topple him to the ground, but when he pounced on him, Shawn bucked him off and rolled, switching their positions.

Shawn's triumphant expression morphed into something dark and ugly. He drew back his elbow, fist clenched.

This would be a prudent time to intervene. Jay liked Tyler's face the way it was, and she would not appreciate Shawn rearranging it. She didn't bother to check her speed. She leaped toward Shawn and grabbed his wrist. In one smooth, rapid movement, she rotated his arm to twist it up behind his back.

"Bitch," he said, struggling ineffectually and hissing when she increased the pressure on his shoulder joint. "Get off me. You want another smack or something?"

"Please," she said. "Do try."

"Fine. I'll get to you when I've finished with the freak."

"In your dreams!" Tyler said, his face tight with determination as he bucked his hips, trying to dislodge Shawn. "You lay a hand on her again and I'm gonna—"

"You're gonna what?" Shawn said. "Sing me a song?"

Jay's vision washed with a bloody red haze that she identified as adrenaline-fueled fury. Humans called this phenomenon bloodlust, or "seeing red". And it was oh-so-very tempting to give in to it.

But at some level, she understood she was defective. There was something profoundly wrong with her. She'd been programmed to defend herself if threatened, but she was not in any danger whatsoever. As much as she might wish it otherwise at this particular instant, her programming did not extend to tearing Shawn limb from limb, or even smashing his face with a clenched fist and ruining the good looks of which he was so very proud. This encounter should not be affecting her in such a way. This annoying, foul-mouthed, *boy* should not have the power to influence her actions. This desire she had to punish him, to exact revenge for his treatment of Tyler, was wrong.

She was malfunctioning, and the consequences of giving in to her rage could be dire.

Jay caged her fury and smothered it with logic. And logic told her the most efficient way to be rid of Shawn's attentions, was to humiliate him enough that he avoided her in future.

She increased the upward pressure on his wrist and shoulder joint, ignoring his vile curses as the pain and the threatened dislocation of his shoulder forced him to abandon Tyler and rise to his feet.

After a brief scan of her surroundings, Jay discounted the trashcans placed beside the bus stop. There was no reason to damage public property.

The dumpster out back of the Chinese takeout? Perfect. She marched Shawn toward it on his tiptoes.

"Hey, Matt!" Shawn yelled, his voice squeaky with growing panic. "Dude, some help, here?"

"She's only a girl," Matt called back. "I'm sure she won't hurt you too bad."

Jay gripped Shawn by scruff of his neck and the waistband of his designer jeans, and tossed him into the dumpster. He landed with a muffled squawk of disbelief and an immensely satisfying *squelch*, signaling that his landing had been cushioned by rubbish sacks full of discarded food scraps.

She sniffed the air. Plastic rubbish sacks by the smell of them. Along with the garbage, they would have contained a higher than normal percentage of air, meaning Shawn would have enjoyed a far more comfortable landing than he deserved.

When she turned back to see how Tyler was faring, she found him staring at her, open-mouthed.

She cut her gaze to Matt.

He, too, gave her stunned eyes. "Uh, nice trick," he said.

Oh. Apparently girls weren't supposed to be able to toss boys into dumpsters. "It's all in the thighs," she said. "Taking out the trash has always been one of my chores."

Tyler's lips twitched upward.

"Did Shawn hurt you?" Jay asked, noting his scraped skin and the bruises that were beginning to form.

"Nah. It's nothing. What about you?"

"I'm fine."

He shook off his shock and dusted down his clothes. "Then let's go, before the trash gets its shit together and crawls out of that dumpster."

Chapter Five

All Tyler could think about was Jay. She was doing his head in. He stared at the lyrics he'd scrawled on his sheet music pad.

Thoughts of you glowing in my heart,
Thoughts of you shining in my soul,
Thoughts of you blazing in my mind,
Thoughts of you, burning.
Thoughts of you,
Burn.

Sheesh. It read like a sappy romance novel. He crumpled the page and tossed it at the trashcan. Then he stuck his guitar back in its case and dragged out his sketchbook. But instead of the graphics project he was supposed to be working on, he found himself sketching Jay's face.

Crap. He had it bad. Real bad.

He closed the sketchbook and grabbed his Bio textbook. And he was still lounging on his bed, pretending to study, when he heard the front door slam.

There was the usual delay while Caro grabbed a snack from the refrigerator, before Tyler heard her footsteps on the stairs.

She was a stomach on legs but she never seemed to put on weight, and her freakish metabolism was the envy of her friends. He waited for her to explode through his bedroom door without so much as a knock, and stick him with some smartass comment. Like she always did.

Wait for it....

The door smacked into the wall with a sickening crunch. "Heard you puked all over the new girl in Bio. Way to go, bro!" Caro stuck her hand palm out, as if expecting to be high-fived.

"Yeah. Thanks." He ignored the gesture and changed the subject to the raw scrape decorating his sister's cheek. "Lemme guess, you tripped over your own two feet and fell on your face during practice?"

"Haha. Very funny. Ashlee clocked me with her heel. She's such a klutz. What's your excuse?" She stared pointedly at his scrapes and bruises. When he didn't rise to the bait she said, "So. Losing your breakfast in Bio. Bet that got her attention, huh?"

"Yeah. Riiight. Puking all over chicks works like a charm. They find it irresistible." He rolled onto his stomach and pretended to be absorbed in the textbook.

Caro snickered, and in a singsong voice said, "You've got it bad for her."

"Don't be daft."

"The way I heard it, she's got it bad for you, too. So bad—" big ole pause for effect "—she treated you to a striptease in the bathroom."

Unease iced Tyler's spine. He'd avoided the social minefield of the cafeteria by hiding out in the music room. Then he'd cut last period English and headed for the library. He'd hoped making himself scarce would dampen the gossip.

Obviously not.

He leveled what he hoped was a nonchalant look at his sister. "Jeezus. I loaned her my shirt so she had something clean to wear. What the hell's wrong with that? And who's doing the mouthing off?"

She gave him "Well, duh!" eyes. "The usual suspects. And you think *that's* bad, you should hear what else the squad are saying about you two."

Tyler gave up on the textbook and turned on his side to better observe his sister's face. "What are they saying?"

She popped the tab on her soda and chugged half the contents before slanting him a look that smacked of pity. "It's bad. Word is, you and Jay also got— How shall I put this? *Intimate.*"

Tyler resisted the urge to dive under his comforter and cocoon himself from the world. He wasn't into risky behaviors like getting wasted, or experimenting with casual sex, but because of what had gone down at Homecoming, loads of kids believed otherwise. They could believe what they liked. Nothing he could say would change their minds. But this? This was something else. Because this time, it wasn't just his rep being dissed and he didn't think he could protect Jay like he'd protected Vanessa.

"How intimate?" he asked.

"Her giving you a BJ intimate."

"Riiight. Like *that* would ever happen. Like Jay would even want to seriously hook up with *me.*"

He forced a laugh. Even to his own ears it sounded tragic, so he flopped back onto his stomach to cover a flush of fury that had him clenching his fists and wanting to hit something. Shit. Shit. Shit. "It didn't go down like that at all," he muttered.

"I know," Caro said. "And I tried to put the lid on the gossip but it's far too juicy for Nessa to let go."

The mattress dipped as she plunked herself down beside him

and reached over to rub the tight, aching spot between his shoulder blades. "I'm real sorry. I don't know what's up with Nessa, lately. She's been acting like a real bitch. And she's really got it in for Jay. Bettina's not exactly pleased to have another contender for hottest girl in school, either. Wouldn't surprise me if she had something heinous planned. Hey, d'you want me to clue Jay in, and tell her to steer clear of you for a bit?"

"God no! Stay the hell out of it, Caro. You'll only make it worse."

He shrugged off her hand to slither from the bed onto the floor, where he propped himself against the mattress, elbows on bent knees, chin cupped in his hands. "I can handle the rumors," he said, as much to convince himself as his sister. He hoped Jay could handle them, too.

"Sure you can." Caro huffed a harsh sigh and joined him on the floor, sitting cross-legged in front of him. "Like you handled them after Homecoming. Look, if you'd just tell me what really happened, maybe I could—"

"Drop it, sis."

She scrubbed her hands through her hair. "Fine. What-freakin'-ever. But you sure can pick 'em, bro. I mean, first day at school and Jay's already attracting the wrong kind of attention."

"Shawn's attention, you mean," he said. And then wished he'd kept his mouth shut when he saw the pain flash across his sister's eyes. Shawn was a dick. He wouldn't know a good thing if it bit him on the ass. It wasn't a matter of *if* he screwed things up with Caro, more like when.

Tyler tried to make amends. "Look, sis, you don't need to worry about Jay hooking up with your boyfriend. She can't stand him. And after the way she dealt to him, I reckon he'll go out of his way to avoid her."

"Oh?" Caro's eyes flashed danger. "And how *did* she deal to him, exactly?"

Tyler went hot-cold-hot with dismay. Ah, crap. When was he going to learn to keep his big mouth shut?

His sister took pity on him. "Chill. I was only yanking your chain. Jay already gave me the whole tragic story about how Shawn wouldn't leave her alone. Some girls might reckon her reaction was OTT, but me? I'm thrilled she kicked his ass. It serves him right. Jerk. Least he could have done was dump me *before* he started hitting on someone else."

He blinked at the bitterness in her voice. "Does this mean what I think it means?"

"That I've kicked Shawn into touch?" Caro smiled in such a nasty way that Tyler shivered and rubbed his bare arms, grateful her huge case of the vengefuls wasn't directed at him. "Not yet," she continued. "First I'm going to make him grovel. And then, just when he thinks he's got me right where he wants me, I'm dumping his ass. Publicly. With maximum humiliation. No one treats me like that and gets away with it."

Tyler half-closed his eyes and clasped his hands together in mock-prayer. "Thank you, Lord!"

Caro scooped a sneaker off the floor and whacked him with it.

"Hey! Settle!" He fended off her enthusiastic attack until something other than the sneaker smacked him upside the head. "Hang on. When did you talk to Jay, exactly?"

She ditched the sneaker and resumed her position on the floor. "On the way home from practice. I spotted her outside Black Angel—you know, that recycled clothing boutique I like? And I made Nessa stop and offer her a lift. I figured it was the least Nessa could do after the way she behaved."

He opened his mouth to enquire how Vanessa had "behaved"

but Caro rushed on. "Jay said she didn't need a lift, so we checked out the new range in store and talked for a bit. And she told me *everything*, by the way."

"Everything?" Tyler felt his face heating as he recalled how he'd ogled Jay when she'd shucked her t-shirt. And how that kiss had made him feel.

Caro arched her eyebrows, trying her best to appear superior. "Yep. Everything. All about how Shawn got royally pissed when she told him she wasn't interested, and he insulted her, and—"

"*Assaulted* her, more like." A surge of anger thrummed through his veins as he recalled the reddened mark Shawn's hand had left on Jay's pale cheek.

"Huh? What did you say?"

Tyler debated whether to zip his lip or spill his guts. And blew out a resigned sigh. Caro wasn't gonna like it, but for better or worse, it was time she realized what kind of guy Shawn really was—like, in case she had a change of heart and didn't dump his ass. "Jay didn't tell you everything," he said.

She wagged her finger at him. "Oh yeah? She told me all about how you came running to her defense and Shawn ended up decorating the dumpster. I wish I'd been there! I hope Matt got the whole thing on vid and posts it online. That'll teach Shawn to—"

"Shawn slapped her, Caro. Across the face. Hard."

His sister paled to sheet-white. "He didn't."

"Yeah, he did. That's why I went for him."

She swallowed a couple of times, like she was trying to digest something nasty. "Sh-she must have really provoked him. Right?"

Tyler's heart went out to her, but he wasn't going to lie to make her feel better and help her justify Shawn's behavior.

"Yeah, she provoked him all right. Threatened to tell *you* what a creep he was, and try 'n convince you to dump him."

"That's *all*?"

"Yeah. Well, aside from that dig about Shawn's daddy buying him a place on the team. And Shawn's flabby ass."

The color had seeped back into Caro's cheeks but she still couldn't look him in the eye. Shawn's shitty behavior had really knocked the stuffing out of her.

"Jay didn't say anything about that," she said. "It's like she hasn't been affected at all. I'd have been gutted! Not to mention, angry as hell. And I'd have ripped Shawn's freaking arm off if he dared lay a hand on me."

Tyler let out a breath that he hadn't even realized he'd been holding. He'd been wondering if Shawn had ever gotten rough with Caro, and angsting over the best way to ask her. "Jay's one tough chick," he said.

"Yeah, she is that." Caro shook her head like she couldn't quite believe what she was about to say. "She didn't even flinch when Nessa punched her and—"

"Vanessa did *what*?"

She clapped her hands over her ears. "Quit yelling."

He pulled her hands away none-too-gently. "Tell me what happened. Now."

"God." Caro bit her lip, staring over Tyler's shoulder at the Eric Clapton poster on his wall. "Poor thing. Talk about shittiest first day ever at a new school. I'd be begging my parents to home-school me right about now. I'm really going have to do some impressive groveling to make it up to her. And boy, am I ever gonna make Shawn suffer."

"Good. About time. He deserves it. Now quit trying to change the subject, Caro. Spill. What happened with Vanessa?"

"It's not as bad as you think," she said. "Well, maybe it is, but—"

He made a rolling motion with his hand.

She slumped. "Okay, okay. When I heard Jay had her sights set on Shawn, I could hardly let it go, could I?"

He kept his mouth shut and after a sideways glance at him from beneath her lashes, Caro exhaled a drama-queen-worthy sigh. "Nessa and I confronted her after last period. She was all, 'Hi, Caro. Wondered when you'd show up.' She was so damn cool I was this close—" she pinched her thumb and forefinger together and waved them beneath his nose "—to giving her hell. Not that I'd ever get physical or anything," she added, when she noticed his outraged expression. "I'd have settled for a verbal take-down. Unlike Nessa."

"Vanessa really punched her? Jeez." Vanessa was more your cheer 'em on from the sidelines, or cower and wait to be rescued, kind of girl.

"Yeah," Caro said, sounding subdued—guilt-ridden, even. "In the stomach. And then Nessa yanked Jay's hair so hard I thought she was gonna tear a hunk from her scalp."

"Jay didn't mention anything about that, either."

"When you walked her home, you mean." His sister's tone was so heavy with innuendo she made "walked her home" sound x-rated.

"It was only part of the way but— Hey, don't try'n change the subject. What else happened with Jay and Vanessa?"

"How do you know anything else happened?"

"Puhlease. She's not the type to stand there and let Vanessa punch her and yank her hair." His brain chose that moment to visualize Jay standing so very still and calm, almost as though she was waiting for Shawn's hand to connect with her face. "Well, maybe she *would* just stand there. Whatever. Tell me, okay? Dying, here!"

He waited for his sister to elaborate. And waited.

When she finally got around to describing Jay's stunt, her voice was hushed with admiration—something Tyler didn't hear very often coming from his sister. Caro was usually the one inspiring the admiration.

"She's way flexible. Do we ever need that girl on our squad. And when she dropped Nessa on her ass and walked off? Priceless!"

"Sounds like Vanessa lost the plot big-time."

"She sure did," Caro agreed. "I reckon Jay's right: Nessa's jealous."

"Vanessa? Jealous? Why?"

Caro reverted to her classic eye-roll. "You are so clueless. Which is why you're so lucky to have me as your sister." She bounced up from the floor, stretched out the kinks in her back, and made a production out of checking her watch. "Goodness. Is that the time? Hey, what's for dinner? Hope there's enough for an extra person."

Tyler groaned and tried to pull off a Caro-style eye-roll. "Please tell me you haven't invited Vanessa. That'd really put me off my food."

"I haven't invited Nessa."

She grinned at him in that smug way which never failed to irritate him, and reminded him of a cat that'd just helped itself to a bowlful of cream. Oh no. This could not be good. He had a bad feeling about this.

He made a grab for her leg before she could disappear on him. "Who, then?"

She swatted his hand away. "Easy on the old knee-joint, bro. I landed hard during practice and it's still a bit tender." She swung her leg back and forth experimentally, still smirking at him.

He lunged, and managed to squeeze her knee before she scooted out of reach. Not too hard—she was his sister, and for all intents and purposes, a girl—but hard enough to make a point.

"Ow!" Caro rubbed her leg. "You've gotten real mean, you know that? It's hardly surprising you've got no friends anymore."

Tyler regarded her sourly. Her comment hurt, but no way was he going to let on how bad. His sister didn't know the full story of why he'd dropped out of the in-crowd. And if he had his way, she wasn't going to know, either.

Hands on hips, she gave him the "You are a lower life form and therefore beneath my notice, but just this once I'll oblige you" glare. "I invited Jay for dinner," she said.

"You did *what*?" He glanced around his room for something to hurl at her. "What the effing hell were you thinking?"

"Chill, bro. Jay turned me down flat when I asked her to try out for the squad, and I want to work on her some more. Plus, I'm feeling real crap about giving her such a hard time over Shawn. So I figured I'd extend the hand of friendship and invite her 'round."

"That's the biggest load of BS I've ever heard." Tyler snatched a pillow from the bed and lobbed it at her.

She ducked the ineffective missile. "Okay, you got me. My own personal feelings aside, I figure she must really like you, or she wouldn't have hung around after you upchucked over her. And I know it'll be a cold day in hell before *you* get up the nerve to ask her out, so I invited her over. What's wrong with that?"

Tyler plucked a tennis ball from the floor and menaced her with it. "What's wrong with that? Everything's wrong with that! Keep your nose out of my love life, Caro. Your last little effort to hook me up with Ashlee was a fricking monumental disaster. Butt out. That clear enough for you?"

She raised her eyebrows. "Crystal. Not that you even *have* a love life for me to butt out of. Yet. You can thank me later."

He ground his teeth and fought the impulse to strangle his matchmaking sister. "You can just un-invite her, okay?"

In a corner of his mind, Tyler noted she was smirking like an idiot. What the hell did she have to smirk about? Didn't she realize how pissed he was with her right now? "Ring her and—"

"Oops," Caro said, pressing her fingers to her lips. "I don't seem to have her number. But feel free to tell her what an interfering beyotch I am, and how you're rudely rescinding my invitation, just as soon as she shows up. Which will be in, oh, fifty-five minutes or so."

Before Tyler could open his mouth to yell at her some more, Caro dived for the door. He threw the ball and missed—much to his disgust. "You'd better get a move on with dinner!" he heard her yell as she sprinted for the safety of her room.

By the time he reached Caro's room, she'd already locked her door. Tyler battered it with his fists. "C'mon out, you freaking coward!"

"Nuh uh," she called. "I'm staying right here 'til Jay arrives. Which should be in about, let me see, fifty minutes and counting. The same time Mom's due home. Isn't that a happy coincidence? What're we eating, by the way?"

"Aaargh!" He howled his frustration. "You are so gonna pay."

"In your dreams," came the muffled response.

Her voice sounded wobbly, like she was….

She was laughing at him? The evil cow! When she unlocked that door he was so gonna—

"By the way, I wouldn't mind knowing what zit cream you're

using."

"Huh?" Tyler leaned his forehead against the doorframe as he tried to make sense of the lightning-fast subject change.

"That huge spot you had on your chin this morning has completely vanished. It must be damn good stuff, bro."

He ran his fingers over his chin. And for good measure, probed the area with his forefinger. Huh. Zit-less. At least something was going right for him today.

"And don't forget dessert," his sister called. "If you have time to make it before she gets here, that is!"

"You… you…. Crap." Beaten—for now—Tyler sprinted downstairs, all thoughts of vengeance and magically vanishing zits smothered by panic.

He glanced at the kitchen clock. Shit! Jay was gonna be here soon. And he felt wired to the max, like a guy going on his first date with a girl he really liked, terrified he was going to screw up and come across a complete loser.

He hadn't the slightest idea what he was going to say to her.

Or feed her, for that matter.

AFTER HER SECOND, far more pleasant encounter with Tyler's sister—if one didn't count Vanessa's glowering, sulky-faced presence shadowing them around the store—Jay had climbed the stairs to her apartment and settled in to do her homework. Some of her teachers had assigned extra work to catch her up with the rest of their students. Regardless, completing her assignments took very little time, leaving her forty-eight minutes before she was due at Caro and Tyler's house.

Jay decided to head to the main shopping district and investigate the only electronics store in town.

Eric's Electronics was stocked with the bare minimum of

basic components, just as she'd expected. But it wasn't a completely wasted excursion. Many of the students at school had iPods. Perhaps owning one of the gadgets would help Jay fit in.

She hesitated over the available selection. Knowing she was expected to choose a color that pleased her didn't help matters. Color was primarily a result of absorption and scattering properties of various materials, and the varying incoming wavelengths of the light that illuminated those materials. It neither pleased nor displeased her. It was simply color.

"Excuse me," she said to a female shop assistant stocking the shelves. "I'm trying to pick an iPod but I'm having difficulty choosing a color."

"For you?" the girl asked.

"Yes."

"Easy. What's your favorite color?"

"I don't have one."

The girl blinked but was too polite to comment.

"What's *your* favorite color?" Jay asked.

Taking the request seriously, the girl scanned the shelf. "Ummm, I quite like this purple one. Pink's too little-girly, you know? Purple's still feminine but more stylish."

"I appreciate your advice. I'll have the purple one, then."

The girl unlocked the cabinet, grabbed the iPod and escorted Jay to the counter. "Rob'll sort you out."

"Thank you." Jay scanned the girl's nametag and remembered to smile. "Michelle."

"You're welcome."

The assistant named Rob shot numerous not-so-surreptitious glances at Jay while he rattled off the store's return policy and the item's warranty conditions. As he rang up her purchase, Jay detected his elevated pulse rate, dilated eyes and flushed cheeks.

She wondered whether he might be coming down with a virus.

"Here you are." He handed over her receipt and the bag containing her purchase. And then he leaned over the countertop to press something else into her hand. "Be seeing you." He threw her a sly wink before turning his attention to the next customer.

"Thank you." Jay left the counter. She extracted the iPod from its packaging and slipped the tiny device and the ear buds in the back pocket of her jeans. The USB cord went in the nearest bin, along with the copious packaging. It would be far more convenient to charge the item by having her body emit a low-level electrical current whenever she handled the device.

As she exited the store, Jay examined the business card the assistant had given her. He'd scrawled a cell phone number on the back. She could only surmise it was his personal number. And that he'd been flirting… with her.

His behavior indicated he found her attractive and would like her to contact him. But why single *her* out, when there had been two other girls waiting in line behind her?

Tyler had responded to Jay's physical form in a similar fashion. So had Shawn, and many of the boys in her classes. But she hadn't deliberately secreted pheromones or groomed herself to attract the attention of young males. What was it about this form that made it so attractive?

It was all very confusing. So confusing, that if she'd been human she suspected her head would be aching right now.

As she walked the couple of blocks to Caro's house, she continued analyzing the incident with the young male in the electronics store, observing and processing new information about the town she'd chosen to hide in, reviewing her class schedule for tomorrow, and pondering the mysteries of human social customs.

Pretending to be human was far more difficult than she had predicted. Nothing in her titanium skeletal structure overlaid with human tissue, her artificial organs and implants, or the complex synthetic neural network that drove her ability to reason, could assist her. She'd been given the capability to alter her outward appearance, to appear to age like a normal human if necessary, but in truth she was nothing more than a supercomputer given human form.

A startling conclusion smacked her, and her head jerked as though she'd been struck in the jaw by some iron-fisted assailant. She was programmed with vast tracts of data about every imaginable subject, and could use the wireless networks to instantly access a huge variety of information. It shouldn't be possible for her to be confused. But she was. The male-female dynamic confused her at every turn.

And this all-too-humanlike confusion was not the only anomaly she'd been suffering lately. The unidentified *feeling*, for lack of a more accurate description, was always there, hovering on the edge of her conscious awareness, waiting. Always waiting. But for what? Some catalyst, some pivotal situation that would provoke a particular action, or reaction, from her?

Jay had no answer. And for a superhuman machine who always knew what was happening inside her, right down to the most infinitesimal process, that was paradoxical.

She kept her gait loose-hipped and relaxed, moving at a steady pace while she considered Tyler and his reaction to what he'd described as her "stunt". He had looked at her differently, speculatively, like she was an unknown quantity. It'd been foolish to toss Shawn in the dumpster and display her capabilities in such a fashion. And it had been completely outside the parameters of her core programming to act without first considering the risks.

She could only trust she would not have cause to regret her actions in the future. And that Shawn would react as predicted, and be too concerned with licking his wounded pride to bother her further.

Pause current thought-thread.

Licking wounded pride. Jay pondered the metaphor. Her own saliva contained enzymes that enhanced the inbuilt healing abilities of her outer dermal layer. If her physical body was injured, she often licked her wounds. Did that constitute irony?

She decided it did.

Resume.

Despite her error of judgment, Tyler appeared to want to be Jay's friend. Caro, too, had made overtures of friendship. Even Matt had chosen not to aid Shawn, and had displayed concern for Jay's physical state.

For now—on the surface at least—Jay was one of them. She belonged. And belonging was excellent camouflage.

She consulted her internal timepiece and continued on her way. If she maintained her current speed, she would arrive exactly at the time Caro had specified. Excellent.

Jay reran her encounters with Caro's brother and chose a pleasing image of Tyler, which she then fixed in her memory banks. Strangely, the chorus of the song she'd overheard him playing resounded again in her mind. And it consumed her.

Thoughts of you glowing in my heart,
Thoughts of you shining in my soul,
Thoughts of you blazing in my mind,
Thoughts of you, burning.
Thoughts of you,
Burn.

Six minutes twenty-three seconds passed before Jay emerged from what humans would term a daydream, to find that she'd halted in the middle of the sidewalk. Unless she ran the rest of the way, she would now arrive later than she had planned. But for some inexplicable reason she did not increase her speed to compensate for the delay.

She turned the corner and strolled up the path toward Caro and Tyler's house. At precisely 18:39 hours she stood before the Davidson's front door.

It felt good—*cool*—to have chosen to arrive late. And, as she rang the doorbell and listened for footsteps, Jay's thoughts were so centered upon Tyler, it didn't occur to her to be alarmed that she felt anything at all.

CHAPTER SIX

JAY WATCHED THE figure inside the house approaching the front door. Viewed through the patterned frosted-glass panes, Tyler's features appeared so grossly distorted that he resembled a cartoon caricature. Once her vision compensated for the distortion, Jay could see him chewing his lower lip, hands fluttering nervously as he tugged his shirt straight and finger-combed his hair.

If she cared to, Jay could eavesdrop and hear what he was muttering beneath his breath. Out of courtesy she tuned out, respecting his privacy. Father had taught her to do that. The old man had habitually muttered to himself, and hadn't appreciated having his words repeated back to him verbatim.

Courtesy aside, some part of Jay dearly wanted to hear Tyler's words. Because some part of her—an alien part, still in its infancy—hoped his mutterings might somehow relate to her.

An ancient station wagon demanded Jay's attention when it jumped the curb before rattling to a screeching halt in the driveway.

Its driver was a woman with the same rich auburn tones to her hair as Caro's. The woman left the engine idling while she fumbled about in her handbag. "Dammit!" Jay heard her say. "Where the heck did I put the darn remote?"

The car's engine hiccoughed and spluttered, and the woman revved it to prevent it stalling. Finally locating the remote, she aimed it at the garage door… which refused to do what it was supposed to do. Namely, open. She closed her eyes, groaned and rested her forehead on the steering wheel for a few moments before jabbing the remote—again with no success.

Tyler jerked open the front door and Jay switched her focus back to him.

"Jay," he said, sounding breathless. "C'mon in."

"Hello, Tyler. Your mother's home."

He stood on tiptoes and craned his neck to look over her shoulder. "Ah crap," he muttered. "Garage door opener's on the blink again. Can you tell her I'll open it manually?" He raced off down the hall.

"There's a pot boiling over on the stove," she called after him.

"The pasta!" she heard him say before another expletive floated to her ears.

Jay walked over to the car. The driver's name was Marissa Carolyn Davidson. Jay knew this because once she'd decided to make Snapperton her home, she'd accessed public records for every Snapperton resident.

Marissa was thirty-seven and mother of twins—Tyler, and Carolyn, who preferred the diminutive "Caro". Five years ago, Marissa's husband had packed a suitcase, walked out of the house, and for all intents and purposes, vanished. Town gossip insisted he'd run off with some unidentified floozy.

Marissa was currently employed as a secretary at the Snapperton Legal Office. Prior to embracing fulltime motherhood, she'd been a registered paralegal, doing everything for her employer barring presenting actual cases in court and giving legal advice. Her skills were underutilized and unappreciated by her current employer. She was barely managing to cover her family's living expenses.

Right now she was taking out her frustrations on the garage door remote.

When Jay tapped on the driver's side window, Marissa jerked in her seat, eyes wide as they raked Jay's face, one hand fluttering at her throat. Her breathing was rapid and her pulse had quickened.

Jay had scared her, and that had not been her intention. She ventured an "I'm harmless" smile.

Marissa rolled down the window of the vehicle.

"Hello, Mrs. Davidson. Tyler's opening the garage door for you. Would you like me to take a look at that remote? I'm Jay, by the way."

Marissa checked her over. "Well, hi there, Jay. You one of Caro's friends?"

"I hope so. I'm also a friend of Tyler's."

"Really." Marissa cocked her head to one side and eyed Jay thoughtfully. "Tyler's friend too, huh?"

Jay nodded. Since Marissa obviously found it strange that Jay would be friends with her son, she chose to volunteer enough information to settle any qualms the woman might have. "I just transferred in. Tyler and I are Bio partners and we have English together, too." That last fact Tyler had yet to discover because he'd skipped English.

She ducked her head and scuffed her sneaker on the driveway, acting as though she was embarrassed about admitting something. "He's very sweet. He helped me get through my first day."

Marissa's expression smoothed, doubts sliding away. "First day at a new high school isn't much fun for anyone."

Jay nodded. "Yes. It was rough. Would you like me to look at that for you?" She held out her hand for the garage door remote.

"You fancy yourself a bit of an expert with electronics, huh?"

"I don't fancy myself an expert, I am one." It was the truth, and Jay saw no reason to make light of her abilities in this instance.

Shrugging, Marissa relinquished the remote. "What the hey. It's not like it's working properly anyway."

Jay pulled a tiny toolkit from her jeans' pocket, selected a screwdriver, and began to disassemble the remote. Noting Marissa's theatrical wince, she said, "It's quite a simple device. It will be easy to find out what's wrong with it."

"Sorry to come across so anti," Marissa said. "Mike—that's Caro and Tyler's dad—fancied himself a bit of a handyman. He was a whiz with computers, but anything else? Let's just say it never ended well."

The garage door creaked open to reveal Tyler leaning on a button by the internal door. "Hi, Mom. Sorry I took so long."

His mother parked the vehicle and cut the engine. It died with a cough, which didn't bode well for it starting up again without a struggle. She got out of the car and slammed the door shut. "Bloody car," she muttered. "Last thing I need right now is for it to give up the ghost."

Tyler beckoned Jay inside. "Caro invited Jay for dinner," he said to his mother. *Hope that's okay?* he mouthed.

His mother hesitated, then gave a quick nod.

Jay pretended not to have seen the silent communication and ducked her head as though intent on the inner workings of the remote.

"And speaking of dinner—" Marissa sniffed the air. "Something smells good. What're we having?"

"Spaghetti bolognaise," Jay said, handing over the remote and pocketing her screwdriver.

"How did you—?" Tyler began.

Too late, Jay realized she'd done something out of the ordinary. A distraction was necessary. "It's my favorite. Everyone knows what his or her favorite meal smells like. Try the remote now, Mrs. Davidson."

Tyler's mother jabbed viciously at the button and watched the garage door smoothly close without any jerking false starts. She blinked, pressed it again and watched it open back up in the same efficient manner. She turned to Jay with a delighted grin. "Gosh, thanks! I take it all back, you *are* an expert!"

"You're welcome," Jay said.

Tyler pried the remote from his mother's hands and used it to close the garage door again before shoving it in her handbag. "C'mon you two. You can play with the remote and do the mutual admiration thing later. Inside and wash up! Pasta will be all gluggy if you don't get a move on."

"Hey, Tyler," Caro screamed from the lounge. "Sounds like something's boiling over!"

"Ah, crap! Not again."

"Tyler!"

"Sorry, Mom," he yelled over his shoulder as he raced off.

"Caro!" Jay heard him howl from the vicinity of the kitchen. "Couldn't you have gotten off your sorry butt and turned the pasta down?"

"Not my turn to cook," his sister yelled back. "Doing important stuff here."

"Yeah. Sure. I know you're watching music vids instead of doing your homework. Oooooh!" He wailed an impression of a popular singer. "Can you handle it? I don't think you can handle it!"

Jay caught Marissa's full-body shudder. "I apologize in advance for my kids," Marissa said. "Siblings. You know what it's like." Her gaze lingered on Jay's shirt.

"I'm an only child," Jay told her. "So this is.... This is a refreshing change." She watched as Marissa seemed to shrug off her fascination with the borrowed shirt.

As a cop from a movie Jay had watched liked to say, "Dodged that bullet." It could prove embarrassing for Tyler if his mother recognized his shirt and asked why Jay was wearing it. Jay didn't believe Tyler would appreciate his mother knowing he'd vomited while watching a frog being dissected. She followed Marissa and the aroma of slightly overcooked spaghetti to the kitchen.

Caro made an appearance as her brother was dishing up. "Oh, hi!" she said to Jay. "No one told me you'd arrived."

"Here." Tyler dumped a large serving bowl full of drained spaghetti into his sister's arms. "Make yourself useful and take this out to the table. And," he said to Jay, "would you mind taking the salad out, please?"

"Why does she get a 'would you mind, please' and I get a 'make yourself useful'?" Caro whined.

"Because Jay's a guest," her mother said. "And besides, you weren't exactly *being* useful, were you?" She assisted her daughter through to the dining room with a firm hand on the small of her back.

Jay followed Caro. "I'm sure you're very useful when you want to be," she ventured, in an attempt to build rapport.

"Typical." Caro plunked her burden on the table. "Ever since Dad left, she always sides with Tyler and—" She broke off, fiddling with the serving spoons. "Anyway. Thanks for coming at such short notice."

"Thank you for asking me."

Caro pulled out a chair and indicated Jay should do the same.

Jay observed Caro carefully. Mimicking Caro's relaxed posture, she slumped forward with her elbows on the table, chin resting on her hands, and legs hooked around the chair's front legs. "May I ask your advice?"

"Sure." Caro assumed what she probably imagined was a worldly-wise expression.

"It's about the behavior of one of the employees in the electronics store. He gave me his cell phone number."

Caro smirked and waggled her eyebrows. "Ohhh! Best not mention that in Tyler's hearing. He'll pitch a fit if—"

"He'll pitch a fit if what?" Tyler was juggling a serving dish of bolognaise and a ceramic tray designed to hold three small bowls, each with its own tiny stainless steel ladle.

"Ooh, fancy!" Caro teased, shooting a conspiratorial glance at Jay. "How come you don't just bring out the dressing bottles?"

"We have a guest," he said, placing everything on the table and fiddling with their artful placement.

Caro rolled her eyes. "Sheesh. Next thing, we'll be using the good linen napkins instead of—"

"Sorry about that, love." Marissa walked into the dining room brandishing four linen napkins that obviously matched the tablecloth. "We use them so infrequently I'd forgotten where I stashed them."

Caro shut her mouth with an audible snap as Tyler carefully folded the napkins and placed one beside each place setting.

"Well, this is nice," Marissa said, beaming first at Jay and then Caro. When her gaze got to Tyler, her smile faltered and became strained. "Thanks for going to so much effort, love."

"No problem, Mom." Tyler didn't seem to notice his mother's tension. He smiled sweetly at her, and then ruined the effect by casting an evil glare at his sister. "It all turned out pretty well, considering Caro only told me she'd invited a guest over for dinner like, *an hour* ago."

Caro shrugged when her mother queried her with raised eyebrows. "I couldn't help it if practice ran over time could I? Now, if I had a cell phone, I could've—"

Marissa buried her face in her hands and pressed her eyelids with her fingertips. When she'd regained her equilibrium she said, "Please, Caro, not now. We've already had this conversation. And no mentioning it to Grandma Davidson, either. I refuse to take any handouts from that old cow after what she said to me when your father—" She flushed when she noted Caro and Tyler's poorly hidden misery. "Well. Anyway, same goes for her giving expensive gifts to you, too, Caro. You are not to so much as hint that you need a cell phone."

Caro's gaze dropped to the tablecloth. She pleated the edge with her fingers. "Sorry."

Tyler let out the breath he'd been holding and passed the pasta bowl to Jay.

"This smells wonderful," she said, because she'd been told by Father it was polite to compliment the cook. In truth, although she could separate out the aromas of every ingredient that had gone into the dish, she neither liked nor disliked the smell. It was fuel. She'd eaten far better meals—and far worse—to maintain her body's optimum muscle tone and keep it functioning at its full capacity. Regardless of what she ate, her system would extract the nutrients required and expel the rest. She could eat things humans would not be able to stomach, things that would make them violently ill—such as the old takeout she'd mentioned to Tyler.

She helped herself to a large portion of his bolognaise.

The tips of Tyler's ears turned pink.

Interesting. Jay wound spaghetti around her fork and took her first bite. As she chewed, she was hyper-aware of his eyes glued to her face, awaiting her reaction to the meal he'd cooked. For her.

She swallowed her mouthful and smiled at him. "This tastes fantastic."

His blush deepened, creeping down his neckline "Th-thanks," he managed.

"Amazing what you can do with a jar of pasta sauce and a bag of salad greens," Caro said, her tone a beautiful example of what the kids termed *snark*.

Tyler's eyes narrowed to slits. His mouth opened.

"I agree," Jay said, before he could utter a word. "It *is* amazing. And I really appreciate the effort you've made, Tyler. It's lovely to have someone cook for me, for a change."

Marissa exhaled a huge breath that reeked of relief. She caught Jay's eye. *Thanks!* she mouthed.

Jay smiled back. As she ate, she examined Caro and Tyler's mother.

Marissa closely resembled her daughter. But where Caro's face was as yet unlined, her mother's showed strain. Fine lines bracketed Marissa's mouth and worry had etched two matching creases between her brows. To Jay's enhanced vision, artfully applied cosmetics did little to disguise bluish smudges of too many sleepless nights beneath Marissa's eyes. Although she put on a good enough show to fool her children, it was obvious to Jay that Marissa was fatigued. And being the sole guardian of two teenagers had to be mentally stressful, too.

It was unnecessary for such an attractive woman to live alone with no male to support her, either financially *or* emotionally. Jay would endeavor to discover Marissa's requirements and introduce her to a suitable man. And perhaps having an adult male in their life again might assist Caro and Tyler, also. In Father's opinion, children benefited greatly by having two parents involved in their raising.

"So, Tyler." Marissa pushed aside her plate. She'd barely eaten anything. Although she made a conscious effort to keep her breathing deep and even—unnaturally so—her pulse rate was elevated. She spoke slowly, choosing her words with the utmost care. "Tell me about those scrapes and bruises."

Tyler's gaze lit briefly on Jay before he discovered something extremely fascinating about one of the arugula leaves on his plate. "'S nothing. Things got a bit rough during Phys Ed."

"Really." Marissa's gaze never left her son's face as she broke off a minute corner of her bread roll, popped it into her mouth and chewed far longer than necessary. "Looks more like a close encounter with a fist caused them, if you ask me."

Tyler's head shot up. His gaze skittered from his mother's impassive face to Jay's.

To Jay, his face read like an open book.

"Would you care to enlighten me?" However politely couched, Marissa's request was an order. Her breathing had now quickened to a pant. Hectic spots of crimson painted her cheekbones.

Tyler contemplated his food, his mouth set in a defeated grimace. "What's the point? It's obvious someone's already ratted me out." He darted an accusing gaze at his sister, but Caro shook her head, pleading her ignorance with wide eyes and a mouthed, *Wasn't me!*

Jay accessed the nearest Wi-Fi network and performed a specific search. When her suspicions were confirmed, her requirement for sustenance vanished.

She arranged her cutlery neatly on her plate and pushed it aside. She had been foolish to provoke Shawn. She had been especially foolish to overreact during the confrontation. The consequences of that foolishness had been exacerbated now that Matt had captured her "stunt" on video and uploaded it to a social networking site.

Chapter Seven

"Who spilled about the fight?" Tyler wondered aloud.

"I believe Matt videoed a certain incident on his mobile phone and the clip has been forwarded to your mother," Jay informed him.

Marissa shifted her stony gaze from her son to Jay. "Smart girl. Someone stuck it on some dating site and—"

"You mean social networking site," Caro corrected.

"I don't care what I mean!" Marissa flared. "What I *do* care about, is Vanessa Ward emailed me a link at work with the subject line 'You need to see this'. And when I clicked on it, I had the dubious pleasure of watching my son beating on the mayor's precious offspring. I'm sure the good folks of Snapperton will be thoroughly entertained when this gets around."

Marissa's expression darkened to something resembling thunderous, and Jay deemed it prudent not to inform her that if the clip was now online, the entire world could be entertained—provided the jaded masses were even entertained by such things anymore. Unfortunately, it wasn't the jaded masses who concerned Jay, but a select group who would be trolling the Internet for just such evidence of her whereabouts.

"Hey, you make it sound like I was winning, Mom," Tyler

said, brightening somewhat.

"It's debatable whether you would have won the fight had I not intervened," Jay told him. "You are more agile, but once Shawn pinned you, his superior weight made it unlikely you would prevail."

"That's not the point!" Marissa said, her voice rising in direct proportion to her blood pressure. Then her face crumpled. Tears brightened her eyes. "God, Tyler. I-I didn't want to do this in front of Jay but I couldn't keep it in any longer. I don't need this right now—not on top of work and worrying about money and... and.... Everything! The last straw will be your grand-mother ringing me to imply I'm a useless mother who can't properly parent my kids, and she should have custody. You shouldn't have been fighting. And especially not with Shawn Evans. His father's not only the mayor, he's on the school board, for heaven's sake. What were you thinking?"

Tyler seemed to physically shrink in on himself. Caro had stilled and was holding her breath.

Jay had heard the expression "you could cut the atmosphere with a knife" used before. She'd never thought it anything more than a fanciful metaphor until now. She decided to diffuse the tense situation by telling the truth—or rather, what small portion of the truth she could safely divulge to these people.

She leaned forward, placing a hand on Marissa's wrist, squeezing lightly to reclaim her attention. "Don't blame Tyler for this, Mrs. Davidson. It's not his fault. Had I not spoken rudely to Shawn and provoked him, it's highly unlikely he would have hit me, and then Tyler wouldn't have felt it necessary to assault Shawn on my behalf."

"He. Did. What?" Marissa spluttered. Her chest heaved like she was having difficulty breathing.

Jay analyzed the sentence. "He" meaning Shawn, or "he" meaning Tyler? The ambiguity of the question disturbed her. As did the glittering intensity of Marissa's stare and the fury vibrating across the woman's body.

"I didn't see *that* on the video clip," Marissa said. "Tell me exactly what happened. Right now."

"Very well." Jay relayed the incident while mulling how best to handle Marissa's evident distress. The woman posed a threat, albeit a minor one. It would be more difficult for Jay to maintain her cover if Marissa demanded to personally speak to Jay's fictional guardian. And she struck Jay as the type of woman who would insist upon face-to-face interaction when it came to a child's welfare—whether her own child, or anyone else's.

Jay did not want to keep on running. She wanted to stay in Snapperton and attend Greenfield High and pretend to be a normal teenager. She wanted to explore the possibility of friendship with Tyler and Caro and—

Most of all she wanted to explore that possibility with Tyler.

She did not know why all this was suddenly so important to her. She only knew that it was. And if she were to have a chance at normality, this present situation must be contained before she tackled the potentially far more serious issue of the video clip. The clip showing Jay tossing a much larger, heavier person into a dumpster as though he weighed nothing. The clip that was now out in the public domain for anyone to see—for *them*, the men who relentlessly pursued her, to see.

"I regret what I did," she said, meeting Marissa's fierce gaze. She assumed an earnest expression, hoping it would help sway the woman if her words didn't. "You should be proud of Tyler, Mrs. Davidson, and proud of yourself, too. You've raised a son who'll look out for his friends and won't hesitate to step in to defend them if they're threatened. Many kids these days are so tied up in themselves, it wouldn't even occur to them to bother to stand up for others."

Marissa stared at Jay, mouth agape for a moment before she gathered her wits enough to shake her head in disbelief. "You have *nothing* to apologize for, Jay. I can't believe Shawn hit you. You poor kid. Are you sure you're okay? Do you want me to take you home and have a word with your parents?"

"I'm perfectly fine, Mrs. Davidson. The handprint can barely be seen and my face doesn't hurt at all. Please don't worry about me."

Marissa tore her gaze from Jay to glare at her daughter. "And that's the boy you've chosen as your boyfriend, Caro? A boy who hits on other girls behind your back and then gets physical with them when they don't return his interest? You need to get your priorities straight, my girl. Good looks, flashy cars, and wealthy parents don't necessarily add up to good boyfriend material."

Jay had to admire Marissa Davidson's interrogation technique. Beneath her steely-eyed regard, Caro broke out into a cold sweat and wriggled about in her chair. "I'm, uh, planning on dumping him first thing tomorrow?" she offered.

"No need," her mother said. "Because I'm ringing Wes Evans right now and telling him what his precious son has done. And then I'm telling him if that boy comes anywhere near either of you girls again, I'm going to—"

"Mom, please!" Caro's face twisted into an agonized expression.

"Yeah, please don't ring Mr. Evans, Mom," Tyler said. "School's hard enough as it is without Shawn *really* having it in for me."

Jay added her voice to the fray. "I wouldn't recommend that

course of action, Mrs. Davidson."

Marissa turned that gimlet eye on her again. Her lips had compressed in a thin, bloodless line. A vein visibly pulsed at her throat.

Jay fought the impulse to quail. Mrs. Davidson would be an asset to any interrogation team. "If you bring this incident to Wes Evans' attention, it will cause him public embarrassment," she said. "And I predict he will retaliate by pressing charges against Tyler for assaulting his son. If the incident with Shawn slapping my face is not included on that video clip you saw, then it will show Tyler attacking Shawn without provocation. It will be Tyler's word against Shawn's."

Marissa's jaw worked but only a strangled gargle came out, so Jay continued. "Since I was the one who provoked this incident, if anyone should be ringing the mayor to complain about his son's behavior, it should be me. And I choose not to take further action. Shawn took an interest in me and believed I would welcome that interest." She paused when she noted Tyler's posture go rigid.

"Of course, he was mistaken," she said, and the breath Tyler had been holding whooshed out as he sagged back against his chair.

Interesting. Could he be jealous of Shawn? Jay hadn't given him any reason to be, but then, most humans weren't particularly talented at reading non-verbal clues.

"I have now made that fact quite clear to Shawn," Jay said. "I believe he will move on and not bother me further. And if I am mistaken, then *I* will handle Shawn in my own way."

Marissa chewed her lower lip. And then nodded. "I see your point. And apparently, from what I saw, you can certainly take care of yourself."

"Yes."

"About that—"

"I've trained under karate and jujitsu masters." Jay shrugged, hoping the gesture would convey the right degree of self-effacement. "It's all in the knees, and using your opponent's momentum against him."

Marissa considered that explanation quite carefully.

Jay noted acceptance sliding across her face and, better still, the beginnings of a smile twitching her lips upward.

"Shawn picked on the wrong girl, huh?" Marissa said.

"Yes, he did."

"I guess I have to respect your decision."

"Thank you," Jay said.

Marissa had to have the last word. "I don't have to like it, though."

Jay held her gaze. "No, you don't. You simply have to accept it. Please."

"Very well." But Marissa still wasn't finished. "And that's another thing, Tyler. Why has this boy got such a problem with you anyway? He's got a rich and influential father, a very sweet stepmother, and everything he could possibly want. Surely he's got better things to do than to make your life a misery?"

Tyler shrugged. "Guess he's still pissed that despite his so-called brilliance, the Raiders haven't won a game since I left the team."

Marissa's righteous anger softened. She sucked in a deep, shuddering breath. "You don't make it easy on yourself, love," she murmured, stroking her fingertips down her son's cheek. "Perhaps if you took up a sport again, rather than immersing yourself in your music? I know it was unfair of your basketball coach to bench you, but that was no reason to quit baseball as well. Maybe you could try out for the school team again? You had loads of friends when you were involved in sports."

Jay watched relief seep into Tyler's body, unclenching his fists and loosening the tightly wound tension in his muscles. "Yeah," he said. "Turned out they weren't real friends at all. And I like coaching the girls' baseball team, Mom. I like coaching even more than playing."

Jay surprised herself by blurting, "You do have real friends, Tyler. You have me, for one."

Tyler tried to hide his embarrassment over her outburst by resorting to sarcasm. "Yeah. Thanks. But might be best to think twice before you get on the wrong side of Shawn and his peeps. It's so not worth the shit-storm afterward."

"Tyler!" Marissa wasn't at all impressed by this declaration.

"Sorry, Mom."

Marissa heaved a sigh that was tinged with a mixture of pride and worry. "So I guess you were only doing what any good friend would do. But regardless of the provocation, it still doesn't look good on video, does it? What if your principal gets wind of it? You know how Ms. Harris feels about physical violence. She won't care you were trying to protect a friend, Tyler. She won't let you coach the girls' team anymore, and all your music room privileges will be taken away."

"The video clip is quite easily handled, Mrs. Davidson," Jay interjected. "I can delete it from the social networking site."

"You can do that?" Marissa gave her big, luminous, hope-filled eyes.

"Yes," Jay said, ignoring the obvious doubt pouring from Tyler and Caro. "I can. All I need is a computer."

"Great! You can use Tyler's." Marissa stood so quickly she set her chair rocking, and began stacking empty plates. "Now all I have to worry about is all the people who've already copped a look at Tyler monstering Shawn."

"I might be able to fix that, too," Jay said. "With a bit of help from my friends."

Marissa brightened and a few of her worry-lines smoothed. "In that case, you three go to it. I'll even volunteer to do the dishes."

Before she left the dining room, Marissa had one more thing to add. "And Tyler?"

"Yes, Mom?"

"Next time, use your brain not your fists. If I hear you've been fighting—whatever the provocation—I'll ground you for the rest of the year. You hear me?"

"Yes, Mom."

"And as for you, Caro. You know what you have to do about that boy."

"Yes, Mom."

"And don't think you're getting off easily, either, Jay. If I hear even the slightest rumor Shawn Evans is bothering you again, I *will* be having words with his father on your behalf. Either you handle it, or I will. Is that clear?"

"Perfectly clear, Mrs. Davidson."

"Good. Now scram—all of you—before I change my mind and stir up a shit-storm of my own."

Caro waited for her mother to exit before turning to Jay. "If Principal Harris sees that clip, Tyler's ass is toast. I sure hope you're as good as you think you are."

Jay didn't respond to Caro's statement. Her gaze flicked to Tyler, but his expression was suddenly as blank as she knew her own could be. She found herself wondering what was going on inside his head at this particular moment, and felt strangely energized by the phenomenon of not knowing, of being clueless… like a normal human.

"You really a computer whiz?" Tyler finally asked.

"Yes," she said. "I really am."

JAY SAT IN the creaky swivel chair at Tyler's desk with her back straight, feet planted flat on the floor, legs slightly apart. Even though she did not feel pain as humans did, she saw no reason to inflict the perils of poor posture upon her body. Her fingers danced over the laptop's keyboard as she searched the internet for the clip. "Here it is," she told Caro and Tyler. "It's not a featured video and it's only had twenty-three views, and no comments. Unfortunately, that's twenty-three too many for our purposes."

"There'll be a heap more tomorrow once word gets around," Caro said.

Tyler peered at the screen, trying to make sense of the username. "NessaSary?"

"That's Nessa's username," Caro said. "*She* must have uploaded the clip, not Matt. Sheesh. That girl really holds a grudge. I'd understand if *you'd* ditched *her* for another girl, Tyler, but she's the one who ditched you for Matt. What the heck did you do to piss her off so bad?"

Tyler's face blanked. "I have no idea what her problem is."

"Liar." Curiosity lit Caro's gaze. "'Fess up."

"Drop it, sis."

She threw up her hands. "Whatever."

Jay clicked on the link and observed Tyler from the corner of her eye.

He winced as he saw himself charging Shawn and whacking him against the side of the car.

Caro socked her brother in the arm with her fist. "How could you do that to a sweet ride like a Miata?"

"Owww!" He rubbed the sore spot. "Stop picking on me, will ya?"

"Baby."

"Brat."

"Wuss," Caro said, then choked back any further insults as the truly interesting part of the clip began—the part where Jay had intervened.

Tyler sucked in a sharp breath as the video version of Shawn sailed through the air, easily clearing the side of the dumpster before disappearing into its depths. "Ho-ly cripes!"

The uploaded clip was short, and had been inexpertly spliced together from two separate source files. But although jerky and at times unfocused, it plainly showed the damning evidence of Tyler making the first aggressive move toward Shawn, as well as Jay launching Shawn into orbit—a feat of strength no teenage girl should be capable of.

"Sheee-it!" came Matt's tinny-sounding whisper. "Un-freaking-believable."

"You got that right," Tyler said. "I didn't realize— Shit, Jay. Shawn's no lightweight. How'd you do that?"

"Yeah, how'd you *do* that?" Caro's question was voiced in a high-pitched squeak.

"As I explained to your mother, it's simply a matter of leverage and training," Jay said.

"Oh. Okay." Caro appeared to have accepted her explanation.

"Martial arts, huh?" Tyler said.

"Yes. It's not difficult to pull off what appears to be an astounding feat of strength if you know the correct techniques."

"Cool," was Tyler's final verdict. "Wouldn't mind you giving me some pointers in case *I* ever have to take out some trash."

"It would be my pleasure," Jay said, meaning it. The prospect of being physically close to Tyler—having an excuse to touch him as she wished, teach him some of what she knew—elevated her heart rate until she was convinced its frantic thudding must be obvious to both him and Caro. She took a deep breath to calm herself.

"Whoa," Caro said. "I still can't believe Nessa posted this clip. 'Boy Wonder Left Wondering'. Ouch. Even the title kinda makes Shawn out to be a dick—remember that suck-up newspaper reporter called him Greenfield High's Boy Wonder?"

"Yeah," Tyler said. "I remember. He took all the credit for our last win."

"And if Shawn's pissed about this," Caro said, "you can bet Bettina will take her cue from him. Nessa might have uploaded this to get back at you, Tyler, but she really didn't think it through at all. B'll probably kick her off the squad." She shook her head. "What the heck is up with Nessa lately?"

Jay wasn't interested enough in Vanessa's fate to bother commenting. She hacked into the site, expertly bypassing the firewalls and all the security protocols. Within seconds she found what she was looking for: the file path for the video clip upload. "This laptop is incredibly slow. I gather you've nothing more powerful?"

Tyler snorted. "You gather right. It's one of Dad's old ones. He was gonna rebuild it for me but—" He puffed out a disgusted breath. "Can't afford anything else. That a problem?"

Jay shook her head. "No. I'll deal with it permanently when I get home. In the meantime, I'll insure no one else can view the clip by making it appear to be a faulty upload."

"If you can do *that*," he said, "why don't you just delete the damn clip altogether, right this instant?"

"I could. But if I use my own computer, I can insure outside interference can't be tracked. I also have a program I can use to trace the views to their point of origin to confirm they're all local."

He considered what she'd said, his gaze so intent, so incisive, Jay could picture it cutting right through her outer shell to search for the soul beneath. Except Jay did not possess a soul. And for the first time since her creation, she felt herself lacking—less than human, instead of more.

She didn't try to hide herself from Tyler. She let him read what he could in her face. And waited for him to ask what he so desperately wanted to ask.

Caro's gaze darted between Jay and her brother, confusion obvious in her furrowed brow and parted lips. "Huh? Did I miss something?"

"No." Tyler managed a smile. "You about done, Jay?"

She turned back to the monitor and began manipulating code. "There." She exited the site. "Caro, try searching and opening the clip now." She relinquished the chair and took a seat on the edge of the bed, leaning back to rest on her elbows.

While his sister was occupied, Tyler chewed his lip and not-so-covertly contemplated Jay. He wandered over and plunked himself down next to her. After a glance at Caro, he leaned in to whisper in Jay's ear. "You're not doing this just for me, are you?"

"What makes you say that?" she whispered back, throwing out the question to test what Tyler thought he knew.

"You gonna tell me why you need to go to all this trouble?" He hissed the question from the corner of his mouth. "Or am I gonna have to employ some devious means of torture to get it out of you?"

A genuine smile ghosted Jay's lips. She liked that he was intelligent enough to figure out she was hiding something, and courageous enough to call her on it. She levered herself up and leaned toward Tyler to brush his hair back from his ear. "Let's just say," she murmured, "there are people out there who have an unhealthy interest in some research my father was doing before he died."

Her lips grazed his earlobe, and he shivered.

Interesting. Or perhaps that should be "cool".

"I get it," he said. "They think you're some whiz-kid who knows all about your dad's research or something."

An ironic statement, given that Jay *was* her father's research. "I'm a computer genius and these people want what they think I know."

"Oh."

"You don't appear bothered by any of this."

He shrugged. "I knew you were something out of the ordinary the first time I saw you."

Jay had never had cause to analyze this degree of intimacy before. It appeared Tyler's physical reactions were in response to her touch rather than the content of what she was saying. To be completely certain, she repeated the experiment, skimming her lips across the sensitive area where his earlobe met his jaw line. "Likewise," she murmured against his skin, inhaling the odor of his hair gel mingling with a particular scent that was uniquely Tyler. "I knew you were extraordinary, too."

The fine hairs on the nape of his neck rose and his breath hitched. "Th-these people. They're like, bad people?"

"They've done some questionable things in the past. I'd prefer them not to know my whereabouts. Can I trust you, Tyler?"

Again he shivered. And his indrawn breath was released in a

series of small shuddering gasps.

She would take that as an affirmative.

As Jay analyzed Tyler's physical reactions, she found herself dwelling on her own. Her pulse and breathing rate had accelerated. She felt—

What did she feel, exactly?

On edge, her perceptions heightened, unnatural warmth suffusing her body. Mildly dizzy, with a peculiar buzzing in her head. Her senses swamped with so much sensory input, she was forced to continually override her brain's directive to enter downtime mode to fully process the data.

And the only catalyst she could think of that might cause such anomalies was the human boy beside her. Tyler. She wondered what it would be like to press her lips to his and kiss him properly, thoroughly, as she'd seen intimate human couples do. She wondered whether he'd let her.

She blinked rapidly, forcing her mind away from his fascinating physical responses. And her own.

Tyler's body, so close to hers, fairly thrummed with the questions he wanted to ask, but he said only, "Yes. You can trust me." He dared a glance at her then, his face upturned, gaze locked with hers as he sought her hand and squeezed it gently. "I won't tell anyone. Not even Caro."

"Thank you."

"Yee-ha!" Caro pumped a fist in the air and whirled her chair to face them. "Tried everything I can think of but the clip won't open. Guess your ass is saved from the toaster, brother-mine."

Caro's glee morphed to a crinkled frown when she registered Jay's close proximity to her brother. And the way Tyler had ducked his head to hide flushed cheeks. A knowing little grin spread across her face. "Would you two like some privacy or something?"

"Shut up, Caro," Tyler said.

"Yes. Shut up, Caro." Jay quirked her lips into a smile to take the sting from her words.

"We need to figure out what to do about Matt and Vanessa," Tyler said, in a transparent attempt to distract his sister. "Bet my right arm the clip's still on their phones. And there're a few choice things I'd sure like to say to them both—especially Vanessa."

Caro favored her brother with a narrow-eyed, thoughtful gaze. "Some secret history between Nessa and you I should know about?"

Tyler dropped his gaze to his sneakers and bent to fiddle with the laces… which were perfectly adequately tied, so far as Jay could see. "I'm just pissed this clip has gone public," he muttered.

"Right." Caro didn't sound convinced but she let it slide.

Jay considered doing some digging into any continuing relationship Vanessa and Tyler might have. She decided against it. It wouldn't be prudent to draw attention to herself by asking questions about Vanessa. Or indeed, any Snapperton resident.

"I'm thinking we need to go at this from another angle," Caro said, her distant gaze and deliberate speech cueing Jay that she was still thinking something through. "It's what's *on* the clip that's the problem, right?"

"Well, duh." Tyler rolled his eyes.

"Got it!" Caro snapped her fingers and pushed the chair into a wobbly spin. "We change the way people think of the original clip."

Jay blinked, unable to comprehend the logic. She stared at Caro, reviewing everything she knew about Tyler's sister in an attempt to understand the girl's thought processes. But Caro's triumphant grin and eager gaze held no revealing clues.

Could Caro, a teenage girl whose test scores highlighted an above average IQ, but certainly nothing in the realms of Jay's abilities, really have conceived the perfect plan to diffuse this situation?

Something fluttered low in Jay's abdomen. An unsettling sensation. How could she have failed so completely? Her systems were in flux, and no longer reliable. What was happening to her?

Tyler groaned, massaging his temples with his fingertips. "I give up. What the hell are you going on about? And I'd quit that spinning 'cause I think the chair's gonna give up the ghost and dump you on your butt."

Jay inhaled and exhaled slowly. Tyler hadn't comprehended his sister's reasoning, either. That was some comfort, at least.

Caro planted both feet on the floor and leaned forward, eager to share her idea. "We make out the whole fight was staged. Like, to showcase Jay's mad martial arts skills. Then no one, not Principal Harris, or anyone, can punish Tyler. Plus, Shawn's sure to go for it, 'cause he won't look like a total dick if he's supposedly volunteered to go dumpster-diving, right? Whaddya think, guys?" Her eyes shone with misplaced enthusiasm.

Tyler appeared to be taking his sister's solution seriously. For all of ten seconds. His gaze skittered to Jay. "One problem, sis. Even if we convinced Shawn to play along with that version, Jay's not so keen on going public with her awesome dump 'em in the dumpster skills."

Tyler understood more than he let on. And for once, Jay was content to sit back and let someone else do the work for her. Father might have called it manipulation. Jay labeled it trust. She trusted Tyler implicitly. His reasoning might be based on incomplete information, but he had her best interests at heart.

"Why not?" Caro was saying, her bottom lip protruding in a pout. "If I could pull a stunt like that, I'd be making sure I was all over the news. I'd be a freakin' celebrity!"

"You'd be a freak, all right." Tyler traced an invisible pattern on the bed's comforter. With visible reluctance, he met his sister's gaze. "Look. Caro. Why should Jay even have to do this for me, huh? She barely knows me. And inviting her for dinner to make up for Vanessa's crappy behavior, hardly makes you two best-friends-forever, either. If Jay doesn't want to turn herself into a public freak-show, then that's that. End of story."

Caro surged to her feet, throwing him a baleful glare. "Leave Nessa out of this. I'll be giving her hell over this stunt of hers first thing tomorrow, you can be sure of that. And if Jay doesn't consider herself my friend, then she'd be straight up and tell me. Right, Jay?"

Jay nodded, intrigued by the dynamics of the argument. "Yes, I'd be straight with you." About that, at least.

"So I don't see what the big deal is, bro."

Tyler levered himself from the bed, his features twisting into a truly impressive sneer that Jay resolved to try to emulate when she was alone with a mirror. Fists clenched at his sides, his lower jaw thrust out, he faced down his sister. "The trouble with you, Caro, is you're so tied up in your own little world, you can't see what an awkward situation we've put Jay in."

This was no case of one-upmanship or sibling rivalry. Tyler was standing up for Jay, trying to protect her. Again. And a part of her, the part Jay's logical brain had labeled a malfunction, was so touched by his gesture that she didn't even consider the irony of a cyborg needing any protection whatsoever from a mere human.

"Tyler." She placed a cautionary hand on his forearm and

marveled at the warmth of him, the concern she could almost see vibrating over his body. "It's all right. I think I need to tell Caro the truth."

"You sure?" He searched her face.

"Yes."

"What's going on?" Caro's gaze switched from her brother to Jay, and back to her brother, unsure who best deserved her fierce glare.

"My father was working on some top-secret research for a private company," Jay told her. "I'm pretty much a genius when it comes to computers, so he co-opted me to collate all his data and research notes and write software programs for him. We were unofficial research partners until he died. And now there's a rival organization who want very badly to get their hands on his research. If I were to be identified on such a public domain, they would be able to track me down."

Caro screwed up her nose as she puzzled it out. "Lemme guess," she said. "This organization thinks you know all about this stuff your father was doing."

"Correct."

"Wow. Your life is starting to sound like an OTT thriller."

"Perhaps. Regardless, it's the truth." Mostly.

"Would it be so bad if you just, like, gave them the research?" Caro asked.

Jay infused her tone with as much emotion as she could summon. "Yes. It would be bad." And it hadn't been difficult to inject fearfulness into her voice because she truly did not want to fall into the hands of the men who pursued her so relentlessly. They would use her as a weapon if they could. And if they couldn't discover how to control her, they would take her apart piece by piece to learn about her, and try to replicate her.

She would destroy herself before she allowed that to happen.

"Not an option, then. Right. Gotcha." Caro accepted the terse explanation without a qualm.

"I like Snapperton," Jay said. "And it's tiresome moving from place to place. Which is why I prefer not to be too noticeable."

Caro chewed her lip. "So, like, if you find out these guys are closing in, you have to take off?"

"Exactly."

"Bummer," Caro said. "That would majorly suck."

Her brother's eyes were round and shiny and envious. Doubtless Tyler found the idea of leaving everything behind and starting all over again exciting. It wasn't. It was tedious—even for a cyborg.

"What about your mom?" Caro asked. "Bet she hates having to pack up and move all the time. Ours would have a cow."

"I've never met my mother."

Caro's eyes rounded. She appeared shocked to her core. "Crap. I'm sooo sorry." And she followed up by lunging at Jay and giving her what would have been a rib-cracking hug if Jay had been remotely human.

Jay patted her awkwardly on the back until Caro released her to ask, "So who's looking after you since your dad died?"

Jay noted Tyler listening intently, despite his apparent interest in the shaft of a tiny feather poking out from his comforter. He eased the feather out and twirled it between his fingertips.

She hadn't anticipated being thoroughly questioned. Even by someone as ingenuous as Caro there was a potential risk. However, there was no time like the present to see if there were any holes in her cover story. "My uncle. Well, he's not really my uncle, he's a guardian my father appointed in his will. He's out of town at the moment."

"Outstanding! What I wouldn't give—"

"To have to do all your own cooking and washing and housework," Tyler interrupted. "Yeah, bet you'd looove that."

Caro snorted a wry laugh. "Not! Okay, so back to the video clip. Tyler's personal problems might not be as huge as yours, Jay, but I don't think he should take all the heat for coming to your rescue. It'd be a crying shame if he had to give up coaching the girls' baseball team. They're doing really well in the league since he took over as coach."

Tyler's eyebrows disappeared beneath his tousled fringe. "A compliment from my sister? I think I just died of shock."

She sniffed. "I tell it like it is."

"And I happen to agree with you, Caro," Jay said. "Tyler should not have to take the blame. But I believe we can kill two birds with one stone. Remember the tracking program I mentioned? It will track all the users who've viewed the original clip, and decrypt their IP addresses so I can verify whether anyone who's likely to cause us problems has viewed it."

"You really are a computer geek!" Caro appeared totally unworried by the implications of a "normal" teenage girl possessing that degree of computer programming skills. Black and white. That was how Caro saw life. How restful it must be to live in such a simple, uncomplicated world.

And now for Caro's brother. The one who hid his true self. The one who had secrets, like Jay did.

Tyler gnawed his lip. "Even presuming all the views have been local—kids from school, Mom's work computer and the like—there're still too many cell phones and laptops and home computers unaccounted for. Either Vanessa *or* Matt could have forwarded the original clips to anyone by now. It's not gonna be possible to hack into everyone's computer, or swipe everyone's cell phone and delete this clip. Basically, we're screwed."

"In theory, it's not impossible to overcome that problem but it's far more likely I'd remain one step behind each new person sharing the video." Jay briefly considered using the device hidden away in her apartment. She'd based it on the same principle as an electromagnetic pulse weapon. Power it up, and it'd affect all electronic devices within a hundred mile radius, rendering them permanently useless.

Of course it'd also bring the entire town, and the surrounding area, to its knees, and more than likely telegraph Jay's whereabouts to anyone who cared to monitor such things. She would not utilize anything so obvious unless forced to.

First she would decrypt the IP addresses, calculate the odds she could be traced to Snapperton, and then decide her future. The problem of the video clip being viewed and then saved on a viewer's personal computer could be neutralized using an IP address-targeted virus. It wasn't a foolproof solution but it was the best she could do under the circumstances.

A mini version of The Pulse would be useful, too—one that would affect only a small, contained area, and was specific to certain devices such as cell phones. Jay wouldn't need to render the devices unusable, merely corrupt specific stored data files. She commenced designing both the virus and the mini-pulse device while she listened to Tyler and his sister.

"So we just have to hope...." Tyler absently stroked the tiny white feather he'd pulled from his comforter. His eyes were shadowed with worries he was reluctant to voice.

"Hope what?" Caro asked.

"The clip hasn't been emailed to anyone who really matters," Tyler said. "Bottom line, if Vanessa's already sent it to Principal Harris, and Ms. Harris decides I'm a bad influence and pulls me as coach, so what? I'll deal with it. In the grand scheme of things, it's nothing compared to Jay having to skip town because these guys have caught up with her."

He scrubbed his fingers through his hair, making it stand up in unruly, gel-assisted spikes. "Shit, Jay. I'm so sorry I've screwed things up for you. I'll be gutted if you have to leave Snapperton because of me. If I hadn't lost my temper—"

"Don't blame yourself. I noticed Matt attempting to video the fight earlier on and merely asked him to put the phone away. I should have insisted he delete the video, and checked whether he'd taken another. It is unlike me to be so distracted."

Tyler seemed more than a little concerned at the implication Jay might be forced to leave Snapperton. She liked that he wanted her to stay. She liked it very much indeed.

"So what are we gonna do?" Caro asked.

Jay swiveled to face her. "Do the students carry their cell phones with them at all times?"

"Duh! What planet are you from? Teachers have hissy fits if they spot a cell phone in class, so everyone keeps them in their bags on silent mode. But during breaks it's text city. Lunchtime in the cafeteria is chronic."

"Good." Jay allowed herself to smile as she explained her plan to Tyler and Caro, and contemplated what humans called "sweet revenge".

JAY DISARMED HER security system and entered her apartment. She didn't bother to turn on the lights—she could see perfectly well in the dark. She walked over to the table and powered up her computer. Given the tedium of the tasks she was about to perform, she instructed her neurological processor to shut down certain bodily functions, and entered a state similar to "downtime", when she recharged and upgraded her systems.

But as with all downtime periods in recent months, while Jay's fingers flew over the keyboard and she remained physically occupied, her mental processes played games. She was ensnared in recollection of the past. A *dream*.

The instant the first task was complete, she emerged from the dream. She shook her head in an attempt to clear the last vivid images from her mind before she began her next task.

Her dreams were yet another anomaly to add to the others affecting her. Cyborgs did not dream. At least, to her knowledge she'd not been programmed with the capacity to dream. But dream she did—recurring dreams about Father's death, which left her questioning everything she understood about herself.

Something was happening inside her. Something beyond the mere tangible aspects of her physical construction. Something profound.

A droplet of moisture plopped on to the tabletop. Jay stared at it, already knowing what it signified but strangely unwilling to confirm it absolutely.

Tears.

She was crying. Again. As she'd done when Father initiated the termination sequence and forced her to end his life.

She wiped her face. Tears. Such a human reaction to pain. But Jay was not programmed to feel physical pain. Ergo, the logical conclusion was that this reaction sprang from emotional distress—the kind of distress that, if she'd been human, might well stem from reliving a loved one's death.

But being distressed over Father's death was illogical. He had chosen to die, and his dying had served two purposes. It had prevented the old man from suffering a slow, painful death from an incurable cancer. And, by taking Jay's command codes to his grave, he had protected her as best he could. Now no living human possessed the commands that would make Jay a servant to their will. She could not be compelled to harm others, or used as a weapon. She was free to make her own decisions.

So why did she feel something she could only identify as sadness whenever she recalled Alexander Durham? And why sadness, when, if she felt anything at all, it should be elation over knowing that no one would command her again. Ever.

What was happening to her?

She ran an internal diagnostic and found nothing untoward, nothing to explain this strange phenomenon. She practiced a shrug in the manner of humans confronted with things they could not change. As Father had been so fond of saying, all would be revealed in time.

She picked up the back-plate, screwed it on to the pocket-sized electronic device she'd been working on, and placed the device on the tabletop. It resembled a cell phone. If anyone saw Jay with it, no one would think it strange or unusual. She didn't bother to test it. It would perform exactly as she'd designed it to.

She turned her attention to the monitor and the lines of data cascading down the screen. As she shifted, Tyler's unique fragrance wafted from the shirt he'd loaned her. The shirt she should have removed the moment she got home from school, and returned to Tyler earlier in the evening. The shirt she was so very reluctant to relinquish because while she wore it, she could pretend that Tyler was here, now, with her.

And then, an overwhelming urge to move coursed over her, through her. She tried to ignore the twinges of her muscles, the prickling of her dermis, as though her outer shell had become too small, too inadequate to contain what was within.

Jay was capable of sitting or standing motionless for hours on end, so this urge was yet another anomaly. Her brain constantly performed multiple tasks at once, so the part that insisted on dwelling upon Tyler was not causing the problem. That part happily analyzed every word he'd uttered in her presence, his every little nuance of tone and expression, while another part analyzed the data the program spat onto the screen.

She stuck it out for another three minutes before she gave in and pushed her chair from the table. The program would alert her if it identified any data outside the parameters she'd set. There was no real need for her to scan the screeds of code.

She spent an hour running through tai chi forms but even that discipline failed to calm her body's unnatural urges. And when the harsh beep of the electronic alert shattered the smothering silence, Jay believed herself grateful, despite knowing the alert heralded unwelcome news.

She quelled her brain's bizarre desire for her body to be continually in motion and resumed her seat to analyze the search results.

The IP address the program had targeted and the accompanying data appeared innocuous enough, but something about it had triggered the alert.

Adrenaline thrummed through her system, causing a flush of an emotion akin to human excitement. She might be what Tyler and Caro termed a computer whiz, and as a cyborg she had a unique advantage, but she was dealing with an extremely talented human, skilled at covering his tracks.

If she was correct in her assumption, she'd encountered this particular human before.

She smiled, anticipating the coming battle with a worthy opponent.

Chapter Eight

SHIT!

The man known to his team as Michael White, whacked his fist on his desktop. Papers fluttered into the air and then settled. Luckily there was no one to witness his lack of control. The building was deserted, the only light source in the darkened office the greenish-hued glow of his laptop's screen. It illuminated his face, throwing gargoyle shadows up the bland gray walls.

He couldn't believe his luck. First, the original clip he'd saved to his hard drive had been corrupted by a very sneaky little virus before he could back it up, and now *this*?

A masked Robin capered across his screen. She'd replaced the original *Boy Wonder Left Wondering* clip with one featuring another Boy Wonder—namely some guy who'd played Robin in the Batman TV series back the '60s.

Michael shook his head and leaned back in his chair. His life might be going down the toilet right now, but at least he didn't have to dress in a red top and green shorts with matching elf boots, and to top it all off, a shiny gold cape, like that poor bastard.

He scowled at Robin and closed his laptop. His fingers drummed the desktop as he considered his options.

His very limited options.

When the uploaded video had first been flagged by his tracking program, and he'd viewed the clip, he'd fist-punched the air. He knew exactly where she was. He could send in an extraction team, and it would all be over. He could say goodbye to chasing rumors and hearsay from one hick town to another. Hell, he might even be able to embrace his old life again, pick up where he'd left off. If his old life would still have him.

But it appeared the kid had been one step ahead of him—again. While he'd been imagining what his life would be like when this nightmare was over, she had been busy covering her tracks. It was a given she would have decrypted his IP address and realized she'd been compromised. It wouldn't be long before she was on the move—again. Or at the very least, planning another little surprise for anyone who dared come after her.

Michael considered keeping this latest development to himself. After all, until he got a hold of the original clip again, he had no hard evidence. But—

He huffed a sigh, grabbed his cell phone from the desktop and made the call.

The instant it connected, he spoke without waiting for acknowledgement. "I got a hit on the kid, sir. And—"

"You mean *it*. You'd do well to remember it isn't human, Mr. White."

Michael winced at the icy-cold tone. "Yes, sir. I got a hit on the cyborg."

"How?"

"A video clip uploaded to a social networking site."

"Send it to me now."

"She's corrupted the source file, and replaced the original clip on the site with another one. She's covering her tracks."

The silence on the end of the line commanded more information. Immediately.

"I'm working on it, sir."

More silence.

A single droplet of sweat rolled down his face, seeping into his shirt collar. "I need more time."

"Call me in the morning when you have something new to report."

"Yes, sir." Michael found himself speaking into the discordant beeping of an already disconnected line.

His employer was not known for his patience, or for anything less than substantiated facts. Which was why Michael had neglected to mention he knew where she was hiding.

Chances of her still being there were slim, he told himself, and—

God. He was torn. He wanted this over but he'd give anything in the world for the endgame to take place somewhere else. And, right now, he was praying she'd act true to type and up-stakes and vanish.

He slumped back in his chair and blotted his forehead with his sleeve. The kid—the *cyborg*—was good. Really good. So good, that even after five years of painstaking investigation, Michael still hadn't untangled the maze of offshore accounts that had absorbed Alexander Durham's considerable wealth after his death.

"They", the faceless, nameless people who comprised the clandestine corporation Michael worked for, had been playing a waiting game for years, hoping Durham's protégé would slip up and make a mistake. Finally she had, by allowing herself to be caught on video. But Michael wanted—needed—to be certain of all the facts *before* he sent in the extraction team. He couldn't risk civilians being caught up in the extraction. Especially not one of the civilians he'd seen in that clip.

If he could have avoided making that call, delayed a bit longer....

No. He'd done the right thing. His employer would find out if Michael sat on the information. He always found out.

Michael rubbed his eyes, rotated his shoulders and flexed his fingers. Regardless of what might prove to be a personal stake in this operation, he had a job to do. And if he valued his continuing health and wellbeing—and the continued health and wellbeing of his estranged family—the deadline he'd been given must be adhered to.

He would think of something.

He always did.

Chapter Nine

The crowd flowed around Tyler like there was a force field shielding him from physical contact. No one spoke to him. No one made eye contact. He might as well have been invisible.

Before Homecoming, he'd been star pitcher for the baseball team, and a top-scoring basketball player. He'd been one of the jocks who'd ruled the school. Girls had pulled all kinds of stunts to get his attention. But after the Vanessa debacle, he'd been demoted to a kid on the fringe who didn't fit in anywhere.

If he had spoken up, defended himself against the lies and rumors, maybe he'd have kept some of his friends. Hell, he might have even knocked the god of jock-straps off his pedestal and shown Shawn up for the piece of scum that he was. But for Vanessa's sake, Tyler had kept quiet. At least, Tyler had convinced himself it was for her sake. Just like he told himself he'd done the right thing, and didn't give a crap what anyone else thought. Now—too late—he understood that by keeping it all locked up inside him, all he'd done was enable Shawn and Vanessa, and alienate most of his peers.

Greenfield High's current social structure was based around cliques. Sad and unimaginative, but true. And because Tyler had been one of Shawn's crew—and a douche-bag to any kid who *wasn't* one of Shawn's crew—when he fell from grace, it was one monumentally big-ass fall. Tyler became a freak, a jock-god accused of something so heinous, not even the jocks had been able to stomach him anymore. Everyone had their place. Everyone knew their place. And after that one incident, Tyler's place was at the very bottom of Greenfield High's social order.

At first it'd felt weird being invisible, but he'd gotten used to it. Plus-side, he didn't need to check in with anyone. He could do what the hell he liked. Downside, he didn't have anyone to watch his back. And at *this* school, life was tough if you didn't have someone on your side.

Tyler didn't want to drag his sister down with him. He made himself scarce rather than put Caro in a position where she might have to choose her brother over popularity. She had enough problems looking out for herself. It was no box of chocolates being on the cheer squad and keeping the likes of Bettina happy, while not losing who you were, and what you stood for. Caro somehow managed to walk that ultra-thin line of being popular, while not succumbing to the temptation of acting like a stuck-up bitch.

Tyler respected that about her. He'd never managed to walk that line. It'd been easier to treat people like crap.

Pity Caro's run of luck might soon be over. And, just like Tyler, she wouldn't fit in with any of the other existing cliques. Mind you, knowing Caro, she'd just form her own. Budget Fashionistas. Yeah. He could see it now.

The grin faded as he steeled himself to run the gauntlet.

Over lunchbreaks, he usually hung out in the music room. Mr. Whaley didn't have a problem so long as no one else had scheduled the room for practice. On the rare occasions Tyler did venture into the cafeteria, he sat way down the back, far removed from the food cabinets and even farther removed from what little natural light pierced the grime-layered windows. It was smart to avoid the prime tables—especially ones with an unbroken view of the lunch queue, from where Shawn would cast his eye over potential girlfriends, and Bettina's squad would loudly critique clothes and makeup, hairstyles and personal attributes, with such consummate viciousness they reduced less resilient girls to tears.

Today, Tyler dared the cafeteria, dared to be noticed, and worse, dared slide into a seat at a prime empty table, right up front. He tried to appear completely unconcerned. He seriously debated leaving Jay and Caro to it—they would manage fine without him—but he didn't want to miss the fun. Unfortunately for his rapidly waning daring, his sister and Jay were nowhere to be seen.

Kids balancing trays of food lurched past his table, nudging each other and whispering. Eyes slanted in his direction. Heads turned. Whispered words floated in the air.

Tyler began to feel like someone had painted a huge target on his back. His spine prickled with unease as he rummaged in his backpack for his packed lunch—yet another reason for the in-crowd to sneer at him.

A hush smothered the cafeteria. And then the elegant squeaks of designer shoes were echoed by the screeches of less desirable rip-offs.

Crap. Tyler knew without even glancing up that Shawn and Bettina and their entourage had just made an entrance. "C'mon Jay!" he muttered. "Where the hell are you?" To hide his agitation, he grabbed a library book from his bag, took a sip from his water bottle, and pretended to read.

The furtive reek of anticipation overpowered even the stink of burgers, fries, lasagna and other supposedly mouthwatering temptations. All the students seemed to be collectively holding their breaths, waiting for Tyler's juicy humiliation to commence.

The type on the page he was pretending to read blurred. He flicked the page over, and hunched his shoulders against whatever form retribution would take. A soda down the back of his neck. His lunch snatched from the table and tossed 'round the room. Maybe his bag upended and the contents sniggered over.

No problem. He could handle that. But perhaps Bettina would come up with something new and original for Shawn to do this time—something that would cause Tyler's control to snap and provoke him to retaliate, like he'd almost done in Bio. Then it'd all be on. He could just see himself wiping that smug look from Shawn's face....

Tyler clenched his fists tight and then relaxed his hands and rolled the tension from his shoulders. It was far too late to dust off the past and rehash it. No one would believe him anyway. Not now.

Whoops of familiar laughter were music to his ears. The girls' baseball team had arrived en masse. They were their own clique. They took crap from no one. Except maybe their coach. And only so long as whatever Tyler happened to be saying made sense to them.

"Catch!" he heard one of his team yell.

He glanced up in time to see Emma, his star pitcher, burst through Bettina and Shawn's tight-knit group, scattering kids like skittles.

Emma ignored their squawking protests, her eyes on the prize. She leaped, plucked the baseball from the air, and then flung herself into the chair next to Tyler... where she shot a hugely insincere smile at Bettina, who stood stock-still and open-mouthed while her group fluttered about her, smoothing their ruffled plumage and exchanging varying expressions of disgust and indignation.

"Gee," Emma yelled across the room. "Sorry, Betty, didn't see you there." She nudged Tyler in the ribs with her elbow. "Nearly got her," she said, eyes twinkling with suppressed mirth. "An inch more to the left and I'd have knocked her down and used her for a cushion—not that she'd make much of a cushion 'cause she's, like, such a bone-bag."

Emma spared a glance for the rest of her teammates, who'd all joined the food line. With a gusty sigh, she took out her lunch, pried open her sandwich and grimaced. "Bologna. My favorite. I'm telling you, Coach, when I get a sports scholarship to some fancy college, I'm never gonna bring a packed lunch again. I swear on my mom's maintenance money."

Tyler took a bite of his own sandwich and wondered what it would be like to have money to burn, like Shawn. Maybe if his dad had stuck around and his mom wasn't in a dead-end job—

"Hey, how come you scored a front table?" Emma asked. "Are you like, not feeling well or something?"

"I just felt like a change," Tyler said.

Emma snorted. "About freaking time. We'd sit with you more often if you got us a decent table."

"Thanks, Em."

She gave him a singularly sweet, sympathetic smile—one that told him she knew exactly why he usually hid down the back. "You know, that sister of yours might look like a top model candidate, but she has skills. We could sure do with her on the team."

Caro had helped out with practice a couple of times when Tyler had been laid up with the flu. She'd even subbed when the team had been down a girl. All the girls in the team liked Caro, and she really knew how to keep them focused. Em was right. Caro would be an asset.

Shame it was so not gonna happen. "We've been through this," he said. "Caro's too tied up with the cheer squad. She turned me down flat when I asked."

Emma smiled at him around her sandwich. "Well, maybe you should ask her again. Because if Shawn has his way, Bettina'll dump Caro from the squad. Meaning she'll have heaps more time up her oh-so-fashionable sleeve."

"Crap," Tyler muttered. "Does Caro know about this?"

"What do you think?" Emma half-rose from her chair, waving to catch someone's attention.

Tyler's breath caught as he spotted the familiar figure poised in the entranceway beside his sister. His face heated. He sucked down a few glugs of water to try and cool his face, wondering how merely gazing at Jay had the power to affect him so drastically.

To his surprise, Caro acknowledged Bettina with a curt nod, but ignored the rest of B's group, including Vanessa. Leaving Jay to join the cafeteria queue, she took the seat across from Emma.

Tyler studied his sister's tense, angry face. "Slumming, huh?"

"The air's not so putrid over here."

"Ah. You gave Shawn the good news, huh? Guessing he didn't take it well."

Caro unpacked her sandwich and took such a vicious bite that Tyler winced. When she'd finished chewing she said, "Jerk tried to make like it was my fault he was horn-dogging around. Like, if I put out, he wouldn't feel the need to get his thrills elsewhere."

"Dick," Emma said. "And speaking of dicks, hope his shrivels up and drops off."

Caro gave her a wan smile. "Thanks, Em."

Tyler reached across the table to squeeze his sister's wrist. "I'm sorry, sis."

"Don't be. I always knew Shawn was an ass. Maybe I thought I could change him. Or maybe I didn't know what the heck I was thinking. To add to my pain, there's Nessa. So much for being my best friend and having my back. The minute I dumped him, she stepped in to 'console' him. She's been all over him like a rash today. It's enough to put me off food for life."

Tyler tossed his own sandwich aside. Vanessa and Shawn? Jeez. What was the girl thinking? "Doesn't he know she's the one who uploaded the clip of him dumpster-diving?"

Caro snorted. "Yeah. He knows. But evidently Nessa talked him 'round. Or something."

Heavy emphasis on the "or something". Caro obviously figured Vanessa was putting out to keep Shawn happy, but Tyler knew there were other things Vanessa could give Shawn to keep him onside.

"Matt's pretty annoyed about being dumped," Caro said.

Since Tyler had been in Matt's place, he knew "pretty annoyed" was putting it mildly. "What about your place on the squad?" he asked his sister. "There've been, ah, some rumors—"

"With regionals so close, Bettina knows she can't afford to drop me from the squad. And the squad means everything to her. So if it comes down to keeping me happy, or keeping her stepbrother happy, guess who she'll choose?" Caro smiled, but it didn't reach her eyes.

"Darn," Emma said. "I was kinda hoping you'd get kicked off the squad so you could come and play for us."

"Aww, that's so sweet," Caro said. "Sorry Em. It's a 'no' from me. It's those uniforms of yours—I wouldn't be seen dead in one. Truly hideous."

Emma shrugged. "Some of us beg to differ. Pity. Guess we'll just have to pin our hopes on some new blood."

Sara, the team's catcher, grabbed a seat, prompting the rest of the girls to follow suit. "Sorry." Tyler dumped his bag on the seat next to him. "I'm saving this seat for someone."

"Someone named Jay, I'll bet," Caro said. "And speaking of Jay, I bet *she's* got awesome ball skills."

"Jay?" Sara said. "Isn't that the chick who dumped Vanessa on her ass yesterday?"

Emma smirked, obviously relishing the memory of Vanessa's humiliation. "Yep. That'd be her. The girl with the long hair, holey jeans, and screamingly red t-shirt, waiting in the queue."

Sara nodded her approval. "She's cool."

"Yanno?" Emma gnawed a fingernail as she gave Jay a once-over."She's got a style all her own. Bet you're itching to make her over, right Caro?"

"The thought had crossed my mind."

Emma huffed on her non-existent nails and pretended to polish them on her t-shirt. "Seriously. Don't muck with perfection, sweetie."

Caro eyed Emma's outfit of baggy jeans and a sloppy, fire-engine-red t-shirt, and wisely took another bite of her sandwich. Tyler bit his lip to keep from laughing at the expression on his sister's face.

A buzz drew his attention. He glanced up, took it all in, and quickly dropped his gaze again. Vanessa and Shawn were deep in whispered conversation, casting dagger-like glances in his direction. Vanessa's gloss-slicked lips were downturned.

"Ah crap," he muttered, as Vanessa stroked Shawn's arm, and then slinked toward Tyler's table. "Here comes trouble."

"AKA the skanky ho," Caro said, loud enough for Emma to

hear and whoop with laughter.

"Well, if it isn't Greenfield High's ex-Boy Wonder." Vanessa fixed Tyler with a saccharine sweet, insincere smile. "I have no idea how you managed to sabotage my upload, but it'll be a wasted effort when I send the clip that's still on my phone to Principal Harris."

It seemed to have escaped Vanessa that Jay's stunt was far more of a conversation-starter than watching Tyler take on Shawn. Vanessa was out to get him—no two ways about it. Ironic considering if he spilled the truth about Homecoming, it'd start a shit-storm… with her taking center stage. God only knew what her reasoning was. It didn't make any sense.

Tyler gave her his widest grin. "Gee, Vanessa. You shouldn't have gone to all this trouble for little ole me. I might end up owing you a favor. Or something."

Her eyes narrowed and loathing twisted her pretty face. "In your dreams!" she spat.

"Nightmares more like," Caro said, glaring at her former BFF until Vanessa flushed and fiddled with the hem of her short-shorts.

"Hey, Nessa," Emma interrupted with a toothy grin.

Uh oh. Tyler knew what that grin heralded. Em had a way with words that was legend amongst her teammates. Vanessa was about to be on the receiving end. This was gonna be ugly.

"I've been dying to know something," Emma drawled. "Are you a skanky ho twenty-four-seven? Or only when there's a penis you feel the need to impress hanging 'round?"

Vanessa opened her mouth as if to reply, frowned, then abruptly turned her back and flounced back to her friends.

"Ouch! That's gotta hurt. Nice one, girlfriend!" Caro high-fived Emma.

Tyler's gaze followed Vanessa's swaying rear.

He waited for the ache of pure yearning to course down his spine. He used to think Vanessa was the prettiest girl he'd ever seen. Even after she'd dumped him for Matt, he'd still thought her model-worthy gorgeous. But today she just wasn't doing it for him. Compared to Jay, she seemed brittle and spoiled and....

Bland.

Bettina and Shawn's peeps were all twittering about their oh-so-important little lives—nothing unusual there. But for once, Vanessa seemed apart and separate from them, as though she'd cocooned herself in her own little world. All her flashy, "look at me!" arrogance had drained away. Her eyes were downcast. She'd wrapped her arms around her middle. She looked entirely miserable, like she was doing her utmost not to burst into tears.

When Bettina prodded her for a response, Vanessa lifted her head and caught Tyler staring at her. She flipped him the finger and turned her back, linking her arm in Shawn's and cuddling up to him.

Tyler laughed but there was no joy in it. More fool him for sticking out his neck and trying to protect her. He should have spoken out and left her to deal.

He spotted Jay approaching and moved his bag, indicating she should take the seat he'd saved. "What's so amusing?" she asked.

"Vanessa. She never fails to live down to my expectations." Tyler glugged the last of his water and wiped his mouth with the back of his hand. "You set?"

Jay patted the pocket of her jeans. "Yes."

"Outstanding." And, seeing a measure of his own glee glinting in her eyes, he grinned. "Hey, guys," he said to his team. "Y'all know Jay?"

"Yeah," Rachel, the team's relief pitcher chimed in. "We all know Jay. She's the one who dropped Vanessa on her chubby ass, and introduced Shawn to the inside of a dumpster."

Caro choked on a mouthful of water. "Looks like your reputation has preceded you, Jay."

"Apparently so," Jay said. "I trust that's a positive thing."

Rachel grinned at her. "Oh yeah. Very positive."

Emma caught Jay's eye. "Wouldn't mind a word with you later. I have a favor to ask."

Jay nodded. "Of course." She picked up her burger, took a huge bite, and wrinkled her nose.

"Whassup?" Tyler asked. "Does it taste off?"

"I don't believe I care for the taste of pickle," she said, sounding awfully surprised by the fact. She fished the pickle out and inspected it. "It doesn't look particularly appetizing, either."

He couldn't help laughing. She sounded like a little kid, disgruntled at being forced to eat her vegetables. "Just as well you don't have to eat it, then," he said.

He was distracted from Jay's amusing pickle issues by Matt approaching their table. What the hell did *he* want?

Matt snagged an empty chair from the next table and loomed over Caro, waiting patiently until she took the hint and inched over to give him some room. He grinned at her as he popped the tab on his soda. "Hey, babe. Whassup?"

She gave him cool, unimpressed eyes. "Oh, you know. The usual. Devil worship, animal sacrifice, bathing in blood on a daily basis—all that woo-woo stuff we boyfriend-less girls are forced to do to amuse ourselves."

Matt choked on a mouthful of soda and spluttered for a bit before it occurred to him she was kidding. He waved his soda in Caro's direction. "Yeah, right. Good one."

Tyler snickered. His sister always had an answer. She'd gotten *that* gene, too, whereas he always thought of the perfect thing to say hours later.

"What are you doing here, Matt?" she said. "Shouldn't you be over there schmoozing with the 'in' crowd? Being seen at our table won't do much for your social cachet."

He scowled. "Whaddya think I'm doing? Same as you. Avoiding certain people so I don't fricking smack 'em into orbit."

Caro didn't appear to have the least sympathy for Matt's plight. She angled her body to give him her back, and ignored him to chat with Emma.

"Hey, Tyler," Matt said. "Can I talk to you about something?"

After the stunt Matt'd pulled with the video, Tyler wasn't feeling particularly magnanimous. "If you feel you have to."

"In private. How 'bout I meet you after school?"

"I'm coaching."

"After practice. I'll give you a lift home."

"Yeah. Okay." He'd take the ride, but it'd be a cold day in hell before he'd help Matt out.

"Thanks, dude."

"Whatever."

Matt rose from his chair and sauntered off.

"What was that all about?" Caro jerked her chin at Matt's departing back.

Tyler shrugged. "Dunno. But I'm curious, so I'll give him thirty seconds of my time—after he's dropped me home."

"Do you think that's such a good idea?"

Before he could respond, Emma tapped Caro's shoulder, demanding her attention again. Tyler followed their gazes. Bettina had finally decided that the next table was worthy of her designer jeans-clad rear. She flicked her wrist at Shawn, and watched with a bored expression while he turned on the charm to oust some star-struck freshmen girls who were only halfway through their lunches.

Emma exchanged a glance with Caro. "Never changes, does he?"

"Nope."

"What were you *thinking*, girlfriend?"

Caro pretended to menace Em with her half-eaten sandwich. "Same thing as the rest of you. More's the pity."

Both girls swiveled in their chairs to look at the "he" in question, who was holding court at his table. As usual.

Caro shook her head, and mournfully contemplated her apple. "He's a looker, though."

Em snickered. "Yeah. If you like Ken dolls."

From the quirk of her lips, Caro was obviously amused by her friend's comment. "I think my next boyfriend will be someone who doesn't take longer to get ready for a date than I do."

"He might be a prize a-hole, but he's got it going on for sure," Sara said.

"Yeah. Stellar bod. Pity 'bout the toxic personality."

"He's one hot himbo and his old man's loaded. Who cares about his personality?"

"Yeah. I sure wouldn't say no to guy-candy that fine."

Tyler couldn't believe his ears. Jeez. Was that all girls cared about? How hot a guy was? How loaded his wallet was?

They all knew Shawn was a douche, but still they admired him. Girls. When it came to boys they were all the same: dumber than freaking mud.

Em redeemed herself somewhat by blowing such a truly rude raspberry, that her teammates quit with the Shawn-fest to roll about in their chairs laughing. "He's a man-slut who can't keep his hands to himself," she said. "We deserve better. End of story."

"You gotta admit, he's a reeeally hot man-slut, though," Sara said.

Em conceded the point. Reluctantly. "Okay. You got me on that one. Malibu Ken is one hot man-slut."

"He knows you're talking about him," Jay said. "See how he's thrusting out his chest, stretching out his legs and angling his body toward us? He feeds off the attention. You should ignore him. That's what I do whenever he bothers me."

The entire girls' baseball team tore their gazes from Shawn to stare at Jay like she was an alien life form.

Jay didn't seem at all fazed. She contemplated a fry. "I observe body language. It's a useful skill to master. Especially when dealing with annoying persons of the opposite sex." She popped the fry in her mouth and chewed.

"He doesn't do it for you?" Sara blinked in a bemused fashion.

"He doesn't do it for me," Jay agreed. And frowned. "These fries seem to be lacking some essential ingredient."

"Salt," Tyler said. "They never salt them enough. You gotta ask for extra. Hey, is Shawn still bugging you?"

She nodded. "Not as much as before, but I wish he'd stop staring at me as though he wants to consume me. I'm afraid that soon I'll be forced to do something drastic, like beat him up."

Sara shook her head in mock despair. "Uh, right. Whatever."

Yeah. Whatever. Tyler was not-so-secretly pleased Jay hadn't been bitten by the Shawn bug. If she'd fallen for Shawn, like any other normal girl, he'd have been gutted.

"So. What's the time, Jay?" Caro waggled her eyebrows in a meaningful fashion.

Tyler bit back a groan. Could his sister be any more obvious?

Jay stuck her hand in her pocket and—

"Wait!" Caro flushed pink when Jay frowned at her. "Ummm. I need to, uh, text Shawn. About a homework assignment. Can I borrow someone's phone?"

Sara tossed over her cell phone. "Use mine."

"Thanks." Caro flushed and scratched the back of her neck when Emma tossed her a how-the-hell-did-you-get-to-be-such-a-loser? look. She flipped open the cell phone.

What are you up to? Tyler mouthed at her.

She winked at him.

He smothered an appreciative grin. Ah, revenge. It was gonna be so terribly sweet.

Caro started texting. "Get ready," she murmured to Jay. "Do… whatever it is you're gonna do, when I give the okay, all right?"

Jay raised her eyebrows and Tyler heard her whisper, "This was not part of my plan."

"Pleeease? For me?"

Jay blinked. "Very well. For you."

Caro pressed Send, then skimmed Sara's cell across the tabletop and settled back in her chair to watch the fun.

Shawn's silver cell phone buzzed. As soon as he picked it up to peer at the screen, Caro whispered, "Go!"

Jay activated whatever device she'd hidden in her pocket.

The cafeteria echoed with blaring ring-tones as every cell phone in the place logged an incoming call. Christmas cracker-like pops mingled with squeals and muttered imprecations from startled students.

Shawn shrieked like a girl and flung his phone away. It skidded across the table and landed on the floor. The shocked expression on his face was absolutely freaking priceless.

Next to him, Vanessa whined and moaned piteously, wringing her hands. "OMG! My phone's died! What am I gonna do now? This is like, terrible! Oh. My. God!"

Tyler gleefully watched Shawn's indecision until Shawn finally got off his chair and scrabbled about on the floor to check his precious phone. He tapped it a couple of times, wrinkled his nose with disgust, then tossed it back on the floor.

Sara bashed her phone on the edge of the table a couple of times in an effort to get it working again. "Dead as. What the hell's going on?"

"A localized signal surge," Jay said. "I believe you'll find it's only affected cell phones within a short radius. May I?" She held out her hand for Sara's phone and checked it over. "Yes. It's as I thought. You'll require a new SIM card but other than that, your cell phone will be perfectly useable. Provided you don't whack it on the table again."

Sara leveled her a narrow-eyed, suspicious glare. "Yeah? How come you know all about this stuff?"

Uh oh. Tyler sought about for something to say that'd make Jay's knowledge seem reasonable. "Uh.... Jay's, um, a—"

"Before we moved out here, my uncle worked for a cellular service provider," Jay finished for him. "I used to help out after school."

Tyler widened his eyes at her, wordlessly encouraging her to elaborate.

"A lightning strike or electrical storm could cause a similar thing," Jay said, taking the hint. She shrugged. "My uncle told me sometimes there's no logical reason, and not even the technicians can figure out how or why such things happen."

Em had a very smug look plastered all over her face. "Shame. Guess this is one time I'm glad I can't afford a phone."

"Darnit!" Sara made a face. "Looks like I'm spending the

weekend reprogramming in all my numbers."

"Awww, poor baby," Em crooned, reaching over to stroke Sara's hand, making like some doting girlfriend until Sara shoved her away.

"They're not the latest models by any means," Jay said, "but my uncle has a box of cell phones at home. You're welcome to take your pick, Emma."

"And me?" Caro clasped her hands prayer-like before her chest.

"Of course. And Tyler, too."

"Thanks!" Caro's delighted expression abruptly clouded. "But won't your uncle be pissed if he finds a couple missing?"

"No," Jay said. "They're just collecting dust. He'll be pleased someone's found a use for them."

Em's freckled face lit up. "Awesome! Thanks, Jay." The bell rang, and she and the team headed off for class. "Hey," she yelled back. "Almost forgot. Meet you at the lockers after next period?"

Jay gave her a thumbs up.

Caro hung back. "Is that stuff about your uncle true?" she asked Jay.

"Partially."

"Which part?"

"The part about the box of cell phones. Don't worry," Jay said. "He won't mind me giving a few away."

Caro hugged her and practically skipped from the cafeteria.

"You've made her day," Tyler said. "She's wanted a cell phone forever."

"And what about you, Tyler? If I give you a cell phone, will it make *your* day?"

He did his best to ignore the pit-a-pat of his heart and the squirming sensation in his gut as he returned Jay's intent gaze.

Cool, calm and collected, that's how he'd play it.

He took a deep breath, and then grabbed Jay's hand and pulled her to her feet. Cradling her face in his palms, he leaned in to kiss her lightly on the lips. "You've already made my day."

As he exited the cafeteria, some instinct made him glance back over his shoulder.

Jay was standing exactly where he'd left her. Her eyes were closed and her fingers rested on her lips.

Whoa. Tyler hadn't expected that kind of reaction. It'd just been a friendly kiss. Nothing for either of them to get worked up about.

Yeah. Riiight.

Chapter Ten

JAY'S LIPS CURVED, anticipating Tyler's reaction. He hadn't spotted her yet. Right now his attention was on Emma, the team's pitcher. The corners of his mouth were curved downward and when he spoke, his voice was gruff. "You're off your game, Em."

Emma slouched over to him, rotating her shoulder joint. "Sorry, Coach."

"What've you done to your shoulder?"

"Hurt it yesterday. 'S only a strain. Nothing serious."

Tyler's scowl deepened at Emma's folly. "Next time, tell me straight up. No point in making the injury worse." He jerked his chin at the bleachers. "Plant your dumbass self over there and rest up for the rest of the session."

Emma jogged over to the bleachers to join Jay. She leaned back and stretched out her legs. "Coach wasn't *too* pissed with me. Reckon he'll give Rachel a turn, then you'll be up."

"Why are you insisting that I do this? If I turn out to be an excellent pitcher, you risk losing your place on the team."

Emma shrugged and threw Jay a lopsided grin. "Can't see that happening. Not unless you're really something special."

Jay quirked her brows. "I can hardly be worse than Rachel." With her gawky, graceless limbs, the team's relief pitcher resembled a flapping seagull—a resemblance that was compounded even more when she lost her balance on the follow-through.

Emma hissed in a breath between clenched teeth. "Rachel, Rachel, Rachel. That's just plain sad. Tragic, even."

Jay analyzed the pitch. Rachel hadn't had anything like the leverage needed to make the ball curve as she'd intended, which was the main reason the ball had stayed up in the strike zone and proved so easy to hit.

Tyler covered his face with his hands and groaned. Loudly. "Rach! What the hell d'ya call *that*?"

Rachel screwed her face into a hopeful expression. "Uh, a curveball?"

"A curveball?" Tyler stood arms akimbo, bristling with indignation. "A *curveball*? You've gotta be kidding me. An extra base hit waiting to happen, that's what I call that! How many times do I have to tell you? Stick with the fastball! No damn point trying anything fancy until you've got the fastball sussed. Which you haven't."

"But Coach, I—"

"But nothing. You haven't mastered it until I say you've mastered it. Which will be when you can throw it for a strike just about every single freaking time. You got that?"

"Yeah, Coach. I got that."

Tyler raked his hands through his hair and Jay could see him tugging on the ends. He didn't look over at the bleachers as he bawled, "Yo, Em! Let's see what this friend of yours has got."

Emma nudged Jay. "Go on. Show him how it's done."

"What happens if I'm worse than Rachel?" Jay wanted to know.

"Guess Coach'll give me heaps for wasting his time."

"We can't have that, now, can we?" Jay allowed a grin to split her face.

"Hey, didn't you bring a mitt?"

"I don't own one."

Emma shook her head. "Borrow mine. Just don't let on to Coach or he'll lecture you big-time."

"Thanks." Jay pulled on the mitt—not that she needed one, but it wouldn't be prudent to attract undue attention.

Tyler did the anticipated double-take as she strolled toward him. He smoothed his expression, hiding his reaction from his team, but Jay spotted his curiosity. And his pleasure at her presence.

"This should be interesting," he said.

"Indeed." Jay put aside her analysis of his fascinating reactions to review the mechanics of pitching.

For the entire duration of her pitch, the pitcher was required to keep one foot in contact with the top or front of the pitcher's rubber—a twenty-four-by-six-inch plate atop the pitcher's mound. This meant Jay could take no more than one step backward and one forward when she delivered the ball. Once she'd released the ball, her foot could leave the rubber.

There were five phases of pitching. Wind-up. Cocking, when the arm was brought back and up in preparation for the forward throw. Acceleration, when the arm came forward in preparation to releasing the ball. Deceleration, when the arm slowed down after releasing the ball. And follow-through. It was important for the pitcher to understand which muscles were used during each phase so injuries could be avoided. During the wind-up phase, for example, the shoulder muscles played only a very small part compared with the leg muscles.

Jay visualized each phase.

Tyler—Coach—gave her a professional once-over as if to

gauge her suitability for the sport. "Em reckons you're a damn fine athlete—just the sort we need on the team."

"Emma presumes too much." Jay held Tyler's gaze. "I'm nothing special."

"Hmmm. Tell me what you know about baseball."

"Quite a bit in theory. But I'm sure we both know all the theory in the world doesn't help when you're out there facing the reality of the game."

He cracked a grin. "Good answer. What's your specialty? Pitching, batting or fielding?"

She shrugged. "I don't have a specialty. I'm sure I can acquit myself reasonably well in all three disciplines, though."

He chewed his lip while he processed her response, perhaps trying to decide whether she was being unduly modest. "Okay, let's see what you're made of. Start by showing me your pitching."

She obliged. Under Tyler's watchful eye, she threw around a dozen fastballs, making certain each one stayed within the expected velocity for a junior female player.

Tyler pursed his lips and tried to appear unimpressed. "Not bad. Let's see what you can do under pressure. Trace!" he yelled at one of the girls lounging in the bullpen. "You're up."

Trace roused herself and wandered up to the plate while Jay debated her next course of action. She wanted to acquit herself well. But not too well.

She focused on Trace, who certainly didn't seem in any hurry to take her place at the batter's box. The girl tugged her gloves, fiddling with the clasps. She stepped in the box and something inside Jay's chest tightened with—

Anticipation. It thrummed though her body, millions of little pinpricks dancing over her skin.

A sixth sense prodded Jay to glance up at the bleachers, where she spotted Matt and Caro picking their way toward Emma.

She glanced toward Tyler, noted him watching her intently.

An audience.

Alien emotions coursed through Jay's veins. A fierce glee, a craving to pit herself against another female. A desire to prove herself worthy enough to win a male's approval.

That she wasn't human, and shouldn't care what any human thought of her physical prowess, didn't concern her at this moment. She was caught up in the heady thrill of the coming confrontation. Pitcher against batter. Nerd against jock. Jay's cyborg ability to gather, analyze and extrapolate data, and then perform a specific task, against this girl's hands-on experience.

The game was on.

And then Trace stepped out of the batter's box.

Jay choked down a guttural cry of protest. She'd been ready, poised to begin a precise set of movements that would ultimately end with the ball being launched. She could almost *see* the fastball she'd been planning whizzing right past the bat and thunking into the catcher's mitt. That ball she'd been about to pitch, its trajectory and curve and speed.... It would have been a thing of beauty!

The heat that'd flushed her skin abruptly drained, leaving her cold and shaking.

Trace took a practice swing, then set her bat down, wedging the knob under her belt buckle as she fiddled with her gloves again.

Jay bared her teeth in a soundless growl. What on earth did this girl think she was doing? How could she spoil the moment with such... such... nonsensical mucking about for no reason Jay could fathom?

Trace took a step towards the box then halted, adjusting her cap before she cast a glance in Jay's direction. A challenging glance.

Knowing slammed Jay—a classically human "aha!" moment. She allowed the tension to drain from her body. This girl—Trace—knew Jay was "on". She might have appeared to be distracted while Jay had been pitching one fastball after another, but she'd been paying attention.

Hitting was all about timing. And pitching was about upsetting that timing, so it might appear the pitcher ultimately held all the power. An intelligent hitter knew better. And Trace was smart enough to know she could slow everything down and perhaps affect Jay's confidence and timing when she pitched. Trace hoped to control when Jay pitched the ball and puncture the momentum Jay had built.

Now she knew what Trace was up to, Jay did not perform any pitching exercises or resort to any petty little delays of her own, such as examining the ball or slapping it into her borrowed mitt. She simply stood in place. Waiting for her opponent. "Take your time. When you're ready," she called.

Trace threw her a curt nod, tacitly accepting the challenge. She stepped into the batter's box and this time her gaze flicked to Jay's right hand, trying to spot whether Jay had changed her grip.

Jay's estimation of the girl rose.

The preferred grip to pitch a change-up was known as a *circle-change*. She would hold the ball deep in her palm with her forefinger and thumb making an "OK" sign. Or she could hold the ball deep in her palm, encasing it with all her fingers in a grip known as the *palm-ball*.

Jay kept her fastball grip, holding the ball loosely at her fingertips. She saw Trace take note of the grip, watched the sly grin curving Trace's mouth as she "read" her pitcher.

Trace tapped the plate with her bat.

"Don't try anything fancy, Trace," Tyler instructed. "Stick to the basics."

Jay would also heed Tyler's advice and stick to the basics so she had a baseline for her opponent's abilities. She pitched her usual fastball at Trace, not even flinching at the harsh *ping* of aluminum bat contacting with the ball. She glanced at Emma, saw her face crease with sympathy for Jay's plight.

"Nice line-drive!" Tyler yelled.

Trace allowed herself a full-blown smirk.

Jay snagged the ball the fielder lobbed at her. She knew she could pitch a fastball that would wipe that smirk off Trace's face and then some. But that knowledge was not enough... even though it should have been.

Jay knew she should stick to basic fastballs and not deviate from her average speed. She knew she should not do anything to stand out. But a deep-seated craving to do the unexpected had overtaken her. She wanted to impress Tyler. She wanted Emma and Matt to launch themselves from their seats and clap wildly. She wanted to beat this batter thoroughly. And to do it was going to require skill—more skill than merely pitching a horrendously speedy fastball.

For her next pitch, Jay kept the traditional fastball grip and pitched a tried and true fastball... except she used her inhuman strength and skill to slow the ball's speed, making it more of a *slow* fastball than a change-up.

Trace swung and missed, her timing completely out of sync with the ball. The wide-eyed shock on the girl's face was Jay's reward.

"Sterrrrrrike!" Tyler yelled.

Trace focused on Jay's handgrip with slit-eyed concentration. Jay kept her fastball grip and held it up for the batter to get a better look. "Don't quite know what happened with that one," she called. "Guess I got lucky."

Her next pitch would be a *sinker*. Just before she released the ball, she turned it over and ever so slightly increased pressure with her index finger. Her sinker dropped seven-and-a-half-inches more than her usual fastball.

Trace swung and hit a ground ball. When she stepped back up to the plate she glared at Jay, as if daring her to try that one again.

Jay didn't bother to take her up on that dare. She checked to make certain Tyler was watching, and wondered whether he would be as impressed as she hoped he might be.

This time, she intended to perform a breaking pitch known as a *knuckle-curve*. Ideally, this pitch would spin like a curveball but wouldn't be as fast. Plus, it would be more deceptive than a normal curveball because the pitching motion was similar to a fastball. It would be far more difficult for Trace to predict and respond to.

Jay pitched.

Trace struck out.

Em's loud whoop pleased Jay no end but her elation died when Sara, who'd muffed the catch, had to scrabble after the ball.

"Sorry, Coach." Jay knew she'd erred.

A breaking ball—a pitch with a sideways or downward trajectory, which didn't travel straight toward the batter like a fastball—was far more difficult for a catcher to receive. In her desire to show up the batter, Jay had let down her catcher. It was not good teamwork. She waited for Tyler to tell her so.

"Fancy yourself a junkballer, huh? Would've been good for Sara to know that beforehand." Tyler scowled as he approached

Jay. And rightfully so.

"I'm not a junkballer. I was showing off. As you are no doubt well aware."

Tyler draped his arm over her shoulder. "Showing off aside, if you can bat as good as you pitch there's a place for you on the team."

Jay glanced over to see Emma giving her the thumbs up. She returned the gesture, then switched her attention to Trace.

The batter threw her a rueful grin. "Rather have you on our team than the opposition's," she called.

Jay considered the offer. She'd enjoyed the physical and intellectual aspects of the workout, the thrill of beating the batter. Perhaps she could do this, share in the camaraderie of belonging to a team....

Provided she reined in her regrettable tendency to show off and didn't draw too much attention to herself. If she wasn't cautious, she would end up pitching far beyond the physical capabilities of a mere teenage girl. If she allowed herself to be caught up in the delirium of the game, who knew what she might do? The provocative thrill of proving her superiority, and the even more intense thrill of performing for Tyler, had overridden all logic and commonsense out there.

Still, despite the risks, Jay was tempted. And then she spotted Rachel, the relief pitcher, slumped on the grass in front of the bleachers. Her hunched posture conveyed her misery and when she lifted her head and glanced quickly at Jay before turning away, so did the expression in her eyes.

If Jay took over as relief pitcher, Rachel would be left as an outfielder. Or worse, a spare who spent each game in the bullpen.

"Thanks for the offer, Coach," she said, meaning it. "But I can't accept a place on the team because I can't commit to a full season. Besides, you've already got two pitchers."

Tyler glanced at Rachel, and Jay knew he understood.

"Fair enough," he said. "Pity. You've got talent. Seems a shame not to use it."

"Perhaps."

Tyler beckoned to Rachel. "C'mon, Rach. Let's see that fastball of yours again. The rest of you, do your drills."

Jay headed for the bleachers to return Emma's mitt. "Sorry to let you down, Em," she said, taking a seat beside her.

"'S all right, Jay. I know why you did it."

"I can't believe you dipped out because of Rachel," Caro said. "Tyler's gotta be pissed."

"He understands. It wouldn't be fair for me to take her place."

"Rach is an average fielder, and an even more average batter," Caro said. "Tyler tolerates her in the team because she's happy to play second string to Em forever. Everyone else knows Em's too darn good. The only chance they'd have to prove themselves is if she was too injured to play."

"Ouch." Emma faked a wince. "That's a mite harsh, even for you, Caro."

"Oh, really?" The challenging lift to Caro's chin dared Emma to disagree.

"She's right," Emma admitted. "If I can't pitch, we're screwed. We could really do with you on the team."

"Sometimes," Jay said, "it's not just about the team."

"Try telling that to Coach if he's ever forced to put Rach on 'cause I'm hurt or whatever."

"You'd better start taking better care of yourself then, Emma," Jay said. "You can't afford to carry an injury."

Tyler had approached them in time to hear Jay's comment. "Yeah," he chimed in. "No more roughhousing with your brothers. You're gonna have to start acting like a lady, Em. For the team." He kicked at a scraggily hummock of grass, spraying dirt in all directions.

Em scowled at him. "Jeez, Coach. Do you always have to be such a smartass?"

Caro grinned. "Yep. He always does."

"I was thinking—" Matt began.

"Don't think too hard," Caro said. "You're only a boy. You might damage something."

He exchanged an amused look with Tyler. "Is she always like this?"

"Oh, yeah. Pity me, much?"

"Envy, more like."

"What?" Tyler rounded on Matt. "You seriously think you want a mouthy thing like *this* for a sister?" He grabbed Caro and tickled her until she was breathless with laughter and had to cling to Em's arm to stay upright.

"Who said I wanted her as a sister?"

Jay interpreted the blush blooming on Caro's neck to mean Caro was not as unappreciative of Matt's attentions as her sneer suggested. She wondered why Matt only hinted at his interest, and did not merely state that he found Caro attractive. And why Caro gave off such mixed signals, as though she was embarrassed to return his interest. Matt was no longer going with Vanessa, and Caro was no longer with Shawn, so what was the issue?

Tyler fidgeted, and Jay guessed he was reacting to the undercurrents flowing between his sister and Matt. "Actually," he said to Jay, in what had to be a blatant attempt to change the subject, "you know that offer of a cell phone? Can I take you up on that?"

"Of course. When?"

"Practice is over, so how about now?"

"Hey," Matt said. "Don't forget I'm giving you a lift home. You might as well catch a lift, too, Caro. Since you're both going the same way and all."

"How very gracious," Caro said. "Perhaps you can offer Jay a lift, too. And Em."

"What am I?" he grumbled. "A taxi service?"

"Tomorrow would be better for me," Jay said. "You and Caro can both come over to my place after school and stay for a meal if you'd like."

"Sounds good." Tyler offered his hand. Jay took it and allowed herself to be tugged to her feet.

"I've got cheer practice," Caro said. "Can I come 'round after that? I'll be an hour and a half—provided I can get through the entire practice without Ashlee doing me bodily harm, of course. If she clocks me again, I'm not sticking around."

"Of course," Jay said.

They all trailed Matt to his car and although he grumbled some more, he seemed more than willing to be a taxi service. Em was first to be dropped off, and then it was Jay's turn.

"You live here?" Caro gazed at the street-level stores.

"Yes. My apartment is on the top floor of this building."

"Cool!"

"Won't be a sec," Tyler said. "I'm just gonna walk Jay to her door."

Matt peered at him over the rims of his sunglasses. "Whatever, dude. Don't do anything I wouldn't do."

"Well," Jay heard Caro say to Matt. "That sure leaves him a lot of scope."

"You can scope me, anytime, babe."

"Oh fergodsakes," Caro said, and Jay could just imagine her rolling her eyes at Matt in mock-disgust.

Tyler reached for Jay's hand as they walked to the entrance of her building. She felt a little thrill course through her body. What would Caro and Matt think if they saw? And what if Tyler kissed her again?

"See you tomorrow, Jay." He squeezed her hand.

Time seemed to slow. And then, just when the adrenaline-fueled anticipation pricking her body became too much to bear, Tyler kissed her cheek.

Heat flowed to that spot, warming her skin, sensitizing it and making her gasp. Her gaze flew to his, and she saw him smile.

His walk back to the car was more of a saunter, as though he knew Jay's gaze would be on him. She waved at him as Matt drove off. And she replayed the scene over and over in her mind, examining every possible nuance of tone, of touch, of possible intention.

If this *feeling* was a malfunction, a product of some anomaly she couldn't yet detect, then Jay wasn't at all certain she wanted to fix it.

She could still feel the warmth of Tyler's hand in hers, a phantom reminder of the boy himself, as she unlocked her door. She was still smiling, remembering, savoring, when she stepped inside.

The emptiness of her apartment momentarily overwhelmed her. That emptiness seemed to take on a life of its own, morphing into a shroud that reared up to smother her in its cold, friendless embrace. And Jay stood frozen in her doorway, stricken by the aching hollowness in her heart.

It took her a full minute to identify the feeling. It was a yearning for something an inhuman creature—a machine—could never have.

Chapter Eleven

Tyler and Caro arrived home with Matt in tow, and discovered their mother had gotten off work early. Much to Tyler's embarrassment, his mom made it abundantly clear she was thrilled to itty bitty pieces he'd brought a friend over.

Matt? A friend? Yeah, right. Not hardly. And Tyler only got his mom to quit plying Matt with cookies and sodas and pointed questions by dragging his "friend" up to his room.

Caro stuck her head through the doorway. "Watch out for that chair," she said to Matt. "It bites." And then, mimicking her mother with a skill that made the hair on Tyler's nape stand to attention, "I think you're mature enough to shut your door when you have a friend over, Tyler."

"Shut up, Caro." Tyler slammed the door and resumed his seat on the end of his bed.

"Your mom's cool."

"Yeah. She is. Now cut the crap. What's with the sudden need to talk to me, Matt?"

Matt scratched his chin. His gaze flitted around Tyler's room, taking in the posters on the walls, the worn carpet, the basic wooden furnishings, finally resting on the guitar case poking out from under the bed. "I didn't send Nessa the video clip of you and Shawn fighting, okay? I showed it to her, sure. But she sneaked my phone and forwarded it to hers."

"Whatever. That all you wanted to talk to me about?"

"Not exactly. Wanted to know the real deal about Homecoming."

"Yeah. Right. Like you haven't heard the story a zillion times already." And acted like you believed it. And let me hang. And like I'm ever gonna confide in you in a million years.

Matt leaned back in the wobbly desk chair and nearly assed over when it tilted far more than it should have.

Tyler sniggered. "Sorry, dude. But Caro did warn you 'bout that. It's on its last legs."

Matt gave him "yeah, sure" eyes. "Shawn's full of shit. I've never believed his version of what went down."

"Gee, Matt. I really appreciate your support. Especially since it's come, like, so many months after Shawn's 'shit' hit the fan." Tyler knew he'd injected just the right amount of sarcasm into his voice when Matt winced and looked all hangdog and guilty and sorry as hell.

"S'pose I deserved that."

"Yeah. You really did." Tyler registered a muffled noise. He put his finger to his lips, cautioning Matt to silence, and jerked his chin at the door.

Matt's brows rose. *Your mom?* he mouthed.

Tyler eased off the bed, tiptoed over to his door and yanked it open. As he'd suspected, he surprised the bejesus out of his eavesdropping sister, who squealed and jumped like a scalded cat. He didn't say anything, simply stood there, glaring at her, until she slunk off down the hallway and disappeared into her room, slamming the door behind her.

"Jeez, she's a pain," he groused.

"Naw," Matt said. "She's cool. Hey, d'you reckon all the attention means she might have a thing for me?"

Matt's tone was so hopeful and so unlike his usual why-bother-with-a-straight-answer-when-a-smartass-one-will-do, that Tyler's glib response died unspoken. "Maybe. It's kinda hard to tell what she's feeling when she's still so pissed at Shawn."

Matt's shoulders slumped. "Yeah. On the rebound and all that, huh? About Shawn. I figure he and Vanessa lied through their teeth about what went down at Homecoming. I reckon you got a raw deal. It really pissed me off when Shawn got you benched. Coach is a spineless dick. He should have told Shawn to stick it."

Tyler snorted. "Yeah. And while he was at it, he should have thanked Shawn's daddy, the *mayor*, for withdrawing his hefty yearly donation. Like that was ever gonna happen."

Matt sighed. "I want to set the record straight. That okay?"

"Maybe. Depends on your motives."

"You don't trust me?" Matt faked being stabbed through the heart. "Wow. That's harsh, dude."

Tyler just stared at him.

"Okay, okay. You got me. I have a motive. I want to take Shawn down. That's why I took the vid of you two beating each other up—was hoping to use it but it kinda backfired."

"Ya think?"

"Yeah. Sorry. But the dude needs one big-ass wake-up call, and I'm hoping to be the one to give it to him. You with me?"

Tyler chewed over Matt's words. Watching Shawn lose his top-jock spot held major appeal. Not even Shawn's influential father would be able to haul Shawn's ass out of that particular fire if Tyler went public with what he knew. But the same reason he'd remained silent and taken the rap in the first place still applied. It wasn't just about Shawn. There was Vanessa to consider, too. Shawn knew that. He'd relied on Tyler's instinct to protect Vanessa—leveraged it and used it to take down a rival.

Bottom line? Tyler *still* didn't want to get Vanessa into trouble. Even if she had morphed into a total bitch lately.

Matt stared intently at him, gauging his reactions. "It's Nessa, isn't it? You're protecting her. You've always been protecting her. Man, I didn't think you were *that* gone on her. Would never have taken up with her after she dumped you if I'd known."

Tyler believed him. They'd once been teammates, and if not close friends, then at least friends. He figured Matt was on the level and there was no hidden agenda.

"I'm not gone on Vanessa," he said. "Not anymore. I mean, I think she's pretty hot and everything. Or I used to. But not now. Not since—" He'd been about to say "Not since Jay" but Matt beat him to it.

"Yeah. That Jay chick's really something. Not my type, but I can sure appreciate what she's got to offer." He noticed the less-than-impressed expression on Tyler's face and warded himself with his hands. "Chill, dude. Sooo not interested, okay? Now, your sister— Don't take this the wrong way, but *she's* my type. The keeper-type. You know what I'm saying? Makes all the other girls seem like practice runs."

Tyler rolled the tension from his shoulders. "Yeah. I know what you're saying."

Matt sagged—slowly and with a great deal of caution—back into the chair. "Back to Nessa. I get you're protecting her. And I figure it's gotta be something real big, right? 'Cause, dude, lately she's owning her inner bitch and you still won't roll over on her. So why don't you spill and we'll figure a way to keep us both happy, huh? Besides, I figure I deserve to know what the frick her deal is."

"Yeah. Guess you're right." And God knew it'd be a huge relief to tell someone the truth after months of keeping it under wraps and having it eat away at him. "But before I spill my guts, you gotta promise you won't go off half-cocked."

Matt's brows knitted into a troubled frown. "That bad, huh?"

Tyler's stomach twisted into a knot. Bile scorched his throat and he swallowed convulsively. He'd thought all this was behind him—convinced himself he'd shucked it off, moved on and all that crap. But now the prospect of telling someone loomed, all the disgust and horror and panic he'd felt that night crashed in on him again.

"Yeah," he finally said. "That bad. So no going all vigilante on me. We'll both figure out what happens from here. Deal?"

"Deal."

Tyler slid off the edge of the bed and planted his butt on the floor. And the more he tried to find the right words, the more he wondered whether *Confessions Of Tyler* was such a good idea.

Aw, hell. He'd just come right out and say it. "Vanessa was dealing."

He snuck a look at Matt's face but Matt wasn't giving anything away. Okay then. "At the after-party, I walked in on her doing a deal with a couple of guys. They freaked and took off. Vanessa must've been on something, because I've never seen her like that before. Talk about OTT. She was all hysterical, begging me not to tell her parents, sure she was gonna be expelled and stuff. She wouldn't listen when I told her I wouldn't say anything if she promised to quit dealing. She offered me drugs. I turned her down—of course. And then she offered something else."

"Sex."

Tyler felt his face burning. Sure he was a teenage boy whose hormones practically owned him, but the shame of that night was still very very real. "Yeah. And shit—" He sucked in a deep breath and let it out real slow. Might as well tell all. "I knew she was with you but I'm only human. So I was tempted. Real tempted. Who wouldn't be?"

"Chill, dude. I get where you're coming from." Matt laughed, but it sounded more wry than anything else. "Nessa can be pretty damn tempting when she puts her mind to it."

"You got that right. Those short-shorts...."

Matt's smirk told Tyler they were both on the same wavelength when it came to Vanessa's taste in clothing.

"Anyway, she threw herself at me. Like, literally. I was trying to calm her down and get her off me, when Shawn walked in." He shrugged. "That's kind of it, really."

"And the reason you didn't rat Vanessa out?"

"It's complicated."

Matt didn't say anything.

Tyler stared at the ceiling. Matt would probably think he was the biggest sap on the planet but— "Because I know what her parents are like. I've seen them look at her like she's the biggest disappointment in their lives. It gutted her. And a couple of times, after they'd given her the big lecture about what a no-hoper she was, she cried all over me about it, you know? She swore if they ever found out, they'd have her shipped off to one of those boot-camps for emotionally disturbed kids. And I could totally see them doing that to her."

Matt picked at a hangnail. "Figures. Nessa's parents are the sort who go in for emotional abuse. 'Specially her mom. She's a real piece of work. And probably the main reason why Nessa's such a screwed up chick in the first place."

"Yeah. You got that right. I couldn't do that to her. So I kept quiet."

"Riiight. That's it, huh? That's the big secret?"

"Yup."

Matt puffed out a disgusted breath. "And you let Shawn tell everyone you'd slipped Nessa something, then tried to do her? *And* let him convince Coach to kick you off the team? Man."

When Matt put it like that, it seemed like a really dumbass thing to have done. Hell, if Shawn had taken it a step further, and if Nessa had been prepared to lie and back him all the way, Tyler could've ended up slammed with a sexual assault charge.

Then Matt surprised the hell out of him by saying, "I probably would've done the same thing."

"Huh? *You*? Puhlease."

"Jeez, dude. Your opinion of me is hardly flattering."

Tyler grinned. "Ya think?" Still, it helped knowing Matt understood why he'd given Vanessa a free pass. It helped a lot more than he cared to admit.

"And what about the Boy Wonder? What the eff was he doing in that room anyway?"

Tyler hit Matt with full on "Well, duh!" eyes. "You even gotta ask?"

Matt smacked himself upside the head with the heel of his hand. "Buying."

"Yup."

"You sure?"

"He walked in waving a wad of cash and telling Vanessa exactly how many AASs he wanted. He wasn't pleased to see me, that's for sure."

Matt jerked in his seat and almost fell off the untrustworthy chair. "AASs?"

"Anabolic androgenic steroids. AASs."

"Dude, I know what they are. I figured it might have been prescription stuff she was dealing. Vicodin or Ritalin or whatever. But AASs? Damn. No wonder Shawn's got such a short fuse. Shit."

And then Matt lunged from the chair, sending it crashing to the floor. "Shit! AASs. Perfect."

Tyler could only describe the expression on Matt's face as unholy glee—an expression he'd often seen on his sister's face. An expression that meant things were gonna start getting real out of hand, real soon. He switched his attention to his chair. Which was now in two distinct pieces. "Yeah. Perfect."

"Big match coming up in a couple of weeks," Matt said, looking all nonchalant. "Word is, there'll be some scouts snooping round. And I've got three more words for you, dude: Compulsory drug-testing."

Tyler groaned and covered his face in his hands, picturing all the drama involved with trying to get Shawn to piss in a cup without him getting suspicious. "Isn't that two words?"

JAY SCANNED HER immediate environs. When she was satisfied all was clear, she leaped from one of the uppermost branches of the large oak, startling the scruffy little dog that had been patiently sitting beneath the tree.

She hushed Fifi, and checked the dog's elderly owner was still napping in his old wingback chair in the sitting room.

He was. Jay could hear his snores over the blaring TV.

She squatted to ruffle the dog's fur. "Thank you for keeping me company, Fifi. It was a most interesting way to spend an hour. I'll see you later, okay, girl?"

Fifi whined and Jay rewarded her with one last pat and a scratch behind the ears. She performed one last scan to confirm she wasn't being watched. And then she leapt the fence and hit the sidewalk at what she considered to be a sedate jog.

Now she knew Tyler's secret—the sordid little trinity involving him, Vanessa and Shawn. What she would do with the information, how she might leverage it, she had no idea.

Yet.

Chapter Twelve

The first words out of Caro's mouth when she barreled through the entrance doors were, "I still can't believe you live in the same building as my favorite recycled clothing boutique!"

Because Caro seemed to expect a response, Jay said, "Yes. I believe I mentioned my apartment is on the top floor."

"That's so cool!"

"It certainly seems that way."

"Do you shop there?" Caro asked. And then, casting her gaze over Jay's jeans and t-shirt, answered her own question. "I guess not."

Jay examined the clothing Caro wore more closely. She'd already mentioned to Jay that she'd purchased the outfit at Black Angel. The ensemble consisted of a black vinyl corset-style bustier worn overtop a blood-red t-shirt, a tattered net skirt, and red leggings. The red-toned eye shadow Caro had dusted around her eye sockets made the contrast of her green eyes all the more startling. They glowed like she was some otherworldly creature. Her lipstick was an unexpectedly deep green that complemented her eyes.

Caro preened beneath Jay's attention. "It's my pseudo-Goth look. I figured I'd wear it today to shock the natives. What do you think?"

"I like it," Jay said. "I presume you didn't practice in that outfit."

Caro snickered. "Of course not. Bettina would've had a cow. I ditched the skirt and corset."

"You should be banned from that store," Tyler said. "You look like you're suffering a bad case of goth-witch-itis."

"Gee, thanks, bro." Caro made a point of sweeping her gaze over Tyler's tatty sneakers, worn jeans, and plain black t-shirt that had been through the wash so many times it was more gray than black. "Coming from you, that really inspires me to make more of an effort with my appearance."

"I think you look amazing," Jay told her.

"All you need to complete the look is a tat," Tyler said.

Caro blinked. "Really?"

"I was joking."

"Still...." Caro heaved a hugely disgruntled sigh. "Like Mom's ever gonna let me get a tattoo."

Tyler snorted. "Like you'd ever handle the pain of getting one. Besides, if you really were stupid enough to get some spider-web tat all over your neck, or face, or wherever, you'd be screwed once this phase wears off. You'd have to save up to get it lasered or something."

"What makes you think it's a phase?" Caro demanded. "And I'm not stupid enough to tattoo my face. I was thinking more the back of my neck, or my hip. Or even the base of my spine."

"Ick," said Tyler. "I'm imagining old, wrinkly pensioners with saggy tattooed skin, just so's you know. Sure doesn't do much for me."

Caro paused to consider that. She grimaced. "Much as I hate to admit it, you got a point."

"I can't imagine you with saggy skin and wrinkles," Jay said. It was the truth. For some reason she had yet to fathom, she couldn't visualize Caro as old. Or Tyler, for that matter.

Tyler laughed. "Happens to us all, eventually."

"Mmmm." Growing old with Tyler—Jay could do it of course, outwardly age her appearance to keep pace with his aging process. Spending the rest of Tyler's life with him.... It was something to consider.

"Hey, sorry I couldn't come over straight after school," Tyler said. "Did you get my note?"

He'd stuck a note in her locker, warning her that his music teacher had asked him to stay after class, so he'd stick around and wait for Caro. "Yes," she said. "Thank you for being so considerate."

He slanted a sly glance at his sister. "We'd have been here earlier if someone hadn't insisted on putting on her finery and redoing her makeup."

Caro sniffed, unrepentant. "Cheer practice is hell on makeup."

Jay led her guests up the two flights of stairs and ushered Tyler and Caro inside.

"Something smells good," Caro said. "What's for—? Whoa!" She whistled as she surveyed the apartment.

Tyler surveyed the space with a more critical eye. "This isn't what I expected."

"What did you expect?" Jay asked.

"I—" His gaze darted from her, to her living space, and back to her. He frowned and gnawed his thumbnail. "Dunno exactly. Just not this."

She paused to consider her apartment from Tyler and Caro's perspective. The area was like a smaller version of Greenfield

High's gymnasium. It had a high stud, with a series of small square windows inset just below the raftered ceiling. Given the lack of windows at viewing height, it would have been a gloomy, closed in space, save for two large skylights that drenched the apartment in light. Jay appreciated them solely because they provided her with an alternate exit from the building.

The space had been partitioned off at one end to form two bedrooms and a bathroom. The rest of the interior was open-plan, with a galley-style kitchen and laundry along one wall. The appliances were yellowed with age but in good working order. They had come with the lease. Jay had furnished the rest of the space with furniture she'd acquired from a deceased estate.

Aligned with the kitchen area was a massive mahogany dining room table with eight matching chairs upholstered in faded bronze velvet. The table was pitted with age but waxed to a high sheen. The lemon scent of the wax Jay had used still lingered in the air.

Beside the dining area, a large Persian rug delineated the living area. The rug was threadbare in patches, the intricacies of its pattern now faded and almost indiscernible. It'd been thrown in at no extra cost because it'd been deemed practically worthless. Jay had taken it because it reminded her of the rug that had adorned the polished floorboards of Father's living room.

Atop the rug, two settees and a matching lounger were arranged around a large, solid mahogany coffee table. The chairs were upholstered in buttoned burgundy leather, now burnished and spider-webbed with age.

Tyler spotted the ornate calligraphy specimen Jay had framed and hung on the exposed brick wall. "*For God so loved the world, that he gave his only begotten son, that whosoever believeth in Him shall not perish, but have eternal life. John 3:16.* What's that about?"

"It was my father's," she told him, a statement which wasn't strictly true. It was a replica of the piece the old man had hung on the wall of his study.

Jay had done the calligraphy herself, then mounted and framed it. This was the third replica of the piece. It wasn't always possible to pack her belongings each time she was forced to move. On more than one occasion, she'd uploaded a virus to wipe her computer's hard drive and left with only the clothes on her back. To Jay, the piece of calligraphy represented the old man's sacrifice for her—the cyborg he'd created in the image of his dead wife. For so long as Jay walked the earth, Mary Durham would live on. And so would the memory of Alexander Durham, Jay's creator.

Jay had also bought the estate's library, and the entire spare wall of the apartment was devoted to bookcases stuffed with books. Despite her efforts, only about a third of the large area was occupied with furniture. She wondered if the emptiness bothered Tyler.

He wandered over to scan the titles in the nearest bookcase. "So you like to read, huh?"

"Yes."

An understatement. Jay *needed* to read. The process of turning each page and disciplining herself to read every single word aloud, relishing the unfolding rhythm as each word segued into a sentence, a paragraph, a chapter, sweeping her inexorably onward until the final page when the author's vision was at last fully revealed.... It grounded her, gave her something in common with the humans she hoped to emulate and live amongst. Let her imagine, at least for the duration of each book she read, that she *was* human.

"Where's the TV?" Caro wanted to know.

"I don't have one."

"You don't *have* one? Oh. Okay."

Caro appeared so dismayed by the lack that Jay felt compelled to add, "I watch a lot of movies and programs on my computer."

Tyler had spotted the huge flat screen monitor and the rest of the computer equipment taking up a third of the dining room table. "That yours?"

"Yes."

He ambled over to check it all out. "Hoh baby! No expense spared, huh?"

"No." He seemed to be waiting expectantly so Jay elaborated. "When my father died, he left me heaps of money."

Some of his enthusiasm diminished. "Shit. Sorry. Didn't mean to, you know, get personal."

She shrugged. "It was a long time ago."

"Can I check out this sweet thang?" He indicated the computer, his gaze hopeful.

"Sure." None of Father's research notes were stored on this computer. They had all been destroyed. The sole remaining copy was encoded within Jay's artificial brain and protected by a verbal password calibrated to her voice pattern. Other than music and eBooks, there were no personal files on the computer, either—why would there be, when Jay herself functioned like a computer and could recall everything of importance? She powered up the PC and input the bios password.

Tyler flopped into the chair and clicked on the media player icon to check the list of downloaded songs in her library. Within seconds *Cold Play's* latest blared from the computer speakers.

"Awesome!" Caro held out her arms and did a three-sixty. Her face broke into a huge grin. "Your system is way superior than Shawn's Bose. He'd be green with envy."

"There's no point listening to good music on bad equipment," Jay said, meaning it.

"The acoustics in this place are incredible," Tyler said.

"You should bring your guitar over one day and check out what it sounds like."

"Thanks. I'd like that."

Both Tyler and Caro seemed to be waiting for Jay to do something. She concluded the "something" was for her to act the host. "Would either of you like a soda?" she asked.

"Cola, if you've got it," Tyler said.

"Diet for me."

Jay knew exactly what the contents of her fridge happened to be at any given time. "Sorry, no diet sodas," she told Caro. "Not that you need diet anything, anyway."

Caro beamed. Her brother sniggered and she stuck out her tongue at him. "Jerk."

Jay snagged the colas from her fridge and tossed one to Tyler and another to Caro. She popped the tab on her can and took a long swig, draining half the contents. Her appreciation for this beverage had only increased over time. She closed her eyes as sugary bubbles fizzed through her system like the nectar of some ancient gods.

Caro interrupted Jay's little sugar-rush. "What're you going to feed us? And more importantly, when? Starving, here!"

"Caro," Tyler scolded. "Don't be so damn rude. Where're your manners?"

His sister smirked at him. "Next thing you'll be digging up napkins, and wanting Jay to set the table with the *good*—" she formed quote marks with her fingers "—crockery. What are you? Our mom?"

"Ignore her, Jay," Tyler advised. "She's practically a savage until she gets fed."

The savage sauntered over to sprawl on the settee. "So what's it to be? Burgers? Pizza? Hope it's pizza. I haven't had pizza in ages." Caro sniffed the air. "Though it doesn't smell like pizza."

Jay quirked an eyebrow. "You don't think much of my abilities as a chef, do you? I thought we'd start off with *San Jacobos*, which are a type of tapas. Then I've made Pork Cassoulet for our main and—"

"Pork Casso-what?" Tyler asked.

"Cassoulet. It's a well-known French dish based on white beans cooked with pork, bacon, sausages and a variety of other ingredients. I realize that it's more winter fare, but it was a favorite of my father's and I wanted to share it with you."

"Uh, right. Sounds pretty fancy."

"And like you went to far too much trouble," Caro chimed in.

"It was no trouble." Jay waved a hand to indicate the slow cooker on the bench. She'd assembled the ingredients that morning, and put the cooker on timer. She lifted the lid to gave the contents a stir, and switched the dial to High. "I simply need to pan-fry the sausages and add them to the cassoulet, then it'll be ready in about thirty minutes."

Tyler wandered over to peer over her shoulder. "Looks pretty good," was his considered opinion. He inhaled, closing his eyes. "Smells even better. And what's for dessert?"

"Little pots of chocolate."

"Little pots of chocolate?" Caro asked.

"I think she means instant pudding," Tyler told his sister.

Jay opened her mouth to explain there was nothing "instant" about her melted chocolate, double cream and egg mixture, which had been flavored with pure vanilla extract and a dash of brandy, and then thought better of it. "Yes," she said. "That's exactly what I mean. There's ice-cream, too."

"Yum!" Caro said, which Jay gathered signified approval of the dessert menu, at least.

"Where're these tapa-thingies?" Tyler asked.

"In the refrigerator on the large white platter. If you wouldn't mind taking them over to the coffee table while I finish up here? Paper napkins are in the cupboard to the left. Don't feel you have to wait for me. If you're hungry then help yourselves."

"Sure thing."

Tyler performed his chores while Jay fished a pan from a cupboard. From the corner of her eye, she noted her guests exchanging mystified glances over the platter of tapas. She considered reassuring them as to the edibility of the Spanish appetizers by listing the ingredients and explaining the cooking method, but decided showcasing her knowledge would only make the situation worse.

Perhaps she should have gone with her first instincts, which had been to provide numerous bags of potato chips. But she'd wanted to cook something special for Tyler. Obviously she still had a lot to learn about acting "normal".

Her guests seemed to have reached an agreement that involved them counting to three, and simultaneously popping an appetizer into their mouths.

"This is really tasty!" Caro sounded so astonished Jay couldn't help smiling. "What are they called again?"

"*San Jacobos.*"

"Fancy name for ham and cheese fried in breadcrumbs?" Caro guessed.

"Exactly. They're often served hot but as I had to make them this morning—" Jay shrugged, and for once the gesture felt natural and not forced. "I'm told they're equally delicious served cold."

Tyler crammed another one into his mouth. "They sure are," came his muffled response.

"You must have gotten up really early this morning," Caro probed.

"Something like that." In truth, Jay hadn't gone to bed.

In the short time it took Jay to brown the spicy sausages and add them to the cassoulet, Tyler had made huge inroads into the tapas. In fact, Caro had taken possession of the platter and adamantly refused to relinquish it until Jay had sampled some.

"You're such a guts!" Caro complained to her brother. "Anyone'd think you got worms."

"I'm a growing boy. Hand 'em over."

"No way. And the only thing growing on you is the moldy crust 'round your barely-used brain. That, and your expanding stomach if you eat any more of these things."

The banter—insults—flew thick and fast, and Jay watched, fascinated. She regretted the silence that descended shortly after she served the main dish and her guests, now confident of her cooking abilities, turned their attentions to the contents of their bowls.

"That was fricking fantastic." Tyler had eaten two helpings. With a groan, he slid back on the settee 'til he was completely horizontal, and patted his stomach. "Don't think I could manage another thing."

"Pity," Jay said. "I've been told my chocolate pudding is heavenly."

"Heavenly, huh? Maybe I could find room for some." He groaned again and closed his eyes. "Just give me five minutes to digest."

Caro threw Jay a mischievous look, cautioned her to silence with a finger to her lips, and edged from her chair. She tiptoed over to Tyler and pounced on him, kneeling on his legs and tickling his ribs.

Jay grinned. Caro Davidson was merciless.

"Gerroff!" Tyler did his best to fend her off but Caro had the advantage. "Dude!" he yelled at Jay. "Some help here?"

Jay shook her head. "I don't think it would be wise for me to interfere with sibling rivalry."

Tyler managed to roll off the settee. Caro threw a cushion at him and the play-fight began in earnest.

Jay's grin grew wider still. She found herself wishing Father had created another like her, someone she could have talked to, confided in, shared dreams with.... Beaten up in a mock fight.

Her grin turned wry. What a ridiculous fantasy. She had been created to be self-sufficient in every way. She had no need of friends. She did not require companionship. She—

The cushion that smacked her cheek was a most effective end to her introspection.

Caro howled with laughter. "Gotcha!"

Jay reached behind her and launched a cushion unerringly in Caro's direction. It caught her right in the midriff.

"Ooof!" Caro wheezed. "Hey, easy on the missiles, Champ! You've got a heck of an arm on you, I'll say that much."

Tyler didn't bother to throw his cushion. He walloped the back of Jay's head with it instead. "Hah! Gotcha, too."

When she turned to face this new threat, Caro took the opportunity to grab another cushion and whack Jay on the back.

"Hey!" Cushion-less and outnumbered, Jay fended off both antagonists with her hands, taking care not to hurt them with her superior strength. "That's no way to treat your host. What would your mom say?"

They merely sniggered and walloped her with renewed vigor. The cushion fight soon degenerated into a full-on wrestling match, with a heap of tickling thrown in. Jay wasn't ticklish, but she crowed with laughter along with her guests. Even though she had to hold herself in check, she hadn't had so much fun since....

Ever.

Tyler's flailing foot knocked the empty platter from the coffee table and Jay, intent on escaping Caro's nimble fingers, rolled atop it. She felt it shatter beneath her and surged to her feet.

Caro and Tyler both froze, eyes wide with chagrin.

"Shit! Sorry, Jay." Tyler reached out to pick up one of the larger shards of crockery.

"Leave it," she told him, concerned that he would cut himself. "I'll clean it up. And don't worry, the platter was old but hardly an antique. No harm done."

"Actually," Caro said, her voice sounding wobbly and strange, "there has been harm done. Look." She'd risen to her knees to point at Jay, but now she sank back against the settee, her face pale beneath her makeup, the pupils of her eyes hugely dilated with shock.

"What's wrong, sis?" Tyler was instantly solicitous. "You not feeling too hot or something?"

"N-not me. J-Jay. She's hurt. Her arm. Oh God. Tyler, do something!"

Jay glanced down at her arm. "Oh."

"Shit!" Tyler stared at her, obviously appalled by all the blood.

Or perhaps it was the large shard of crockery piercing Jay's biceps.

Chapter Thirteen

Jay yanked up her sleeve to better examine the injury. She extracted the shard from her flesh and let it drop to the floor. The slash bled freely. Blood dribbled down her arm.

Caro made a strangled noise and Jay glanced up. Caro had turned an even paler shade of white beneath her makeup. "Call 911," she told her brother in a voice that was husky with shock and fear.

"Unnecessary," Jay said.

"You're so gonna need stitches," Caro insisted.

"I won't. I'll be fine."

"No freaking way will you be fine!" Tyler yelled.

Jay pinched the wound together with her fingertips. "The bleeding will stop soon."

They both stared at her, disbelief staining their eyes, creasing their faces, hunching their bodies. "I could do with a soda, though," she said, not because she was thirsty but because she hoped to break the tension.

"Get Jay a soda, Tyler." Caro's gaze remained fixed on Jay as her brother leaped to do her bidding. "You really should get that seen to," she said, visibly shaking off her shock and trying her best to assume a parental role. "If you've got some phobia about hospitals or doctors, and you're scared to go on your own, we'll come, too."

Jay smiled gently at her. "Thank you, Caro. But it's not that I'm scared of doctors, it's that I truly don't require the attentions of one."

"Bullshit." The slight tremble in Caro's voice betrayed her.

Jay gave her wound one final squeeze with her fingers before performing an internal diagnostic. Given the depth of the wound, it'd take a couple of hours to heal completely but it was hardly a serious injury. Turning aside so Caro couldn't see what she was doing, Jay licked her fingers to coat them with saliva and brushed them down the already knitting slash. Her saliva would further speed up the healing process and insure that her dermis healed without scarring. She swiped the blood from her skin with her fingers and then licked them clean.

She heard a muffled imprecation and glanced up to see Tyler's horrified face. He'd seen her administering to her wound. He'd noted how quickly it was healing.

Wordlessly, he handed Jay the soda and then joined his sister, dropping to the floor by the settee and leaning against Caro's knees. He appeared to draw comfort from the physical contact.

Jay considered the situation, running various scenarios and options. Logically, she knew she could—and should—provide some feasible explanation for what Tyler and Caro had witnessed. But her programming stuttered when factoring in the human equation of friendship. And trust.

She ignored her programming. Again. "You should make yourselves comfortable," she said, popping the tab on her soda. "Both of you. I have something to tell you."

In eerie unison, Tyler and Caro levered themselves up onto the settee. They sat very close together, knees touching, united in the face of something strange and disturbing.

Jay envied them their closeness. She'd shared some of that today—enough to know she'd give all she possessed to have more. But once she told them her secret, their freely offered friendship would die, to be replaced by fear and loathing.... Loathing of *her*. And everything that she was.

Jay wouldn't taint their friendship by lying about what they'd seen. She would tell the truth. And then she would do what she always did: Cover her tracks and run. A pall mantled her at the thought of leaving this town—of leaving Tyler, giving him up. Even Caro now held a place in what Jay had come to think of as her heart. She liked having a female friend to "hang with".

She gazed about her apartment, the place she'd tried to make a home. And wondered whether she had injured something more than merely her arm, for everything about her abruptly seemed drab, colorless, lifeless. She felt....

What did she feel? She analyzed the waves of unfamiliar emotion. And was forced to conclude what she felt right now was similar to what she'd felt when Father had sacrificed the remaining few months of his life to protect her. Immeasurably sad, as though she'd lost something precious.

But why did she feel sad? Why did she feel anything at all?

That, she could not answer. So she drank off her soda and crumpled the empty can in her fist, shaping it into a sphere with her fingertips. Without looking, she lobbed it over her shoulder.

The missile arced towards the stainless steel bin Jay had placed next to the kitchen counter for recycling purposes. It hit the domed lid at precisely the correct angle to set it swinging open. The can popped through the opening, landing with a tinny thud before the lid swung back. "Slam dunk," she said.

"Impressive." Tyler's calm, even tone belied his too-pale complexion.

Jay saw it in his face—the little tic in the muscle by his left eye, the wide gaze fixed on hers like she was dangerous and he didn't dare take his eyes off her. She detected it in the wild pounding of his heart, smelled it on his suddenly sweat-dampened body.

Fear. Of her.

His gaze dropped to the wound on her arm, which now appeared to be merely a surface scratch.

He'd guessed.

Caro dragged her gaze from the recycling bin and cocked her head, staring at Jay. Tyler's sister was now more curious than worried for her safety. Caro was not afraid—not yet.

Jay walked over to the bin. Picking it up, she turned to face her audience. She held the bin lightly between her palms. And then she crushed it, and its contents, as easily as a human would crush a flimsy aluminum can.

CARO LEANED FORWARD, and to Tyler she now seemed more curious than afraid. "So what *are* you, Jay?"

He wanted to laugh at his sister's casual phrasing of that oh-so-crucial question. But he knew that if he started, he might not be able to stop.

"Have either of you seen *The Terminator*?" Jay asked.

Omigod. No. She couldn't be. Tyler had been thinking more along the lines of genetically enhanced human but—

Oh. My. Freaking. God. Jay wasn't *human* at all.

His sister nodded enthusiastically. "Yeah. Great movie. I love that scene where the cyborg gets munched and—" Her eyes rounded still more as she made the connection. "That's you?"

"Correct. Titanium skeleton, artificial organs and implants, all overlaid with living human tissue."

"You're a *robot*?" Caro squeaked.

"Cyborg is a more accurate definition for what I am. Aside from the now obvious quick healing of most injuries, I can think and reason. I can mimic humans. I even have the capacity to appear to age if I so desire."

"Outstanding!" Caro's eyes shone. She didn't sound fazed at all. In fact, she seemed fascinated—tickled pink by the revelation.

Tyler's limbs twitched and jerked with the powerful desire to leap from his chair and hurtle from the apartment. He wanted the hell outta there. His heart was thumping fit to burst from his chest, and his body felt hot and cold, as though he was burning with a fever and kinda frozen all at the same time. A roaring sound like a thundering waterfall filled his head. His brain forced his body to suck in oxygen but still his head spun and silvery splotches danced before his eyes. He stared at the black blobs that his sneakers had become, and fought to keep it together.

Jay was a cyborg. She was dangerous, inhuman, "other"—a fictional creation straight from the script of some Sci-Fi movie suddenly come to life. No wonder people were after her.

"Hey, so who made you?" Caro asked, her tone light and airy, like she'd asked for a bowl of Jay's chocolate pudding.

"My father gave me life," Jay said.

"Not your real father, though, right? Because you were, like, *created*, not born."

"My creator *was* my father. He was as real to me, as your father is to you."

Tyler's head jerked up at that. When Jay spoke about her father there was real emotion and hurt throbbing in her voice. She sounded all too human. But that had to be another lie. She must have been around someone who'd lost a parent, someone whose reactions and emotions she could mimic.

Or she wasn't pretending at all and the hurt was real.

Yeah, right. Impossible. Or perhaps a miracle?

His gaze abruptly snapped into focus but Tyler couldn't immediately make sense of what he was seeing. When his brain and body were again in sync, he found he was staring fixedly at the trash can Jay had molded into a round, shiny ball. Beneath his bewildered gaze, it sprang into fluid motion again.

God. She was tossing it from one hand to the other, like any normal kid might do with a baseball.

He managed to work enough saliva into his mouth to form actual words. "Our father gave up the right to be called 'Dad' when he upped and left us."

"Regardless, he's still your father," Jay said. "Just as in here," she tapped her temple, "and here," she tapped her chest, "the man who created me will always be mine, even though he's dead."

Tyler blocked off the words—the lies—and focused on *it*. The… the… *thing* who called herself Jay.

It stood there, perfectly relaxed, in the kitchen area of its apartment. It sounded like a normal girl, what with all this talk about absentee fathers. It even looked like your average teenage girl—

All right, not exactly average-looking. Anything that looked like Jay could never be average. But it looked just like the girl who'd been kind to him, the girl he'd trusted. The girl he really liked. And had hoped might become something more than a friend.

It looked human. Sounded human. Acted human….

But it wasn't human.

His gaze slid to the bloodied shard of crockery.

She—it—saw the direction of his gaze. And walked over to grind it beneath the heel of its sneaker.

Tyler shuddered. It could probably have ground the shard to powder just as effectively with its bare foot.

He might have been able to reason away the abnormally fast healing of what he knew had been a deep gash, but he couldn't ignore the "ball" it still toyed with. It had crushed the metal trashcan like some flimsy aluminum soda can. It could crush him and Caro if they got in its way. Or did anything to jeopardize its secret.

He moaned, sick to his stomach at the mere thought of what this cyborg could have done to Caro and his mom. They had invited it into their home. And it could have killed them all—destroyed their bodies and vanished, leaving only that incriminating video clip as evidence this inhuman thing was capable of so much more than your average Snapperton teenager. But….

But it hadn't harmed them. It had even gone so far as to reveal its secret to him and Caro. It trusted them. And now it was waiting to see what they did with that trust.

He watched it observing him closely, waiting for him to say something, make a move, react.

Tyler tore his gaze from the cyborg and fixed it instead on his sister's open, trusting face. Surely Caro could see how dangerous it was? Surely she had some doubts?

But no. From her wide grin and shining eyes, his sister thought its revelation was too freaking awesome for words. Typical. No help there.

"Tyler."

Its quiet, controlled voice rolled over him, commanded his attention. "I would never hurt you," it said.

"Too late. You already have." Before he ducked his head to hide his anguish, he glimpsed confusion marring the smooth perfection of its face.

"How have I hurt you?" it asked.

"He's hurt because he, uh, *likes* you," Caro explained when Tyler refused to answer.

"I like him, too," Jay said.

Tyler's chin lifted. He couldn't stop himself. He had to see the expression that went with those words, had to see if the lie was reflected in its expression. Had to see whether there even *was* an expression.

Caro rubbed her hands over her face, smearing her eyeliner. "Let's be clear about this, okay, Jay? Tyler *likes* you. You know, I-wanna-be-your-boyfriend type of like."

"I would have liked that very much," it said, sounding so wistful it tore at Tyler's determination to distance himself by thinking of the cyborg as an unfeeling thing, incapable of emotion.

"Would have?" Caro pounced on its phrasing.

Tyler couldn't find it in him to appreciate his sister's support. He wanted nothing more than to wipe the last ten minutes from his mind. Pity whomever had created it wasn't around. Anyone who could build a cyborg that was so very humanlike, probably had the skills to mind-wipe this nightmare from Tyler's brain, too.

"It's hardly likely now he knows what I am," it said.

Was it his imagination or was that desolation he heard in its voice?

It smacked of the same desolation *he* felt. But it couldn't be desolate, could it? It wasn't human, didn't have feelings. Not real ones.

Caro made a gurgling noise that was somewhere between a snicker and a chortle. If Tyler had been able to make his legs work properly, he'd have leaped at her and stuffed a cushion in her mouth. Instead, he sat there, overcome with self-pity like the pathetic loser he was.

"Seems like a perfect match to me," his sister said when she quit with the gurgles. "Two freaks together. You're practically made for each other."

That was going too damn far. "Oh har-de-har-har!" Tyler tilted his chin to fix his sister with a blazing glare that he dearly wished could melt the rubber soles of her trendy boots.

"That's better." Caro's tone had that insufferably smug edge he knew so well. "Now you've stopped wallowing in self-pity we might actually get some answers."

"Answers?" He hit her with his most dire frown, willing her to shut the hell up.

"I don't know about you, bro, but I've never had a super-strong, cybernetic, computer genius of a friend before. This is, like, the most majorly awesome thing ever!" She gasped, and slapped her forehead. "OMG, Jay! No freaking wonder you could toss Shawn about like that—and pitch like that. And no freaking wonder you walked away from the team. I completely understand where you were coming from now. You've got morals, girlfriend. This is why those people are after you, right? Because they know what you are?"

"Yes." Something that smacked of uncertainty twisted its face and shadowed those incredibly beautiful, inhumanly blue eyes. "Do you still want to be my friend, Caro?"

"Duh!"

Caro's answering grin almost split her face, like she'd practically invented the whole ear-to-ear thing. And seeing that uncensored grin, Tyler knew absolutely that whatever Jay was, human or otherwise, Caro truly considered her a friend. And that was the end of it so far as his sister was concerned. Black and white. Cut and dried.

"I'm guessing you don't really have an uncle, huh?" Caro probed.

"No, I don't."

"Excellent. I predict some awesome parties in your future. Give me five, girlfriend!"

The cyborg blinked, hesitated, and then smacked its palm against Caro's.

Huh. Why was he even surprised his sister had accepted the cyborg so readily, and was willing to remain friends despite the lies. But he wasn't so gullible as Caro. He didn't stay friends with kids who lied. And pretending to be human had been the biggest lie of all.

"I'm dying here!" Caro bounced in her seat like some hyper little kid. "You're super strong, super quick, and you can even eat and drink, too. What else can you do? C'mon, Jay, spill!"

"Well, I'm an excellent mimic. That's how I pass as human. I mimic you to fit in."

It reeled off a list of its abilities and Tyler tuned out. He didn't need to hear anything more. The only ability that really mattered to him—the one that really had him tripping—had already been revealed.

It was a mimic. A damn good one.

This thing chatting away to his sister didn't feel. It just *pretended* to feel. And everything it had made *him* feel about it was pretense, too.

On a purely intellectual level, Tyler realized he was being irrational. It could hardly have walked up to him on its first day at school and said, "Hi, I'm Jay and I'm a cyborg. I think you're hot. Wanna be my boyfriend?" But emotionally, he didn't give a crap. He felt like being unreasonable, figured he deserved to indulge.

He was also angry. Even more than that, try betrayed. Try gutted.

Ridiculous, he knew. But he couldn't help it. This inhuman creature had made itself important to Tyler, made him feel something for it, something strong and pure and so much more than he'd ever felt before. And now it wasn't even bothering to lie. It was clearly stating, no BS or trying to hide the truth, that it was all pretense.

The sunlight winked out, extinguished by clouds scudding overhead. Tyler shivered. He felt cold, so very cold. But there was always his anger to warm him. He let it coil through his belly and worm its way up his spine. He embraced its poisonous heat. And when it reached his heart, he let it jerk him from his chair. On legs that felt too weak to be his own, he let it force him toward the thing that was Jay.

As if sensing his mood, it stilled. And even Caro, her mouth open to ask another question, subsided.

Tyler halted directly before it. He raised his hand.

"Tyler, no!" Caro's horror-filled face and her outstretched hand blurred. They had no power to affect him. Only Jay's face—the thing's face—mattered.

With all the strength he could muster, he slapped its cheek.

It absorbed the blow. Its head didn't move, not even a tiny bit. It just stood there, feet planted, staring up at him with those mesmerizing blue eyes.

The skin of its cheek bloomed bright with a perfect imprint of his palm.

Its cheek had felt like a rock. And the pain hit Tyler in a stinging, throbbing rush that made him gasp.

He cradled his hand. "You bitch," he hissed, ignoring Caro's shocked squeak of protest. "Pretending to like me, pretending to give a crap—it's all bullshit! Just like all your talk about feelings is bullshit. You said it yourself: You're a clever mimic. How can you possibly understand, how can you possibly care what you've done to me?" His voice had risen to an anguished shout but he didn't give a shit. He didn't care if anybody else in the building heard. He didn't care about anything anymore.

"You're wrong," it said. "Something's happening to me, something I don't understand. And although it's impossible, I.... I *feel*!"

Its words, the anguish in them that matched his own, pierced his heart. They took up residence in his muddled brain. "You really can *feel*?"

It nodded. "I'm not programmed to feel. I shouldn't be able to but...." A tiny frown creased its forehead and to Tyler, who was examining every tiny nuance of expression on its face, it appeared genuinely confused, lost.

"When I—" It squeezed its eyes shut, and then opened them again. "The night Father died, I cried for the first time. I didn't even realize what they were at first, the tears. I didn't truly understand what they meant, either. And ever since then I've begun to feel. Not physical pain—" its hand went to the cheek he'd slapped "—but here." Its hand drifted to its head, tapped its temple. "And here." It formed a fist and punched its heart.

Or where its heart would be, if it possessed a real one.

It must have plucked Tyler's thoughts from his mind. It stepped closer, took his hand and placed his palm on its chest. "I do have a heart, Tyler. And as you've seen, when I bleed my blood looks the same as human blood. Just because my heart is artificial and more efficient than a human's, doesn't negate the fact I have one. And right now, even though it shouldn't be at all possible, my heart is aching."

"Why?" he whispered, his own heart stuttering.

"Because I've hurt you." Its brilliant gaze burned with conflicting emotions.

They were emotions he recognized. Shame. Fear. Hope.

He wanted to lash out at this thing with his fists, pound it for making him like it, for making him believe it might care for him. He wanted it to wrap its arms around him and hug him close. He wanted it—Jay—to be human. But those were his issues, his crap—nothing to do with it.

It was alone in the world. Men were after it and God only knew what they'd do if they caught it. Dissect it? Like it had dissected the frog in Bio?

He shuddered, rubbing the chill from his arms, picturing this incredible creation, this almost-human work of art, lying on an operating table, its beautiful eyes dulled and lifeless as it was taken apart piece by piece.

Tyler knew what it was like to be alone and friendless. He knew what it was like to be rejected, too. His own father had taught him that. And Vanessa, his first serious girlfriend. Likewise, the guys he'd believed had his back. So if it truly *could* feel, he couldn't hurt it further by rejecting it. No matter what it was, no matter how it had unintentionally hurt him, it didn't deserve that from him.

To Tyler, Jay-the-cyborg ceased being a "thing" at that moment. She was just Jay. She couldn't help what she was. And she'd tried so hard to fit in, to be normal. To be human. "Duh," he said. He even managed a crooked smile.

And she smiled back at him. Tentatively at first, then fully, brilliantly. She held his gaze and the genuine joy in her smile thawed the frozen little lump his heart had become.

"Friends, then?" she asked.

He nodded. "Friends."

He knew he should apologize for the slap. Hell, he should prostrate himself at her feet and beg forgiveness. But he couldn't bring himself to say he was sorry. Besides, she hadn't felt the blow anyway.

He consoled himself with that thought as his sister's disappointed, judgmental gaze raked him. And then dismissed him as a lost cause.

"I could go dessert right about now," Caro said, breaking the awkward silence.

"Of course," Jay said, ever the polite hostess. "And afterward, I'll show you the cell phones and you can take your pick."

"Sweet! Can I pick one for Em, too?"

"Of course you can."

"You, girlfriend, are the best!"

Jay seemed content to play hostess. Tyler's sister seemed more than willing to accept her in that role. Both girls carried on like the world hadn't changed at all.

But for Tyler it had. It'd changed forever.

This couldn't be happening. He pinched his thigh. Hard. But everything remained the same. The truths didn't dissipate into the ether. The anguish lurking in his soul didn't subside.

He ducked his head, staring at his sneakers, wondering how the effing hell he'd gotten into this mess. He'd finally found a girl who didn't have an agenda, who really liked him, who could see past his outer shell to the real person beneath. And she wasn't even human.

He'd gone and fallen for a cyborg.

Hard.

Shit. Caro was right. He was such a freak.

Chapter Fourteen

TYLER WAS IN the bathroom, trying to get his hair to behave, when Caro cornered him. After she'd quit laughing at his efforts and restyled his hair to her satisfaction, she said, "When're you going to quit feeling sorry for yourself and give her a chance?"

"Don't know what you're talking about."

"Oh, come on. Don't give me that. You barely speak to Jay. And when you do, you're so terribly polite it's like you've got Miss Manners shoved up your butt. You even made her partner Matt in Bio. Which I gotta say, is just plain shitty, because even though Jay's a freaking genius with computers and stuff, she hasn't a clue how to deal with guys like him. Quit being such a moody a-hole. Jay needs us. She needs *you*. And she needs to know you're on her side."

Tyler stared at his reflection, thrusting out his chin to check for eruptions. There were none, of course. Hadn't been since Jay had somehow healed that zit on his chin. Wow. Freaking amazing what a cyborg could do for a guy.

"She's got *you* on her side, Caro. She doesn't need me."

Caro vented her frustration with a gusty sigh that dragged Tyler's reluctant gaze to hers. She rolled her eyes toward the ceiling in her signature gesture of not-so-mock despair. "She's hurting,

Tyler. Real bad."

"That's crap and you know it. She's a cyborg. She *can't* hurt."

"And you know it's *not* crap. Jeez! She's all confused because feelings, and this girlfriend-boyfriend stuff, are all Greek to her. But do you cut her a break? No. Of course not! You tell her you're still her friend but do you act like her friend? No. Of course not. Noooo, instead you make like an angry ex-boyfriend, like she's played you and broken your freaking heart. It's pathetic! What am I going to do with the two of you?"

She scrubbed her hands through her immaculately styled hair, grabbed a couple of handfuls and yanked. Hard enough for her to blink and twist her face into a pained grimace. "Look, Tyler, I know you're upset but Jay can't help what she is. And regardless of what she is, she really likes you. So why can't you just—"

"What?" He whirled to confront his sister. "Be boyfriend and girlfriend? Get married? Live happily ever after in a nice house with a white picket fence, and have little Terminator babies? Yeah, like that's a possibility." He turned back to his reflection, trying to ignore her slack-jawed dismay at his OTT reaction.

Crap. He might have over-played that one. Caro wasn't stupid. If he wasn't careful, she might actually suspect the truth: He wanted so badly for Jay to be human that it hurt.

He stared into the mirror with a truly pathetic attempt at mess-with-me-at-your-freakin'-peril eyes. "Get real, Caro."

To his dismay she didn't take the hint. She palmed his shoulders. "Listen up. Jay's in trouble."

Tyler's stomach flip-flopped and finally settled with a sickening lurch. "Well, duh. She's a cyborg and bad men want her."

"Quit being obtuse."

"Obtuse. Now there's a big word. You been reading Mom's word of the day calendar again, huh?"

"Tyler!" She dug her fingernails into his shoulders and shook him so hard it snapped his head back on his neck.

"Ow!" He glared at her in the mirror's reflection. "Quit shaking me."

"I'll quit shaking you when I've shaken some sense into you, and you stop being such a smartass and hear me out!"

She was mega-serious. She meant it. And Tyler couldn't keep up the pretense that he didn't care deeply about Jay any longer. His shoulders slumped beneath her grip. "What's happened?"

"Do you remember that tracking program she ran? The one that was tracking IP addresses of the people who'd viewed the clip?"

"Yeah, I remember."

"One of them wasn't local."

His stomach lurched again. He swallowed, trying to work some moisture into his suddenly dry mouth. "So?"

"So, it was suspicious. Jay did some further digging and she says the guys who're after her have tracked her down. They'll be coming for her. Soon."

Tyler's world came to a screaming halt. His heart galloped. "What's she gonna do?"

Caro didn't say anything.

"Is she gonna run?"

She released him and headed for the door.

"Caro! What's Jay going to do?"

"Ask her yourself," his sister said. "You owe her that much, at least."

THE MORNING DRAGGED. Even art class failed to hold much pleasure. Tyler found himself sketching Jay's face, trying to capture her essence—that part that was uniquely Jay. And wondering what it meant when he couldn't quite manage it as well as he'd like.

"Excellent work, Tyler."

His art teacher's voice made him jump.

"May I?" Mr. Sands took possession of his sketchbook before Tyler could protest, and examined the drawing more closely. "Is she someone you know?"

"Uh, yeah. She is."

"The eyes are truly stunning. The way she's staring out from the page…." Mr. Sands held up his sketch, waving it to catch his students' attention.

Tyler scrunched lower in his chair and thought seriously about crawling under his desk.

"I want you all to take a look at Tyler's sketch," Mr. Sands told the class. "See the way he's used different techniques such as crosshatching? And that slinky stroke we talked about last week, to get this dark shading here and here? And the way he's highlighted the eyes so the face seems to leap from the page—excellent technique!" He droned on, ignoring the titters from a couple of girls who'd recognized the subject of Tyler's portrait.

Good going, dude. Way to feed the gossip.

Tyler groaned. Was he a complete idiot? Only saving grace was, Caro couldn't draw to save her life, so she wasn't in this class. If his sister ever copped a look at that sketch she'd be on his case big-time.

When his teacher returned his sketchbook, Tyler studied the drawing. He wasn't inclined to agree with the glowing assessment. Beneath his critical gaze, Jay's face appeared soulless, almost inhuman. Which of course she was. And seeing the truth of Jay leaping out at him, so starkly captured in pencil lines and smudges on a page, scared him.

Scared or not, the truth didn't stop his stupid heart and head from liking her *that way*. It didn't stop him from dwelling on how he'd practically stopped breathing when she'd kissed him, either. Or how she'd looked that time in the cafeteria—stunned and pleased and very vulnerable—when he'd glanced back and caught her touching her lips after he'd kissed her. Whenever he closed his eyes, he saw her. And, in his mind at least, it was easy to tell her how he felt about her. And show her. By kissing her… properly, this time.

How pathetic was that?

How pathetic was he?

He growled to himself. And scowled a mind-your-own-freaking-business scowl at the guy sitting in front of him when he turned around to check whether Tyler had morphed into a wild animal.

Tyler brooded for the rest of the class. When it was over, he ripped the page from his sketchbook. And as he left the room, he tossed it in the trash.

By lunchbreak, his head ached from trying to work it all out. He couldn't handle going to the music room and working on his songs. He dragged his feet to the cafeteria and ran the gamut of whispers and nudges before plunking his butt in a seat at the back.

His own choice, of course. He could have sat with Em and the other girls from his team. Caro would be there, too, avoiding Vanessa and Shawn. And pretending to ignore Matt, who had apparently decided Caro was still worth pursuing and sat at her table every lunchtime. But that would also mean Tyler sitting with Jay, confronting his feelings for Jay, trying not to give in to Jay's mesmerizing, too-sad, totally miserable gaze.

That would mean telling her how he felt for real. And he

wasn't ready for that. Not yet.

Maybe not ever.

He rummaged in his bag for his packed lunch and unwrapped a bologna sandwich. He choked down a single bite, gave up and packed it away again. He ignored the sticky, grungy tabletop, and laid his aching head atop his arms, tuning out the rest of the world.

Someone placed a hand on his shoulder.

Tyler jumped at the sheer unexpectedness of the touch. His head jerked up and his wild-eyed gaze met Jay's electric blue one.

"May I join you, Tyler? Please?"

"Uh. Sure!" His heart tripped and that warm feeling he got whenever she looked his way infected his brain, driving away all good sense. He shook it off, tore his gaze from her face, even managed a shrug. "Whatever."

She slid into the chair next to him and maneuvered it sideways until she sat angled toward him. Even though Tyler kept his gaze strictly front and center, he knew she was watching him intently. He felt it—felt *her*, her closeness. Her need.

"What do you want?" he finally asked, unable to bear the silence any longer. He thought his voice sounded strange, hoped it didn't sound laden with all the hurt he was trying so desperately to hide. But if he hadn't pulled it off, he hoped she didn't notice.

Shit. Who was he trying to kid? This was Jay. Of course she would notice. Hopefully, she would be too polite to acknowledge it.

"I want to ask you a favor," she said.

Oh no. No way. He opened his mouth and a bunch of crap he didn't mean spewed out. "Sure. Anything. We're friends, right? And friends do favors for each other."

"Are we friends, Tyler?"

He slanted her a quick, assessing glance. Huh. Just as he'd thought. It was a sincere question. And it deserved a sincere answer.

"Sure." He scraped a piece of dried food from the surface of the table and flicked it away with his fingernail. "Sure we are."

"Mmmm. I might not be human, and I might not know all there is to know about friendship, but somehow I doubt we *are* friends."

God, she sounded so sad. Tyler dared examine her face. And he didn't turn away, not even when he spotted the hope lighting her eyes—hope that he was going to dash to itty bitty irretrievable pieces, because he couldn't bring himself to be completely honest with her.

He could hardly tell Jay that he really liked her—maybe even more than liked. Not that he could possibly know what love felt like, 'cause he'd only recently turned seventeen. But if love was feeling like total crap when Jay wasn't around, if it was feeling like his entire world brightened when he caught the merest glimpse of her in a hallway, if it was feeling as though he wasn't truly complete without her, then—

OMFG.

He couldn't be.

"Are you all right, Tyler? Is something wrong?"

He tensed all his muscles to keep from shaking. "No! And of course we're friends, Jay. What else could we be?"

What else, indeed.

"You've sure got a crap way of showing it," she muttered.

"What did you say?" She'd sounded so human, so almost Emma-ish, that Tyler couldn't quite credit his ears.

Maybe a bit of Em's smart mouth was rubbing off on Jay? Horrible thought. He suppressed a shudder.

"Nothing," Jay said. "Look, Tyler, I'm planning on leaving soon because of—" She seemed to recollect she was in a public place and lowered her voice. "You know why. But before I take off, I wanted to throw a party—a farewell party. Caro's idea, of course."

He snorted. "Of course. Any excuse for a party. But won't that be dangerous? I mean, if these people are looking for you, wouldn't it be better to, like, disappear in the dead of night?"

She grinned. And her expression was so mischievous, so *normal*, it warmed him… and almost made him forget what she was.

But not quite.

"That's the beauty of Caro's plan," she said.

"My sister actually came up with a plan? Whoa. Frame it and hang it on the wall. Wonders will never cease."

Jay gave a bark of surprised laughter. "I've missed your way with words, Tyler." Some of her joy seemed to dim as she swept her gaze over him. "I've missed you."

"Oh, come on." He tried for a scoffing tone. He thought he pretty much pulled it off, too. "We've only known each other for a short time. And it's not like we were dating or anything. It's not like we—" he curled his fingers into little pretend speech marks "*—broke up*."

"Seems that way to me. You go out of your way to avoid me, you barely speak to me at all, you won't look me in the eye." She tapped her temple with a forefinger. "Classic after break-up behavior, according to my databases. And haven't you heard the gossip around school?"

"I refuse to listen to gossip," he said.

She quirked an eyebrow. "Yeah. Riiight."

Whoa, she really was beginning to sound like both Caro *and* Em. "Fine. What gossip?"

"Thought you didn't—"

"What. Gossip?"

She smirked. Actually smirked! "You really sure—?"

"Spill," he said.

"You asked for it. Word is, you really *did* convince me to blow you in the boys' bathroom. And I was totally into you, but you're just, like, a coldhearted a-hole who doesn't give a crap about me now you've gotten what you wanted. So you've given me the brush-off. And now I'm pining. 'Cause you're, like, sooo totally hot, I'm just gutted and I can't get over you." She scratched her head, frowning. "Did I get it right? Uh, yeah, that was it. Kinda."

Tyler's jaw sagged. "You have got to be freaking kidding me."

Jay's mouth curled into a smug smirk. "Yep."

He couldn't help his burst of laughter. "You got me good. That was totally Caro-worthy."

"Yep. Your sister has definitely been influencing me—in a good way, I hope. Evidently I don't sound quite so nerdy and uptight, now. Did I really sound uptight before?"

He bit his lip, trying not to smile. "A little. You were a bit too, um, *polite* before. But I didn't think too much of it until I found out, uh—"

"What I am?"

"Yeah. What you are."

"Mmmm." She nibbled her lower lip, processing that statement. "Well, I'm hoping what I've learned will help me integrate myself into human society a bit more efficiently next time."

Next time. Tyler's heart plummeted to his toes. He didn't want to think about Jay finding another home. Another school. Another boyfriend.

He pretended to fumble in his bag for a non-existent something. God. He really had it bad.

When he'd composed himself, he asked, "What was that favor you wanted?"

"I'm having the farewell party at my place tomorrow night. Cover story is, my uncle rang, and he's had a job offer that's too good to turn down. So he's staying on to finalize the arrangements while I—"

"Throw a huge party and trash the joint? Sounds like something Caro would come up with."

Jay snorted. Another of those very human-like mannerisms. "I was going to say, while I pack up and arrange to fly out and meet him," she said. "I thought it was a pretty sound plan, actually. Believe me, Tyler, it won't be long before the people after me come sniffing 'round, asking about me. And let's just say, some kid throwing a farewell party while her uncle is out of town, isn't quite so suspect as a kid who disappears without trace in the middle of the night and sets the entire town fluttering with dire predictions about her demise. Throwing a party is hardly something a cyborg would be likely to do, is it? With any luck, my pursuers will arrive in Snapperton, immediately verify I'm not here and leave without bothering anyone."

"Here's hoping. Not that I'd tell them anything, anyway."

She reached over and squeezed his hand. And kept hold of it. "If they ask, tell them the truth."

"And what truth would that be?"

"That you don't know where I've gone. Don't volunteer any other information. And for your own safety, don't admit you know what I am."

A chill stroked his spine. This wasn't a game. This was real. And things could get nasty. "I'll be okay. I'm a pretty good actor."

"Yeah," she said. "You are. And you fool most people, too.

But beneath that I-don't-give-a-crap façade, there's someone I care about very much. So please, if you spot any strangers asking questions about me, keep a low profile. Be safe, Tyler. Promise me?"

"I will."

He felt himself flushing beneath her concerned gaze. He'd never had much of a problem with blushing until she showed up. "About that favor," he said, as much to distract himself as her.

"Oh yeah. The favor. So, I'm having this party Saturday."

"Yeah, I kinda got that," he said.

"And *I'd* kinda like you to come. As my date."

Chapter Fifteen

THE DUST-SMOTHERED TRUCK jolted over a wicked pothole, causing Michael to bounce off his seat and whack his head on the roof. He let loose with a vicious tirade that was completely out of proportion to the relatively minor pain. He swore when he was worried. And he was far more concerned about this little escapade than it warranted.

He rumbled to a halt outside one of Snapperton's two motels, this one on the very outskirts of the town. From habit, his gaze flickered about, gauging potential threats without seeming to show any undue interest in his surroundings. He forced himself to relax. This wasn't a retrieval. Hell, it wasn't even a sanctioned operation. No one knew he was here.

At least, Michael hoped no one knew.

He climbed down from the truck and paused to stretch out the kinks in his back before reaching in to grab his bags.

When he was halfway to the motel's reception area, reality smacked him so damned hard he rocked back on his heels.

It was just as he remembered. The sign still proclaimed "*Snapp to M tel*". The missing letters had been painted in at one stage, but the paint had soon flaked and peeled. The motel's frontage was still a listless blue, teetering on the edge of shabbiness and crying out for a decent lick of paint. The garden still needed a few more shrubs to fill in holes where plants had died off and been yanked out, but not replaced. Even the outside lights illuminating the reception area still buzzed like ravenous mosquitoes. Sure as eggs, the interior of each room would be clean and neat as a pin, though. And any guest with a hankering for some hearty home-style cooking, could still wander over to the on-site café and be served with the best damned pie they'd ever tasted.

And the worst damned coffee, too.

About ten years ago, he and Marissa had farmed the kids out to friends and stayed the night here. They'd been so hard up they hadn't been able to afford anywhere more fancy but they hadn't cared. And Marissa....

Michael smiled at the memory his wife picking up the phone and coercing I-don't-do-room-service-Earl into bringing them an entire apple pie, a carton of ice cream and two spoons. One kiss on the cheek and that sunny smile of hers, and she'd had the motel owner wrapped around her little finger. And after she'd shooed Earl out the door, they'd lounged in bed and scoffed the lot. It'd been one of the best nights of his life.

He shook his head in wonderment. He'd bet his next slice of apple pie when he walked inside, Earl would still be lounging with feet up on his desk, popping gum, one eye on the door and the other on his portable TV.

He pushed open the door.

Yep. Earl was still manning the desk. He looked just as Michael remembered, beer belly, comb-over and all. Seemed nothing in Snapperton had changed.

Except for him.

He doubted even Marissa or the kids would recognize him now. Amazing what a shaved head, fake glasses and a thick, droopy moustache could do for a man. And not necessarily in a good way.

Earl tore his gaze from the small television and wadded his gum into his cheek with his tongue. "Help ya?"

"I'd like a room, please."

"How long you staying?"

"Couple of days."

"Yeah?" Earl cut his beady little eyes from Michael's faded jeans and worn boots, to his laptop bag. "Got some important business in our fair town, huh?" He sniggered at his own pathetic joke.

"Didn't want to leave this in the truck," Michael said, brandishing the laptop bag in an embarrassed fashion. "Boss'll make me pay for it if it gets swiped. I'm just passing through on the way back from a sales conference. Figured I'd try and catch up with some old drinking buddies I haven't seen in a few years. Know any good places round here?"

Earl leaned forward and beckoned Michael closer. "Don't let the Missus hear me telling you this, but I might be able to direct you to a particular establishment that'd make your hair curl. Whoooweee!" He fanned his face.

Michael pretended to be mightily impressed by Earl's description of the "particular establishment". It was all part of building rapport. In the last five years, he'd perfected the art of being amiable and not too memorable. And the fictional "old drinking buddies" gave him an excuse to stay out half the night without Earl thinking anything of it.

By the time he'd signed in, paid the deposit, and pocketed the key, he knew his disguise would hold. Earl hadn't recognized him, didn't suspect a thing.

Michael was confident no one else would, either. Excepting

perhaps his wife.

He checked his watch. It was nearly four. Marissa had recently started working Saturdays as cashier at the local Save-Mart. He'd been gutted to discover she'd taken another dead-end job to make ends meet. Ironically, *he* had money to burn but no way of getting it to her without raising suspicions—hers, and his employer's.

She'd be finishing her shift soon. It crossed his mind he could visit her workplace on the pretext of needing groceries, just to see her again. Just to confirm that she, too, hadn't changed a whit.

Too risky.

Like it was too risky to swing by his house and front up to the kids he hadn't seen or contacted since he'd upped and vanished from their lives. Not that he cared about risking his own hide, but he sure as hell cared about risking Marissa and the kids.

He wanted to see them, though. So damn bad it hurt.

Five years. They would both have changed. Grown up. Done so much without him. It wounded him to think of all the milestones he'd missed.

His already shaky composure was completely sunk when he opened the door to his motel room and realized it was the same room he and Marissa had been given ten years ago.

Michael threw his laptop on the table, slumped on the end of the bed and covered his face with his hands as he remembered… and was again forced to confront what he'd given up.

Eventually he got it together, and resigned himself to doing what he did best: hiding away in some darkened room and ferreting out information.

He was ninety-nine percent certain the "Jay Smith" who'd registered at Greenfield High and was currently residing in an apartment not far from here, was Cyborg Unit Gamma-Dash-

One. But he told himself gathering information was the sole reason he'd come to Snapperton: He merely wanted to eyeball the target—be one hundred percent certain before he sent in an extraction team.

He told himself he was risking his employer's considerable wrath because it made sense to have all the facts. And having all the facts minimized the risk of casualties if the target set a trap for them—as she had done when they'd gone after her at Durham's house. She'd beaten them down good and proper that time. And, in the deepest darkest recesses of his heart, damned if he hadn't applauded. But this time the stakes were too high. This time, he couldn't afford to think of her as human. She was the target, nothing more.

Michael told himself again what he'd told his employer: Only the mission mattered. And when fear clawed through his belly at the thought of Marissa or Caro or Tyler coming to harm, he knew he was lying to himself. Like the man he worked for had lied to him all along.

Chapter Sixteen

FOR THE UMPTEENTH time, Tyler wondered what had possessed him to agree to be Jay's "date" for her farewell party. If he hadn't known the truth about what she was, it would've been dream come true material. He'd have been blissed out to the max. Over the freaking moon. Period.

But knowing what he knew, knowing what she was....

What made the whole situation miles worse was having Caro, his normally über-cool sister, swan around the house with such a dopey grin plastered over her face that anyone would think *she* was the one going on this date.

Even his mom sported a dewy-eyed, proud-parent-type smile.

Tyler eyed his reflection in the mirror and scowled. It was a killer scowl, absolutely perfect in every way. And if he'd been able to produce it for his mom or his sister, it would've wiped the dumb expressions from their faces for sure. No doubt about it. Pity he couldn't seem to summon anything other than a goofy grin whenever they brought up the "date" subject.

He couldn't figure out Caro's deal. What was her stake in having her brother date a *cyborg*? She was his sister and although he loved her to death, the inner workings of her mind were a constant mystery. And his mom? She was a whole 'nother scary-ass story. What the hell was *she* imagining? The whole hearts and flowers thing? Her son finally dating a "nice" girl?

He snorted. No such freaking thing. Girls weren't nice. They messed with your head and screwed with your heart.

Vanessa had seemed *nice* at first. Sweet. And totally hot, which of course had been a definite plus. But it'd all been a lie. She'd dumped him the minute Matt looked at her sideways, because Matt had his own car. And then, at the first opportunity, she'd dumped Matt for Shawn, moving on up the food chain without a backward glance.

If Caro ever found out what Vanessa had done that night, his sister would pitch a fit of monumental proportions. A drug-dealer for a BFF and an ex-boyfriend who was popping steroids like candy? She'd wig out. She'd never forgive Vanessa and Shawn. Or Tyler, for not telling her the truth.

And Jay.... God, Jay might do more than dump Vanessa on her ass this time. And, if he asked her, she'd treat Shawn to more than just a dumpster-diving session.

He indulged in a daydream where Shawn got his face rearranged. A couple of black eyes and a swollen, bloody nose. And if not losing a couple of teeth, then maybe enough damage that he'd need a retainer for the next year. Oh yeah. Niiice! Vanessa wouldn't be too keen on flaunting her Boy Wonder if that happened.

Secrets. Gah. Tyler was plain fed up with them and all they stood for. Maybe he should 'fess up and tell Caro what'd really happened. She was strong enough to deal. Hey, maybe he should just start a tell-all blog and have done with it.

As appealing as it was to fantasize about airing his dirty laundry, Tyler had one secret he could barely admit to himself. It was a big-ass scary secret. And one he prayed would never, ever, be discovered by anyone: If Jay were human, she'd be The One.

He scooped up his new cell phone and shoved it in his jeans pocket. He was halfway out of his room before he decided to grab one more thing—a thumb drive for Jay. He didn't know whether or not he'd give it to her. He'd play it cool and see what happened.

Tyler's mom was oohing and aahing over Caro's cell phone when Tyler clomped downstairs. "Are you sure Jay's uncle is okay with this?" she asked for the umpteenth time.

Caro groaned. "Yes, Mom. He's got, like, a box of them. Perks of his last job. How many times do I have to tell you this? And they're pre-pays. So we'll be using our allowances to top them up, okay?"

"Well, I suppose it's all right then. But—"

Tyler cut his sister a break and interrupted before their mom could air any more doubts. "I'm ready," he announced from the doorway. "Let's go. We promised Jay we'd get there early and help her set up."

"Bye, kids. Midnight curfew, as usual."

"Just this once can you make it one?" Caro wheedled from the doorway.

"Fine. Just this once. Have fun."

His mom's pleased face was the last thing Tyler glimpsed before he pushed Caro, who was still trying to figure out how to disable the predictive text function on her phone, out the front door.

They walked in silence. His sister kept slanting him quick glances, which he studiously ignored.

About halfway to Jay's place she couldn't keep her peace any longer. "What gives?"

He stared straight ahead. It was on the tip of his tongue to fob her off with some flippant comment. At the last moment he couldn't do it. He hoped she didn't laugh in his face.

"Tyler? You still with me?" She'd halted and grabbed his arm. Now she shook him gently.

"Yeah. If I tell you something, will you promise not to laugh?"

Her gaze raked his face. She obviously recognized the vulnerability lurking there, for she merely nodded, as if she didn't trust herself to speak without screwing it up.

He sucked in a deep, bracing breath.

It didn't help. When he spoke his voice cracked like he was on the verge of losing it. "She could have been The One, you know?" He ground his heel into a weed sprouting from a crack in the sidewalk. "But she's not even human. And now she's taking off and I'll probably never see her again."

"Ah, shit." Caro grabbed him and pulled him into a bear hug, ignoring his squawk of protest. "It'll be okay. You'll get through this. I promise."

Tyler suffered her awkwardly patting his back. He knew she really *did* get it. And it helped.

A piercing wolf-whistle shattered the brother-sister moment. "Get a room, guys!"

Caro released Tyler like he'd burned her and visibly struggled to compose herself. She pulled it together fast, and he envied her the ability. "You're such a dork, Matt," she drawled.

As Matt drew level with them, the cheeky grin slid from his face, replaced by stunned, open-mouthed, male appreciation. "You, uh, look amazing, Caro."

"I know." She smoothed her silky dress over her thighs and fussed with the tie of her cardigan-wrap. Then, grooming complete, she plucked Tyler's arm. "C'mon, we better get going."

Matt's gaze dwelled on her for a long moment before he finally turned his attention to Tyler. "You going to Jay's party?"

"Yep. You?"

"'Course. Off to Bob's Burgers for a feed first, then I'll head over. See ya 'round." He made a point of catching Caro's gaze again before he took off.

She glanced back over her shoulder at exactly the same time Matt did. She waved and he did the same.

Tyler threw her a lopsided grin.

"What're you smirking about?" she said.

"Nothing."

JAY WIPED TEARS from her cheeks. She pressed her fist against her heart, trying to keep the overwhelming pain at bay. She didn't want to leave him. She didn't want to vanish from his life as efficiently and carelessly as she'd entered it. She didn't want him to forget her, even though she knew that, eventually, he would.

She would never forget him, though. He was etched in her memory forever. Even if she erased all her memories, she knew that she would always carry this pain in her heart. It was such a human condition, this anguish. And she cherished it.

After running all manner of diagnostic tests, extrapolating all available data, she'd been forced to conclude she was suffering no anomaly. There was no part of her that was in any way, shape, or form, defective. Father had planned this, had designed Jay to evolve in this manner. All that had been needed to set her on this path was the right catalyst.

Tyler had been that catalyst.

Father had created her to be the daughter he and Mary Durham had never been able to conceive. He'd even used Mary's genetic material to create Jay in her image. But in doing so, he'd never considered the long-term consequences to himself. Every time he'd looked at Jay, he'd seen his dead wife. And only now did Jay understand how profoundly it must have pained Father to be forced to look at her, and interact with her, every single day. Jay was, in effect, a carbon copy of Mary, but she could never *be* Mary. And Father had never been able to bring himself to love Jay, and assist her to fully evolve.

It seemed grossly unfair to finally find that missing part that made her so almost-human the difference was negligible, only to be forced to give Tyler up.

Jay expelled her breath in a wistful sigh. For the first time since she'd been given life, she examined herself critically.

Who was the pale, smooth-skinned creature staring back at her in the mirror?

Was she Cyborg Unit Gamma-Dash-One, Mary Durham's cybernetically enhanced clone, or plain Jay Smith?

She knew who she wanted to be. And she could pretend—she was extremely good at that. Maybe when Tyler looked at her this time, all he'd see would be "Jay". And maybe, just maybe, it would be enough.

With shaking hands, she opened the shopping bag. Makeup. Hair products. Even a brush and comb. According to Caro, everything Jay needed to look her best.

First she tackled her hair. It proved no easy task. She'd never tried to style her unruly mane before. In the end, she stuck her head under the faucet and rinsed all the gunk from her hair with warm water.

She assessed the damage as she squeezed the water from it and dried it as best she could with a towel. Her nose wrinkled of its own volition. There was nothing for it but drastic action. She slathered on some gel, slicked the mass tightly back from her face, and tied it into a ponytail.

The wet-look do was such a startling change that she blinked, and then blinked again, because the girl staring back did not look like her any more. But there was no time to wonder whether she was doing the right thing.

Five minutes later, Jay stalked from the bathroom. The only makeup she'd used was the barest smudge of purplish shadow on her eyelids, a hint of blusher on her cheekbones, and a pink-tinted gloss on her lips. She'd been too overwhelmed by all the different products, too scared of overdoing it, to attempt more. The result was a wholesome girly-girl look. And if that wasn't the right "look" for her then too bad.

Back in her bedroom, she dragged on the new jeans and a deep-plum-colored scoop-necked tee she'd bought with Caro's approval. She added silver hoop earrings, a silver-tooled cuff bracelet and matching necklace.

The only concession she made to her former self were her old black sneakers. They were comfortable and familiar, and she needed a heavy fix of familiar right now.

Would her altered appearance even register with Tyler? Would he realize she'd done it for him and appreciate this mask she had applied, these clothes she'd purchased specifically for this occasion? Did the way she looked really matter *that* much?

So many questions she couldn't answer.

She heard a rap on the door. She knew who her visitors were even before Caro called, "Hey, it's us. Open up!"

Jay's stomach twisted and she covered her mouth with shaking fingers. It was too late to hide.

Chapter Seventeen

"WHAT TOOK YOU so long?" Caro's gaze was glued to her precious new phone. "Gahhh! How the heck do you turn the predictive text off on this thing?" She stabbed a few more random buttons.

"Jay." Tyler cleared his throat and tried again. "You look—"

Jay tried not to react to the stunned expression on his face. She sucked in a deep breath and held it, letting it out ever so slowly when the O of his mouth stretched into a smile.

"Got it." Caro finally glanced up from her phone. "Hey, you look amazing!" she blurted, seconds before Tyler gave his final verdict—the word no girl wanted to hear in relation to her appearance: "Nice."

An awkward silence descended. Jay shifted from one foot to the other, illogically discomfited at being the center of attention. Vulnerable, despite having applied a physical mask of cosmetics to hide behind.

Tyler stared at her.

Hot-cold shivers scuttled up and down Jay's spine, goosing her skin. She'd made a huge mistake. If this was *his* reaction, what would all the other kids think? What would they do when they saw her like this? What would they say?

She must have looked like she was about to bolt because Tyler grabbed her arm. "Sorry 'bout the dorky compliment. I wasn't expecting you to— You caught me by surprise, is all." He bent to kiss her cheek. "You look wonderful."

Jay's breath caught in her throat and all she managed was a breathy, "Thanks."

"Can we come in?" He didn't wait for a response. He placed his hands on her shoulders and gently pushed her inside. She couldn't even be annoyed with him because her legs had turned to Jell-O and without some physical prompting, she might have zoned out and stayed put, basking in the warmth of his admiration.

The apartment was now almost empty. The bookcases were gone, as was all the furniture except for a stereo system, and the two trestle tables Jay had pushed against one wall, groaning with an assortment of sodas and snack food. She'd scattered numerous large cushions and beanbags around the outskirts of the room. For decorations, she had crisscrossed the ceiling with strings of colored lights.

She pulled herself together, flicked a switch and the room lit up, flashing like some psychedelic fairyland. "What d'you think?"

"Outstanding!"

Caro gave her a hug and Jay had to hold herself still, tensing her muscles against the need to cling and seek comfort.

"It's gonna be some party," Caro said. "What can we do?"

"iPod's on the bench," Jay told her. "Why don't you check out the playlist and test the speakers?"

"Sweet!" With a flick of her skirt, Caro sauntered off.

Jay was as alone with Tyler as she'd ever be this evening, given fifty or so kids would be showing up in a half-hour. She bit her lip, feeling awkward. But from somewhere—some emotional reservoir she'd never before needed to tap into—she found the courage to show Tyler how she felt. She captured his face with gentle fingers. Gentle or not, she gave him no choice but to tip his face downward to meet hers. She pressed her lips to his, and her eyelids drifted shut as she savored him.

His hands clamped her upper arms, hesitated, and then tensed to push her away. She was far stronger than he. It was her choice that she broke the kiss and stepped away, not his. And her heart felt like it had shattered into a trillion tiny pieces and would never be whole again.

"What in the freaking hell d'you think you're doing?" he hissed, hyper-conscious of his sister in the background, hunched over the iPod and oblivious. For now.

His screwed up face and startled eyes were almost comical. Almost. "Kissing you," Jay said.

"You're leaving tomorrow."

"Yes. I am. I have to."

"Then why? Why kiss me?"

"Because I wanted to."

"Oh? And what about what I want?"

She cocked her head to one side and frowned, trying to read him. "What *do* you want, Tyler?"

"What do I want?" His laughter boiled up from between teeth so tightly clenched his jaw must surely be aching. The anguish in his voice hurt Jay like a physical blow never could. And that anguish told her exactly what he wanted.

He wanted her to stay.

He wanted her to be human.

But he settled for the only truth he felt he could safely confess. "I want the impossible," he said.

He backed off, distancing himself, protecting himself. A beautiful human emotion Jay believed she might finally understand enough to return in kind, flashed briefly in his eyes before he gave her blankness. His jaw worked, and for one heart-stopping moment she believed he might ask her to stay.

For one heart-stopping moment she believed she *would* stay, that she would find a way. For him. But then he turned on his heel and stalked over to Caro.

Jay exhaled the breath she'd been holding very slowly. She stood there, alone, in the middle of the vast space. She watched Tyler talking to his sister, sharing some joke, arguing over song choices, acting like nothing had happened.

Right. If that's the way it's got to be, then that's the way it's got to be.

She wandered over to the table to get herself a soda—not because she was thirsty, but because she needed something to do. She wondered how she was going to make it through the evening. And wished she'd never agreed to this farce.

EMMA AND THE REST of the team were first to arrive, providing Tyler with a welcome diversion from his solitary brooding.

Emma made a beeline for him, plunking her butt down on the nearest beanbag. She glanced around the room. "Whoa!" She had to yell to make herself heard over the music. "Some place, huh?"

Tyler nodded. "Yeah. Get you something to drink?"

"Cola, please."

He returned with two colas and a bowl of pretzels. Em seemed quite happy to chat with him rather than join her teammates, who were skidding about the place in their socks, playing some weird form of human dodgems and yahooing every time someone got floored.

He allowed himself to be charmed by Em's attentiveness. Beat the hell out of wallowing in misery and pretending not to watch

Jay.

This was not how he'd imagined spending his last few hours with her. He glanced over at the girl in question and spotted her deep in conversation with Rach, the team's relief pitcher. Rach was, as usual, emphasizing everything she said with her hands. Just as Sara moved to join them, Rach flung out an arm and managed to knock the soda right out of Sara's hands.

Tyler winced in sympathy. And tried not to react when Jay's hand shot out and caught the soda before it could hit the floor. But instead of Rach's usual hangdog expression when she made a dork of herself, she had a huge grin plastered all over her face. She looked totally buzzed, more excited than Tyler could ever remember seeing her.

"What's up with Rach?" he asked Em. "She looks like she's won the lottery."

Em's gaze swiveled in time to witness Rach pull Jay into a hug. And Jay hesitate just a moment too long before returning the gesture.

"Jay's been giving her some pitching pointers," Em said. "Girl's style is now total weirdness but somehow it works. You'll see. She'll surprise the hell out of you next practice."

"That so?" Tyler wondered how Em felt about her relief pitcher's dramatic improvement. But Em was Em. Doubtless she'd be pleased—both for the team's sake and Rach's. Em loved the game but she didn't much like the stress of being the team's main girl, too often their only chance of scoring a win.

Had Jay squared it with Em first—asked how she felt? And had Jay decided to help Rach solely because she felt sorry for the girl? Her motivations were interesting. Fascinating, even. But he couldn't afford to be fascinated by her any more.

"Hey, Tyler, can I ask you something personal?"

He gave his undivided attention to Em. It was safer. *She* was safer. "Sure."

"I thought you and Jay were, you know, an item."

He choked on his mouthful of soda and she thumped him on the back. "We're, uh, just friends," he managed. "Why?"

"Oh. No reason." She drained her soda and rolled from the beanbag to her feet. "Another drink? This one's on me."

He shook his head. "Nah, I'm sweet."

Jay sauntered past on her way to greet some more kids and Tyler had to force his gaze to halt mid-swivel. He was not gonna pine after her like some lovesick puppy. No freaking way.

When Em returned, she stuck her soda on the floor, grabbed Tyler's hands and yanked him to his feet. When she overcompensated for his weight and almost overbalanced, he steadied her with his hands on her waist. Her warmth seeped into his skin—so very different from Jay's coolness.

"I love this song! Dance with me?" Em's gaze was fixed on his face, her own expression the slightest bit anxious as she waited for his response.

Tyler blinked. And looked around. No one else was dancing.

Em gave him a sheepish smile. "Someone's gotta be first."

"Uh, okay. Sure." Tyler didn't mind dancing. What he did mind was being stared at. What he minded even more was the slit-eyed gaze and what appeared to be an actual snarl on Jay's face when she spotted him with Em.

She was leaving tomorrow, fergodsake! She had no claim on him. Not anymore.

He turned his back on her and threw Em the most brilliant smile he could summon. She smiled back in a dazed kinda way. And his battered heart ached with guilt. He was using Em. He knew it, but he did it anyway.

More kids arrived. Someone cranked up the volume to ear-drum splitting level. Caro and Matt, and a bunch of other kids joined Tyler and Em.

Tyler relaxed. He even gave himself permission to have fun with Em. She had to know he wasn't interested in her that way. He'd never given her any reason to believe otherwise. They were just friends. Having fun. Isn't that what friends did?

Someone elbowed Em aside—a girl with bleach-blonde hair, glossy pink lips and violet-tinted shades. She lunged and shoved Caro backward. Hard—so hard, Caro lost her balance and fell on her butt.

"Hey, watch it!" Caro yelled, glaring up at the offender, who took off her shades and sneered down at her.

Vanessa.

Great. Just freaking great. Another drama—so not what Tyler needed. And things were gonna get pretty damned dramatic real soon if the pissed-to-the-max glint in Nessa's big blue eyes was anything to go by.

"What the fuck are you doing here, Vanessa?" he said. "Get the hell out!"

He reached for her, but Em held him back. "Not your fight," she said. "Let Matt and Caro deal with it."

Tyler shook off her hand but did as she suggested. For now.

Matt "dealt with it" by grabbing Caro beneath her armpits and hauling her to her feet. She promptly launched herself at Vanessa, reaching for her long, bouncy ponytail and yanking hard.

Vanessa's eyes widened with shock. She screeched like a banshee, both hands going to her hair as she tried to escape Caro's grip.

Tyler grinned. Way to go, sis.

Matt peeled Caro's fingers from Vanessa's hair and pulled her backward into his arms, hugging her tightly to prevent her escaping. "You okay?" he asked.

"I'm fine. Let me at her!" Caro struggled in his arms.

Vanessa lunged for Caro again, but this time, Jay intervened by stepping in front of her.

Tyler bit back a sympathetic "Yeow!" as Nessa smacked into what must have felt like a solid brick wall. And when Jay grasped Nessa's shoulders and shook her until her head snapped back on her neck, he wondered whether he should step in.

Naw. Nessa had it coming. And Tyler didn't believe Jay would actually damage anything except Nessa's pride.

"Listen to me, you stupid little bitch," Jay said. "It's obvious to anyone with half a brain you're high on whatever else you're dealing along with the steroids, otherwise you wouldn't have dared show your face here." Her voice had risen to a roar that could be clearly heard over the music… which was abruptly cut off. This little drama was way more entertaining than whatever was currently playing on the iPod.

"So before I call the cops and point them right at your chubby, drugged up ass, why don't you slink back to Shawn?"

Vanessa's mouth opened and closed like a demented goldfish.

"Not that I give a shit about Shawn," Jay continued. "But I'm sure he's not exactly thrilled his walking steroid supply has gone AWOL and snuck off to gatecrash my party. We've all had enough of your crap, Vanessa. No more lies. No one's gonna take the rap for you anymore. And if you think Tyler's gonna shield you this time to save your precious reputation, then you've got another think coming. You hear me? Enough!"

"Jay!" Tyler didn't know whether to laugh or be shocked by her tirade. She sounded just like your average, mega-pissed-off teenage girl.

Matt caught his eye. “Well, that’s not exactly how I’d imagined taking Shawn down. But hey, works for me.”

Tyler agreed. Even the rumor of steroid use would be enough for Principal Harris to crack down hard and launch an investigation. Chances that someone who was watching this little showdown didn’t grasp the perfect opportunity to make trouble for Shawn and run bleating to the principal? Nil. Shawn had pissed off too many people.

“What the eff is going on?” Caro twisted around in Matt’s arms and peered up at him. “Is Nessa really dealing drugs? And Shawn.... Steroids? Are you kidding me?”

“I’ll explain it all to you later, babe.”

“You’d better.”

Jay thrust Vanessa away like she was toxic, and Jay couldn’t bear to touch her. “Go home. You hear me?”

“Yeah, I hear you.” Vanessa straightened her top, patted her hair, and pulled a sneer at the sight of Caro held snug in Matt’s embrace. “Dude, you were so better off with me,” she said. “At least I know how to show a guy a good time. Shawn told me that one’s nothing but a cock-teaser. And she—”

Jay’s hand snaked out, so lightning fast that it was a blur. And when Tyler refocused on her arm, it was back at her side, like he’d only imagined the movement. Except he hadn’t, because Vanessa’s left cheek sported a crimson handprint.

“Don’t you ever, ever speak like that about my friends again,” Jay said.

“You freaking slut!” Vanessa shrieked, cradling her cheek in her palm, her pretty face twisted with loathing.

“And you would know all about being a freak *and* a slut,” Jay said. “You’ve caused enough trouble, Vanessa. It’s time for you to leave. Go back to Shawn. Dealer and user, and both of you liars with all the morals of pond scum. The two of you deserve each other." As she had once done with Shawn, Jay expertly manacled Vanessa's wrist and twisted her arm up behind her back.

Tyler decided to step in. But only because after witnessing this delightful little scene, he wasn't entirely sure Jay could control herself if Vanessa provoked her again. "I'll help you walk her to the door," he said. With heavy emphasis on "walk". Like, in case Jay was thinking more along the lines of "toss her out on her butt".

"Let me go," Vanessa screeched, leaning backward, trying to dig in her heels. "You're hurting me!"

"Tough." Jay marched her through the silent crowd, who all stepped aside.

"Get your hands off me!"

"No."

"When Shawn hears about this—"

"You'll be lucky if he doesn't wash his hands of you. Now shut up or I'll toss you down the stairs, simply for the pleasure of seeing whether you bounce."

"Jay." Tyler placed a cautionary hand on her arm. "She's not worth it, really."

Jay shoved Vanessa through the doorway and leaned against it. The music started up again as she watched Vanessa totter and sway down the first few steps.

"Oh for God's sake!" Jay screamed. And before Tyler could stop her, she ran toward Vanessa, swung her up over her shoulder, and sprinted down the stairs.

"Shit." Tyler followed at a run. And when he hit the first floor landing, he was more relieved than he could possibly have believed to see Jay had reached the bottom of the stairs without doing something drastic. Like kicking Vanessa into orbit. Instead, she set Vanessa down outside the building and turned her back on Vanessa's shocked face.

Vanessa took to her heels.

Jay let her go.

Tyler waited at the landing as she climbed the stairs toward him.

She glanced up at him, and the anguish on her face hit him like a physical blow. She doubled over, gasping. Her legs folded.

Tyler scooped her into his arms and sat on a stair, cradling her in his lap, rocking her and stroking her hair while she shivered and shook. "What's wrong?" he whispered.

"Isn't it obvious? I'm having a human meltdown. Because I don't want to go. I don't want to leave you. I can't bear the thought of never seeing you again."

He brushed the hair back from her temple and pressed a kiss to the tiny vein throbbing beneath her cool skin. "I wrote a song for you, you know. I recorded it on a thumb drive. I was going to give it to you tonight. To remember me by."

She muffled her face in his shirt. "Sing it to me. Please?"

He sucked in a deep breath and launched into an *a cappella* version of the song.

"I wake in the dead of night,
And you're not there.
I call your name,
But you don't answer.
You're gone,
And I'm lost.
Half of what I am is yours.

And I'm lost without you.

Thoughts of you glowing in my heart,
Thoughts of you shining in my soul,
Thoughts of you blazing in my mind,
Thoughts of you, burning,
Thoughts of you,
Burn.

I walk into the room,
And you're there.
I tremble like a lunatic,
But you only smile.
I'm gone.
And I'm lost.
Half of what I am is yours.
And I'm lost within you.

Thoughts of you glowing in my heart,
Thoughts of you shining in my soul,
Thoughts of you blazing in my mind,
Thoughts of you, burning,
Thoughts of you,
Burn."

"It's beautiful," she said.

"Like you."

She was silent for a moment. "What's it called?"

"Lost Without You."

A sob escaped her. And then another. And Tyler held her while she cried.

Footsteps echoed through the stairwell, getting louder, heading toward them.

Tyler didn't move, content to hold Jay for as long as he could. He hoped whoever it was would take the hint and continue on up the stairs.

The footsteps paused and he felt Jay go very still. He glanced up at the intruder and saw it wasn't Vanessa returning, or some other kid who'd turned up late. It was a bald guy with a 'stache.

Jay heaved a sigh and lifted her head from his chest. "Good evening, Michael," she said. "You're early. How very tiresome. If you'd waited a few more hours, I would have been safely away."

The man—Michael—laughed softly. "This wasn't exactly how I'd planned it, either. But hey, I'll run with it. Might be a good idea if your boyfriend made himself scarce, though."

That voice.... So very familiar. Hauntingly familiar.

"Perhaps you might like to reconsider your options," Jay told the guy. "In fact, I know that very shortly, you will do just that."

She crawled from Tyler's lap and clamped her arm around his waist, holding him tightly against her side as she drew him to his feet. She sounded completely unlike the girl he knew. Or the cyborg he knew, for that matter. She sounded too sure of herself, too adult. She spoke to this stranger like she considered herself his equal. Or perhaps even his superior.

"Tyler," Jay said, "I'd like you to meet Michael White. Not his real name, of course. But unless I'm very much mistaken—which of course I'm not—you know him quite well."

Tyler frowned at the stranger.

The guy frowned right back. Fiercely. And then his jaw sagged open and whatever he'd been about to say ended up a strangled, "Shit."

"Ignore the walrus moustache," Jay said. "Ditch the fake

glasses and imagine him with hair. You're an artist, Tyler. Don't be fooled by outward appearances. Go deeper. Look at the eyes, the facial features, bone structure."

Tyler gazed into the man's eyes and his world tipped on its axis. Again. Because he *did* recognize this man with the dorky 'stache and shaved head and stunned eyes and shock-frozen face.

Except, to his knowledge, no one except Jay had ever called him Michael. Not even his wife.

Everyone knew him as Mike.

Mike Davidson.

Tyler's father.

Chapter Eighteen

"SON," TYLER'S FATHER SAID. "Listen to me. I want you to move away from her and come stand by me. Now."

"Don't call me son," he managed to say.

"Tyler, please."

This was no joke. Tyler's father had spoken tersely, his voice tense and strained. He was scared, scared of what Jay might do.

But Tyler knew she would never hurt him. Or at least, not physically.

Before he could even decide how to react, in one fluid movement Jay threw him over her shoulder and bounded up the stairs to the top floor landing. He struggled and she set him back on his feet but kept him close with an arm about his waist. "He'll be far safer with me, Michael. For the moment."

Tyler's father blew out a disbelieving snort. "I don't think so, Gamma. The first time you singled him out for attention, you put him at risk. They'll target him for interrogation. And I can't let that happen. I *won't* let that happen. Let him go. I can protect him. I can make sure he's safe and—"

"Can't you sense them, Michael? They're deploying themselves around this building as we speak. He didn't trust you so he had you followed. And you've led them right to everything you hold so dear. Do you truly believe they'll care who gets hurt in the crossfire? Or are you truly that naïve?"

Tyler's father stilled. He cocked his head, considered Jay through narrowed, intense eyes. He obviously heard something Tyler couldn't because he visibly paled. And then he sprang into motion, pivoting to rush headlong down the stairs.

"What the hell is going on, Jay?" Tyler's head was whirling from everything he'd witnessed. He was kinda grateful for her arm about his waist. Without her supporting him, he might have toppled down the stairs and landed at the bottom in a gibbering, useless heap.

"Your dad's done a stupid thing and now it's come back to bite him on the ass. I need you to trust me and do exactly what I say. Can you do that?"

He nodded. Then he had a really terrifying, paralyzing thought. "Will…?" He choked back his fear. "Will they hurt Mom?"

Jay shook her head, her bright blue eyes gleaming in the dull gloom of the stairwell. "I don't believe she's in any immediate danger. As always, they appear to have their priorities sorted. And, as always, their first priority is me."

Michael raced back up the stairwell, taking the stairs two at a time. "Shit. You're right. Full extraction team armed to the teeth. Tyler, where's your sister?"

"Caro's upstairs, Michael." Tyler ignored the pain in his father's eyes at the way Tyler had addressed him. Michael had walked out on them five years ago. He didn't deserve to be called "dad". "She's partying with a whole bunch of other kids in Jay's apartment."

Michael scrubbed his hands over his shaven scalp. "Shit." He stared helplessly at Tyler. "Shit!"

Cold, sick dread coated Tyler's skin. "What the hell kind of people are you working for?"

"A ruthless bastard who'd do anything—and I mean anything—to get his hands on this cyborg."

Jay smiled. "Gosh, it feels wonderful to be loved."

Michael stared at her, like he couldn't believe what he was hearing. "If you're thinking of using my son and daughter as hostages—"

"Don't be an ass, Michael," she said. "I love your son. And your daughter is my best friend. I'm hardly going to endanger them to save my own skin."

"Huh?" Tyler heard himself squawk. "What did you say?"

Jay pressed a hard, possessive kiss to his lips. A kiss that left him entirely breathless, and hot and tingling all over. She reached into her back pocket and handed him a credit card in his mother's maiden name, Marissa Rowen. A black American Express card. "Unlimited funds," she said. "And I mean, unlimited. All payments are handled by one of my offshore account agents. When it's safe to leave the building, tell Marissa to take you and Caro and leave. Don't pack up, don't take anything. Just hire a rental, and go. This card will buy you anything you need. Car, house, anything at all. Tell her I'm sorry. It's the best I can do. If I had more time—if there was any other way...."

Michael approached warily. He paused, then grabbed Tyler and hugged him so tight he could barely breathe.

"Take Tyler inside, Michael, and shut the door behind you. Input this code, 3-7-9-6-5-1-4-5, on the interior keypad by the door. The door is reinforced and the code will engage the deadlocks. Do you have it memorized?"

Tyler's father muttered the numbers beneath his breath and nodded. "3-7-9-6-5-1-4-5. Got it."

"For the release code, add one to all the digits: 4-8-0-7-6-2-5-

6. Give it thirty minutes. This will all be over by then."

"What are you going to do?" Tyler knew his voice was scratchy with fear and worry but he was unable to hide it from her.

Jay's gaze locked on to his. "Whatever it takes to keep you and your sister and Marissa, and yes, even your misguided father, safe."

Michael stuck out his hand, wincing slightly when Jay grasped it. "Thank you. And I'm sorry."

"I know, Michael. You were lied to from the start and you were only trying to keep your family safe. If you've got any sense, you'll make yourself scarce, and go on that extended holiday, too. Marissa will need your help. And if you get down on your knees and beg, you might even convince her to accept it. I've considered all the available men in this town, analyzed all the available data, and in my not-so-humble opinion, no one else is good enough for her."

Jay's features smoothed, blanking until it seemed to Tyler that she'd shucked off her humanity and he was gazing at something manmade. Something inhuman.

"Go," she said to him. And launched herself down the stairs without a backward glance.

Michael yanked open the door and pushed Tyler inside. The instant before his father slammed it shut behind them, Tyler heard the unmistakable sound of breaking glass.

Chapter Nineteen

Michael punched in the code Jay had given him and waited until the deadbolts slammed into place. "Just act normal," he told Tyler. "We don't want any of the kids panicking."

But acting normal, like he wasn't locked in an apartment with a bunch of other kids to protect them from madmen with a terrifying agenda, and no qualms about collateral damage, was gonna be the hardest thing Tyler had ever done in his life. He hoped Caro didn't spot him. God only knew what he'd blurt if she asked what was going on.

Tyler squinted and dabbed his watering eyes with his sleeve. After the gloom of the stairwell, the bright flashing lights seared his eyeballs. From what he could see, none of the partygoers had heard anything untoward over the booming music. And no one seemed to bat an eyelid at the adult who'd suddenly joined them. They were all too intent on dancing, drinking, eating, talking, and doing what teenagers did at parties—even necking in shadowy corners, by the looks of it. All were oblivious to the danger Jay had put herself in for their sakes.

Michael shadowed Tyler as he headed for the nearest window. Which was just plain stupid, really, since all the windows were set so high up the walls he couldn't possibly see out without a ladder.

A ladder…. With a ladder, he might get out through a skylight and onto the roof. But wasn't like there was one conveniently lying around the place. Tyler stared up at those tantalizingly unreachable panes of glass and fisted his hands. Better that than scream his fear and frustration, which sure as hell wouldn't be acting "normal".

"What do we say if someone wants to leave before Jay gets back, or—" Tyler didn't want to think about the alternative. Couldn't. "What do we tell them?"

"We say the locks are jammed and Jay's gone to get a locksmith," Michael said. "It's only eleven. Can't imagine any of these kids wanting to leave so soon. Not when there's plenty of food and drink to keep them happy." He slumped against the wall and slid down to the floor. He sat with knees bent, chin propped on his hands. Tyler joined him.

"If I didn't know how impossible it was," Michael muttered, "I might actually believe she cared deeply for you."

The flashing lights painted Michael's face with lurid rainbow slashes. He looked alien, implacable. Hard. Completely unlike the man who'd raised him and Caro—the father Tyler had once believed could do no wrong.

"Why is that so impossible to believe?" he ground out. He knew what Michael meant but it hurt all the same. "Am I so unlovable? Is that why you left?"

Michael White, AKA Mike Davidson, his *father*, turned pain-filled eyes on him. "No! Of course not. Don't be an idiot, Tyler. It's just…. You do know what she—Jay—is, don't you?"

"Yes. She told us—Caro and me. Showed us, actually."

Michael blew out a relieved breath. "So. You understand why she didn't mean it—why she couldn't mean it. She's a cyborg,

Tyler. A machine. She can't love anybody. She pretends. She's an outstanding mimic."

Tyler burst out laughing, but it was a mirthless laugh laced with despair. "But she *did* mean it. She told us something was happening inside her, something not even she could comprehend. She did have feelings. And emotions—human emotions. I saw her crying. So I know she really could care for me. I know in here—" he thumped his chest with his fist "—in my heart, she really could love me."

"Tyler. Son—"

"Don't call me that, *Michael*." His father flinched back from Tyler's vicious emphasis of his name. "You lost the right to call me that when you took off five years ago."

"You'll always be my son. And no matter how much you hate me for leaving you, I'll always be your father."

Tyler sighed, his anger draining away, leaving him cold and bereft and very, very sad. "Funny," he said, his voice cracking, "that's what Jay said about *her* father."

Michael snorted. "She might look human, Tyler, but she was created in a lab. She didn't have a father, she had a creator. And she killed him."

"She *what*?" The blood chilled in his veins.

"She killed him. Broke his neck minutes before our team got to him. From what they could tell from his medical records, the old man was dying, anyway. Incurable cancer. But she's dangerous, Tyler, a killer. And now there's no one alive who knows the sequence to override her inbuilt safeguards and command her obedience."

Tyler closed his eyes. His mind whirled as he thought hard, winnowing through and discounting the myriad possibilities, trying to justify Jay's actions. She wouldn't have killed her father.

Not the Jay he knew, the Jay who'd been so gutted when she talked about his death. She couldn't have killed him—not willingly, anyway.

"It's a good thing he's dead," Tyler said. "If he'd been alive when you came for him, you'd have tortured that sequence out of him so you could command Jay and use her as a weapon. But now you can't. No one can."

Michael frowned as he processed Tyler's words, absorbing the surety, the belief.

Tyler's gaze drifted to a blank space on the wall. Something had hung there recently. He could still see the picture hook. A psalm. Yeah. That was right. Something about sacrifice and eternal life—

And he was hit by a moment of pure clarity that left him struggling to catch his breath and give voice to the words that had formed on his tongue. "He used the command sequence on her. He forced her to kill him so they wouldn't get their hands on him. God. No wonder she cried when he died. No wonder she was so damned gutted. Shit. Being forced to kill your own father. What a fucking awful thing to have to do."

Michael made a strangled noise of protest.

"You don't get it, do you?" Tyler stared into his father's eyes, willing him to understand. "To Jay, her creator *was* her father. She even called him Father. She loved him. Just like she loves me."

Michael blinked. He opened his mouth as if to say something, then shut it with a snap. His face was all tight and pinched, like he'd eaten something gross.

"None of it matters now," Tyler said. "Doesn't matter how I feel about her, or how she feels about me, or even whether you believe she can feel anything at all."

"It matters," his father said, staring off into space. "Believe me, it matters more than you realize."

"Whatever." Hope joined the churning mass of emotions battering him. "So what are you going to do? What's your plan?"

A bitter little laugh erupted from Michael's mouth. "I don't know quite what you think I've become, Tyler, but I'm simply a computer geek who caught the attention of the wrong people, and got caught up in their schemes. I'm a button-pusher, not an action hero. I'm unarmed, and even if I wasn't, I'm no match for those mercenaries out there."

Tyler searched his father's face and knew Michael spoke the truth. His heart twisted. Jay was on her own.

Caro spotted him just then. She stood on tiptoes to wave at him over the crowd of bobbing heads. And then she frowned at his companion. She started to drag Matt through the dancers, and from the look on her face she was all set to give Tyler the third degree until he got an unexpected reprieve. The iPod cut off mid-song and the lights died, plunging the room into darkness.

Over the squeals and excited laughter, Tyler whispered to Michael, "What do you think's happened?"

"My guess is they've used the new EMP combo weapon they've developed."

"EMP? What's that?"

"Electromagnetic Pulse."

Tyler had a really bad feeling about that. "Like in the movies? When everything electronic gets fried?"

"Near enough," his father said. "The first one they developed had no effect on her whatsoever, so they went back to R and D and started from scratch."

"That's not good. Is it?"

"Maybe she'll be—" Michael seemed to think better about trying to sanitize the situation for him. "No. Probably not."

Tyler began to wish his sister *had* made it over before the lights went out. Because he really needed a hug right now, and if he didn't watch it, he'd be asking for one from the man he'd convinced himself he despised. "What Jay said about you only trying to keep us safe—did those people threaten to hurt us if you didn't do what they said?"

"Among other things. I left because I had no choice. I left the way I did, without saying goodbye, because I had no choice. I did it because I needed to keep you all safe. And if I had to make the choice all over again, I would do the same thing." Michael was silent for a long while. And then he asked, "Does that make any difference?"

Tyler thought about it. "I think so. It doesn't make it hurt any less but at least now I understand why you left."

"Good."

They waited in the darkness, Tyler hoping, praying….

And Michael? He didn't have a clue what his father was thinking or worrying about. And that was okay, 'cause right now, Tyler only had the strength to worry about one person.

Jay.

"What's that humming sound?" he asked.

Lights flared, the music blared to life, and loud chatter resumed. Within seconds, the party was in full swing again. It was as if nothing had ever gone wrong.

"Huh," Michael said. "She must have hooked the electrics up to a petrol-powered portable generator that automatically kicks in after a few minutes. Smart kid."

Tyler unclenched each quivering muscle and crawled to his feet. His father input the release code and stuck his head out the doorway. He ducked back in to say, "You stay here with your sister. I'm heading downstairs to check it out. I'm locking you back in, okay? In case anything happens, do you remember the release code?"

Tyler nodded. "Yeah. It's 4-8-0-7-6-2-5-6."

"Good boy. If I'm not back in ten, call the cops. Tell them you heard shots or something, so you locked the door and you're too scared to come out. That ought to do it. Then promise me you'll do whatever it takes to convince your Mom to leave town, okay?"

Tyler swallowed. "Okay. Be careful. Dad."

His dad grinned and ruffled his hair. "I will." And he disappeared through the doorway, leaving Tyler to face the wrath of Caro, which was bearing down on him like a small and very determined, but very stylishly dressed, tank.

His sister confronted him, hand on hips. "What the eff is going on, Tyler? Where's Jay? I haven't spotted her in a while. And who was that guy I saw you talking to just now? And—"

"It was Dad."

Her brows drew together in an ominous frown. "Have you been drinking, Tyler Davidson? What the hell would our AWOL father be doing at Jay's farewell party? And where is Jay, anyway?"

"She.... She had to leave. In a hurry."

Caro paled and Tyler gripped her arm to steady her when she wobbled. "Shit. What happened, Tyler? Is she all right? Tell me!"

So he did.

And he was just finishing up when the door opened and Michael entered the apartment. "Looks like a bomb site outside," he said when he spotted Tyler. "Couple of cars toppled on their sides, broken windows, one storefront completely demolished and— Shit. Caro?"

She glared at him, lips thinned to a tight white line, eyes glinting with tears. "Don't you ever walk out without saying goodbye again, you big dumbass."

Michael blinked.

"Well, aren't you gonna give me a hug?" And with that, Caro threw herself into his arms.

Over her head, Michael swept his gaze across the melee of frenetically bopping kids. "We should go. Before the police get here."

"What about Matt? And Em? And everyone else?" Caro had rallied from the shock. "We can't leave them here. We can't just leave."

"This lot are all safer up here than down on the street," Michael said. "And when the police get here, they can get these kids home far more efficiently and safely than we could. We have to go. Your mother—"

"Caro, we need to get Mom." It was killing Tyler not knowing what had happened to Jay. He had to get downstairs, see the destruction for himself, see if there was any chance she might have gotten away. And, if she was as good as he believed she was, then he wanted to stand out in the open where she could see him. He wanted to give her the opportunity to emerge from wherever she'd hidden and come back to him.

"Caro," his dad said. "We can't afford to get anyone else involved with this."

She stared at them for what seemed like forever, and then reality bit and her shoulders slumped. "Okay."

Michael slipped from the apartment, with Tyler and Caro following close on his heels. No one uttered a word as they trooped down the stairs and burst through the street doors.

Tyler skidded to a halt. He gazed at the damage. Rubble,

shards of glass, cars on their sides and on their roofs, parts strewn everywhere.... "Oh. My. God."

"The kid sure put up a fight."

"What do we do now?" Caro asked. And Tyler was grateful she had, 'cause he wasn't capable of anything much right now. He felt head-to-toe numb. He couldn't think straight. He could barely breathe.

A siren sounded in the distance. Someone in one of the nearby buildings must have called the cops.

"*We* aren't doing anything." Michael's tone brooked no argument. "Tyler's going to take you home, and you're going to explain everything to your Mom, and pack up the car."

Tyler tried to muster a protest but his dad was having none of it. "I'm not kidding around, son. These guys play for keeps. You need to keep your mother and sister safe for me. I can't lose you all over again. Can you do that for me? Please?"

When he nodded, Michael let out his breath with an audible whoosh. He visibly sagged. "Thank you."

"What are you gonna do, Dad?"

"I'm going to have a quick look around and see what I can find." He paused, obviously seeing the doubt in their eyes. "Tell your mother.... Tell her—shit, I don't know. I'll be back as soon as I can, I promise. We'll sort it all out then, all right? Now scoot. Before the cops arrive and start asking questions."

Tyler nodded. He grabbed Caro's unresisting hand and took off at a loping jog, tugging her along beside him. Only when they'd rounded the corner and were a block away from Jay's apartment, did he slow to a fast walk to let her catch her breath.

They walked in silence. What more was there to say? There was only speculation and hope—something Tyler was rapidly losing.

Chapter Twenty

The garage door opened. And as his mom reversed the car out into the driveway, Tyler glimpsed the man standing on the path leading up to the front door. A frisson goosed his skin. He knew exactly who it was. His dad had kept his promise.

Mike Davidson had finally come home… in time to see his family leave.

Tyler and Caro had prepped their mom—as much as they could, anyway. How'n the hell could you explain to someone why the person they loved, the person they'd married and raised children with, had walked out and stayed away for five whole freaking years to keep them safe? Not to mention now he'd come back, he was so worried for their safety he insisted they leave town. The whole "Jay is really a cyborg" thing was more than enough to do his mom's head in without adding all the stuff about his dad.

Tyler thought she'd taken everything in. He hoped so. But it was difficult to tell. His mom's face, usually so open, with that wonderful quality that made you instantly want to be her friend—just like Caro's—had changed with each new revelation. By the time they'd finally finished telling her everything they knew, his mom's face had been wooden. Shuttered. Secretive.

His mom closed the garage door and got out of the car.

Tyler exchanged a glance with his sister and they both wound down their windows. He couldn't hear what his parents were saying, though. Their voices were too muted. Still, at least it wasn't full-out screaming, which had to be a good thing.

His dad tossed a small bag in the trunk, came around to the passenger's side, and hopped in, leaving his mom to take the driver's seat. "Got everything you need, kids?"

"Yep." Tyler had grabbed a change of clothes and his guitar. That was all he needed. Caro, too, had packed light—just a backpack with some clothes and makeup. She hadn't even argued about leaving her cell phone behind because maybe it could be traced. And their mom.... Well, the bag in the trunk of the car was full of photo albums, which about said it all. She hadn't bothered with much else except a change of clothes. And although she'd taken the AMEX card, glanced at the name on it, and muttered something about spending up large, her heart hadn't been in it.

She revved the car and reversed out into the street.... And Tyler suddenly remembered something important. Something he needed to do. "Wait!"

She slammed on the brakes. "What?"

He opened the door and jumped out.

"Where the hell are you going?" his dad yelled, fumbling with the passenger-side door.

Tyler delved in the back pocket of his jeans as he ran to the side of the house. He squatted to lever a potted plant up from the dish it rested on, and placed the thumb drive next to the spare front door key.

"What the hell do you think you're doing?" His dad's voice came from behind him, tight with fury.

"It's a song I wrote for Jay. I'm leaving it here. Just in case."

"Nothing else but the song, right? Nothing that could tell those bastards I worked for where we're headed?"

"Nope. Just the song. If she got away, she'll find it. I know she will."

A hand squeezed Tyler's shoulder. "I'm sorry, Tyler."

"Yeah. Me, too."

His dad followed him back to the car.

When his mom drove off, Tyler didn't look back. If Jay got away, she'll find me. I know she will.

TYLER ROLLED ON TO his back and stared at the ceiling of their fancy hotel suite. "What do you mean you're sorry? What are you trying to say?"

His dad heaved a heavy sigh. "I was trying to pick the right time to tell you this, but I don't think there's ever going to be a right time.

"Tell me straight."

"I don't think she made it."

"Jay?"

"Yeah. All I found was this." He held out something wrapped in a towel. "I wasn't going to give it to you but your mom said I should."

Tyler sat up and took the offering, laying it in his lap. His dad sat next to him on the couch. Tyler slanted him a sideways glance. He looked tired, worn out. Dark rings beneath his eyes, deep lines bracketing his mouth. He'd ditched the moustache, thank God. Must have shaved it off last night before he hit the couch.

Tyler was sharing a room with Caro. Their mom had the other room to herself. Their dad was sleeping on the couch. It was an arrangement both seemed content with, and for that, Tyler was grateful. At least his mom hadn't slung her estranged husband out on his ass.

Tyler contemplated the lumpy whatever-it-was, cocooned in the grubby frayed towel. He had a bad feeling about what it could be. But he had to know.

He unwrapped it.

It was bad, all right. Real bad.

Waves of sickly heat washed over him. He drew in a breath and then another. And another. And still he couldn't get enough oxygen.

Enough. Suck it up, dude. Deal.

His internal pep-talk worked. He stared at the severed hand. At first glance it appeared to be human. He steeled himself to pick it up, take a closer look.

There was no blood. It'd been completely washed clean. And the closer he looked, the more fascinated he became. Its construction, the metallic-looking bones, the tendons—all encased in smooth, pale, humanlike skin.... It was miraculous. A work of art.

He rewrapped it carefully. It was a part of her, of Jay. The only part left. "Where did you find it?" he asked, proud of how steady his voice sounded.

"I tracked the extraction team to a house—vacant, thank God. The place was completely wrecked. There'd been an explosion. It was professionally done, set to cause maximum damage. I can only presume Jay was responsible."

"Or maybe it was the extraction team," Tyler said, thinking aloud. "If they couldn't capture her, they might have decided to eliminate her."

His father rubbed his chin. "A possibility," he finally conceded. "They'd cleaned up and gone by the time I arrived, but I think she got a few of them. I didn't find anything on site and I figured they'd taken her. And then I spotted something in the pool by the filter. It was the hand."

"Jay's hand."

"Tyler, I'm ninety-nine-point-nine percent certain Jay deliberately blew herself up in that explosion. And for some reason, her hand was the only part of her that wasn't obliterated. I'm sorry."

"I know." Tyler met his eyes. "What're you gonna do, Dad?"

"About the people I work for?"

Tyler nodded.

"I got a message from my employer. Before Jay—" His dad raked his hand through his still non-existent hair. "Somehow, Jay convinced him it would be prudent to cut me loose. I'm not privy to the details. Nor am I going to try and find out what she said to them. I'm not that morbidly curious, just grateful as hell. Now Jay's gone and her creator's research along with her, with any luck that'll be the last I hear from the unholy bastard. That's what I'm hoping, anyway. Just like I'm hoping that we can all go home very soon."

"And if not?"

"You're stuck with me. I won't leave my family again."

"Glad to hear it," Caro said, from her prone position on the other couch. She rolled to her feet and wandered over to flop onto the seat next to her dad. "How's Mom taking all this?"

"Mom's taking it just fine."

Their mom padded into the sitting room and perched on the arm of the chair. "Mom'll take it even better if she's clued in on what's going on in her kids' lives in future. And her husband's."

"Duly noted," said the husband in question.

Caro yawned and stretched. "It's been a rough couple of days. I know it's early but I'm off to bed.

Her mom smiled. "Me, too. We've got a shopping expedition tomorrow."

Tyler thought his mom looked tired but pleased. Content. Like whatever had been missing in her life had been found. And it had, of course, the instant her husband had walked back into her life like some returning hero, begging her forgiveness, and promising he'd never leave her again.

If only Tyler could have Jay back to fill the empty hole she'd left in his own heart.

"Tyler. Ah, love, I'm so sorry. I know how much she meant to you." His mom slipped into the seat next to him. And hugged him while he tried not to cry like a girl.

A WEEK AFTER Jay's farewell party, Tyler and his family returned to Snapperton and settled back into uneasy normality. They buried Jay's remains under a tree in the backyard. No one said anything. No one had to. Jay had touched all their lives. Everyone understood how Tyler had felt about her. Regardless of his parents' personal feelings about his non-human almost-girlfriend, they respected his.

Caro walked to school with him on Monday. They'd both have preferred not to go to classes at all but their dad insisted they act as though everything was normal. Normal....

Yeah. Riiight.

Tyler was going to have to face up to the fact Jay was gone. Just like he was going to have to face up to the fact he'd used Em to make himself feel better, and then discarded her without a thought when Jay needed him. He liked Em—as a friend. And he didn't have a clue what he was going to tell her.

He'd have preferred to walk alone, lost in his own thoughts, but Caro was having none of that. "Do you reckon Shawn will still be top-dog?" she asked. "Or do you reckon the rumors and the lies will have finally caught up with him, and he'll be the one sitting at the back of the cafeteria?"

"Dunno. Don't much give a crap, either."

"Yeah. It all seems so trivial. But it'd be cool if you were reinstated as one of the top-jocks again. Right?"

"I'll never be that person again, Caro. And yanno what?"

"What?"

"Way I see it, Jay was interested in me because I was a freak. So if I hadn't gone through all that crap with Vanessa and Shawn, I'd have been just another popular guy. Nothing special. Probably a real douche-bag to boot. And then she wouldn't have wanted to know me. So I'm kinda glad. 'Cause I feel privileged to have known her."

He ducked his head, concentrated on scuffing a stone from the sidewalk and sending it bouncing onto the road, not wanting Caro to see the expression on his face. "Suppose I sound like I'm wigging out big-time, huh?"

"Nope." She gave him a quick hug.

IT WASN'T UNTIL Tyler got home from school and discovered his parents weren't home that he realized he'd left his door key on his desk in his room. Crap. But the spare key would still be in its hiding place under the potted plant, so it wasn't like he had to sit on the doorstep and wait for his sister.

When he tipped over the pot, he found the key. He also found something that'd been missing, something he'd believed had died forever. He found hope. Because the thumb drive he'd left for Jay was gone.

Epilogue

He was the last one to scramble off the bus. The driver threw him a grin. "Daydreaming, huh?"

Tyler grinned back. "Nightmare, more like."

"First day, is it?"

"Yeah."

"Don't worry. They're a good bunch, these kids. You'll do just fine." The man winked at Tyler and waved as the bus drove off.

The day was looking up. But as he wandered through the front gates of Appleton Performing Arts School, Tyler's high spirits began to fray a little around the edges. A new town. His first time away from home, living on his own. His first day on campus. A chance to make new friends—if he could be bothered.

The prospect of any of the aforementioned was daunting, but all of them in the space of a couple of weeks was enough to do his head in.

He strolled up the paved pathway, admiring the landscaping. Lush swathes of grass and meandering paths were interspersed with large shade trees, under-planted with flowering shrubs. Nice. Maybe he'd sit out here and eat lunch rather than braving the cafeteria.

He halted to examine the architecturally designed building that housed the main wing of the school. It'd been rebuilt about a decade ago and won some fancy award. He could see why. Where possible, the architect had retained the original façade, skillfully and seamlessly melding old-fashioned charm with modern convenience—all without making the building look like hot mess.

Sucking in a deep breath, Tyler pushed through the front doors and made a beeline for the Admin area.

As he neared the office, he slowed mid-step. Another new student was already waiting at the desk. And something about her, some indefinable quality, demanded his attention—

Whoa. He eyed her beneath his lashes. Tall. Willowy. Nice ass—real nice. She wore faded jeans that rode low on her narrow hips, an old checked flannel shirt over top a worn t-shirt of indeterminable color, and sneakers that were more holes than sneaker.

As if aware she was being eyeballed she glanced his way.

The chestnut hair gave him pause. Then his stomach flip-flopped. Her eyes were the most shockingly intense shade of blue he'd ever seen.

Her smile turned his brain to mush. He tried to look away, act all nonchalant, but he couldn't.

Her gaze absorbed him from head to toe. She winked at him and he just stood there, gaping at her. Elated. Disbelieving. Hopeful.

Her lips curved as she sauntered over to him. "Hi. Have we met before?"

"I reckon so," he said, matching the lightness of her tone even though his heart was racing, and damned if his knees hadn't turned to Jell-O.

"My name is Jaime. But *you* can call me Jay."

"Pleased to meet you, Jay. I like the new look, by the way."

Her smile was pure wickedness as she did a campy twirl for his benefit. "Really?"

"Yeah."

"How about meeting me for coffee after your class?"

He couldn't help glancing down to check she wasn't missing a hand.

She noticed—of course—and flapped both appendages in his face. "Don't be silly. I'm sure I mentioned to you once before what I'm capable of."

"We have a lot of catching up to do," he told her.

"Yes," she agreed, her hand creeping to her throat and toying with the thumb drive she wore on a sturdy silver chain around her neck. She cocked her head to one side, gazing at him in that particular way she had. "We sure do."

~*~

About the Author

MAREE ANDERSON WRITES paranormal romance, fantasy, and young adult books. She lives in beautiful New Zealand, home of hobbits, elves, and kiwis—both the fruit and the two-legged flightless variety. Her first novel for young adults, the multi-award-winning *Freaks of Greenfield High,* was optioned for TV by Cream Drama, Inc., Canada, and currently has over 2 million reads on Wattpad. She recently released the third book in the *Freaks* series, and is working on a second book in the *Liminals* series.

For more information about Maree's books, please visit her website at: http://www.mareeanderson.com

Other books in the Freaks series

FREAKS IN THE CITY

FREAKS UNDER FIRE

~*~